The Auction

A Reverse Harem Romance

Krista Wolf

KRISTA'S VIP EMAIL LIST:

Join to get free book offers, and learn release dates for the hottest new titles!

Tap here to sign up: http://eepurl.com/dkWHab

* * *

~ Other Books by Krista Wolf ~

Quadruple Duty
Quadruple Duty II - All or Nothing
Snowed In
Unwrapping Holly
Protecting Dallas
The Arrangement
Three Alpha Romeo
What Happens in Vegas
Sharing Hannah
Unconventional
Saving Savannah
The Christmas Toy
The Wager
The Ex-Boyfriend Agreement
One Lucky Bride
Theirs To Keep
Corrupting Chastity
Stealing Candy
The Boys Who Loved Me
Three Christmas Wishes
Trading with the Boys
Surrogate with Benefits
The Vacation Toy
Nanny for the Army Rangers

Wife to the Marines
The Switching Hour
Secret Wife to the Special Forces
Secret Baby for the Navy SEALs
Given to the Mercenaries
Sharing Second Chances
Baby for the Mercenaries
Best Friends Never Kiss
The Auction

Chronicles of the Hallowed Order

Book one: Ghosts of Averoigne
Book two: Beyond the Gates of Evermoore
Book three: Claimed by the Pack

~ 1 ~

AUTUMN

Putting yourself up for a singles charity auction wasn't something you aspired to, it was more like something that just happened. And it didn't seem real, to be honest. More like the type of thing that only occurred in sappy rom-coms, developed in the cheesiest parts of Hollywood.

Only right now I actually *was* in Hollywood.

And I was actually going through with it.

"One hundred dollars?" the voice beside me called into the microphone. "Anyone?"

The auctioneer smiled weakly, his hawk-like eyes scanning the well-dressed crowd. Forty-five minutes ago his voice had been cheery and boisterous. But now, with mine being the last date auctioned off, he just sounded tired.

"Ninety perhaps?"

I grinned through clenched teeth, trying to look pretty while silently cursing my lifelong best friend. Kinsley had ushered me up here spur of the moment, or at least it seemed that way. Right now she grinned supportively from the crowd just below the stage, sipping on her fourth glass of champagne and intermittently clapping to encourage more men to bid me up.

Only nobody was bidding.

"Seventy-five then," the auctioneer conceded, wincing a little as he said it. The mustached man in the thousand-dollar suit cast me a nervous glance. "I mean gentlemen, just look at her. She's lovely. And in fact—"

"I *am* lovely," I spoke loudly, deftly swiping the microphone from his tired hand. "*Very* lovely, and you'd be lucky to have me. But seventy-five dollars isn't going to cut it, gentlemen. Charity or no charity, this New York girl knows her worth."

The crowd that had been so attentive at the beginning of the auction had devolved into milling around, talking amongst themselves. But now a hush settled over them again. Apparently something interesting had happened.

"I'll bid on myself if I have to," I said, stepping forward to the edge of the makeshift stage. "After all, this *is* for a fantastic cause. The animal shelter needs every penny it can get. The poor dogs and cats still looking for homes are depending on you."

I shot a quick glance downward, at my friend. Kinsley's whole face had lit up. The bubbly brunette was smiling ear to ear, giving me the 'OK' sign with her free hand.

"Kinsley is my best friend," I went on, "and as you know, she's the manager of the place. The building is run down. The roof is leaking. There are too many animals, and not enough space. It needs our help."

I turned sideways in my borrowed red dress, showing myself off. Letting the men in the crowd know what they were about to miss out on.

"You all came here to support Cozy Noses," I said admonishingly, "or at least I thought you did. Back on the east coast there would already be a bidding war for this." I slapped a playful hand on my hip and angled it their way. "Apparently though, none of you sun-kissed valley guys can handle a date with me."

There was some intermittent laughter in the crowd, even scattered applause. I smiled back at them and winked.

"Which is why I'm bidding five-hundred dollars for a date with myself," I finished glibly. "And when I win, I'll take my *own* ass out to a nice dinner."

With that, I thrust the microphone back into the auctioneer's hand. There were looks of shock and surprise from the women in the audience, but from the men in the crowd, it was mostly comical appreciation and excited chatter. Apparently they weren't used to someone talking this bluntly. And if my New York accent hadn't slapped them in the face, my heavy Long Island accent had nearly bludgeoned them to death.

That said, the applause I received afterward was equivalent to a good mic drop.

"Holy *shit!*" Kinsley hissed, from somewhere just beneath me. She was clapping her hands together, her champagne forgotten. "Autumn, that was amazing! YOU were amazing! I can't believe you—"

"GENTLEMEN!" the auctioneer called loudly into the microphone, silencing the chattering crowd. He was finally awake and alive again. "You all heard the lady! The bid right now is five-hundred dollars!"

I spun around slowly, holding my hand out like a game

3

show host. The fund-raising event my friend dragged me to had been mostly dull, if I were being honest. But playing the crowd was suddenly fun.

"Will you let this gorgeous woman *shame* you into taking herself out to dinner?" the auctioneer teased, grinning. "Or will one of you step up and—"

"A thousand dollars!"

All heads turned, including mine. A blond-haired man with striking green eyes stood with one hand raised. And those piercing emerald eyes were locked on me.

Now we're talking.

"One thousand dollars!" the auctioneer repeated, as the crowd erupted in applause. "For a date with this strikingly beautiful and *vociferous* woman," he shot me a sideways glance, "who is apparently from New York."

It was already more than most of the other women — and men, of course — had gone for. And to think I'd almost balked when Kinsley suggested I get up here to help out the shelter. Right now I was smiling at the selfish notion they'd saved the best for last.

"This 'vociferous' girl thanks you very much for your generosity," I curtsied, leaning into the microphone this time without taking it from the auctioneer's hand. I made sure to stare directly at the hot, green-eyed stranger who'd just bought himself a date with me. "I'm sure you and I will have an excellent time tomorrow night, before I have to fly—"

"TWO thousand dollars."

Another voice, this one deeper and more resonant, echoed loudly above the noise of the crowd. I turned my attention to the opposite side of the room, where an exceptionally tall man stood a full head and shoulders above the rest of the room.

"Two *thousand!*" the auctioneer swore. He raised an eyebrow. "Seriously?"

The tall man nodded slowly. He was impeccably dressed, with model good looks and thick acres of gorgeous dark hair. His expression was stoic, but with a hint of mischief. Best of all his handsome face was shrouded in sexy dark stubble; the kind that I was always a sucker for, whether or not it was good for me.

And historically, it wasn't.

"Two thousand dollars then, for a hot date with the beautiful girl from New York!" the auctioneer shouted. "Thank you sir!"

Hot date? I repeated silently, mouthing the words to the auctioneer. The man only laughed and shrugged.

"Hey, you wanted to help the shelter, right?" he asked, covering the mic with one meaty hand.

"Yeah, sure. But—"

"Two thousand going once!" he stepped forward, ignoring me completely. "Two thousand going twice..."

"Twenty-five hundred!" another voice called out.

Everyone whirled their attention back to the original bidder. Only it wasn't the original bidder. It was the man standing *next* to him.

What the—

The new bidder's arm was still raised, much to the dismay of what apparently looked to be his blond friend with the green eyes. He had beautifully-tanned skin. Chocolate brown eyes. And of course, as fate would have it, even more sexy stubble.

"You really struck a nerve with these guys," the auctioneer swore under his breath.

"I... I didn't—"

"TWENTY-FIVE HUNDRED!" he boomed. "A most generous donation, for a very lovely—"

"Three thousand."

The tall man's voice was so naturally strong and commanding, it drowned out the excited murmurs of more than two hundred other people, even from the back end of the room. The crowd gasped. Kinsley choked. The auctioneer swung his arm left, pointing back at the new highest bidder. Before he could open his mouth, however:

"Thirty-five hundred!"

The blond man's hand was raised again. I noticed it was tattooed. He looked lean and strong, with an intensity about him that seemed oddly dangerous. But only to his enemies. Never to friends.

How the hell I knew all this without knowing anything about him was a complete mystery

"FOUR."

The tall man bid again, directing everyone's attention back on the two apparent friends. The men conferred with one another, and their exchange got quickly heated. A moment later, the Italian-looking man elbowed his friend.

"Five thousand!" he shouted, before his friend could recover.

The auctioneer glanced at Kinsley. She nodded in shock.

"FIVE THOUSAND DOLLARS" the man shouted into the mic, "is the maximum bid allowed! Therefore sir, I declare you the winner of—"

"BULLSHIT."

The tall man near the back of the room took several steps forward, the crowd parting as he made his way to the stage. He had an undeniable aura about him. A raw charisma I could feel from up here.

"You never said there was a maximum," the man declared as he got closer. "I'd have bid five thousand right from the jump."

The auctioneer looked abruptly panicked. He lowered the mic.

"I'm sorry sir, but—"

"And I would've done the same," the blond man interrupted. He appeared beside the stage so suddenly, he might as well have teleported. "You should've told us from the beginning," he seethed. "What kind of auction has a maximum bid, anyway?"

"The kind that can only accept individual donations in certain amounts," Kinsley stepped in. My friend's eyes blazed with a defensive fierceness I knew well. "If you really wanted a date with her, you would've outbid your friend over there. But you didn't. And so..."

She paused mid-sentence, her shrewd eyes scanning away for a moment as an idea suddenly occurred to her. Just another one of her mannerisms I knew especially well.

"Wait," said Kinsley. "What if you *all* took her out?"

By now even the winner of the auction had made his way over. The three men looked at each other in confusion, then back at Kinsley.

"What do you mean?"

"I mean technically you could *all* be the highest bidder," my friend went on. "Three of you, three dates, three separate bids. Fifteen thousand dollars for Cozy Noses. Everyone wins."

Still standing over all of them, my mouth dropped open. "Wait a second..."

"Done," said the tattooed blond. "Count me in."

"That works for me also," the tall man nodded. He scanned me, top to bottom, beneath a pair of heavy, dark brows. "As long as I get my date."

All eyes fell on me. I was still in shock.

"Umm... would you do that?" the auctioneer asked hopefully. "Would you go on three separate dates?"

I was totally on the spot. I shrugged.

"Yes, but—"

"Then it's settled!" he smiled, uncovering the mic with his hand once more. "I'll declare all of you as winners, and—"

"Did you forget I'm *leaving* the day after tomorrow?" I nudged Kinsley. "I can't go on three dates!"

My friend frowned. So did the others.

"My flight back to New York leaves in thirty-six hours," I reiterated. "I'll go out on a date tomorrow night for sure, if it helps out the shelter. But after that—"

"What about a triple date?"

Kinsley's eyes flared as she blurted the words. She still hadn't worked out the details yet, that much was obvious. My friend's brain was always working its ass off to keep up with her mouth.

"What are you talking about?"

"I mean all three of you should take her out," she said, matter-of-factly. "Autumn and I were supposed to hang out together before she left, but I can give that up. You can have the whole day with her."

Once again the men glanced at each other, unsure of what to say. None of them were willing to show weakness, however. Not one of them wanted to give in.

"C'mon," Kinsley urged. "What do you say? It's just a *charity* date, really — you know, to support the shelter. That's why you all placed bids in the first place, isn't it?"

Two of the men — the sexily stubbled ones — scratched at their chins. Begrudgingly, they nodded.

"It's not like it's a 'date' date," Kinsley went on. She paused awkwardly. "Unless you *want* it to be. Or one of you happens to hit it off with her." She grinned up at me and winked. "I mean, my friend *is* pretty awesome. The three of you would be crazy not to jump at the chance to—"

"Okay."

The answer came from my handsome blond savior; the one who'd bid on me in the first place. He cleared his throat and said it again. "Alright, I'm in."

"Sure," his friend added immediately. "Me too."

The dark-haired giant paused for a moment, as if weighing his options. I could tell he was calculating everything at once; me, Kinsley, his apparent rivals. The incredible amount of money the shelter would receive. In the end he reached up and loosened his tie, which had been fixed in a Windsor knot, and not the easier, 'even your wife could tie it' version.

"Fine," he said at last. "We'll all take her out tomorrow. But I pick the restaurant. And also—"

"Done!" Kinsley said, clapping her hands.

The auctioneer's smile returned. He lifted the microphone again, apparently to announce all three extremely generous donations to the very patient crowd. As he did, Kinsley motioned me down to her level with a frantic hand.

"Autumn!" she hissed excitedly. I could tell by her expression how much this meant to her. "You *are* okay with this, aren't you?"

I laughed bitterly. "You're asking me *now?*"

"No!" said Kinsley. "Well, I mean yes, but not really. I mean—"

My expression softened as my best friend damn near bit her tongue off trying to make everything right again. I let her off the hook with a smile.

"Yeah, sure," I conceded. "It'll be fun, right? Just like you said?"

"Three times the fun," Kinsley winked again.

It was that wink that always got us in trouble. That same wink that had started entire *wars* back in New York, while the two of us were growing up.

"Besides," she added, just before the crowd's applause drowned out everything else. "You're going home the day after tomorrow, anyway. How much could possibly happen?"

~ 2 ~

AUTUMN

I couldn't remember the last time my best friend had brushed my hair, but that was exactly what was happening. It had to be high school at the very least. I was probably getting ready for a date back then, too.

"You *sure* you don't think this dress is a little too much?"

As with the rest of her wardrobe, the studded black dress Kinsley lent me walked the tightrope between slutty and sexy. It fit well though, and hugged my curves in all the right places. Maybe a bit too much.

"Are you kidding?" my friend laughed. "They're going to eat you up!"

"I'm doing this for the shelter!" I frowned at her in the mirror. "I am *not* going to get eaten up."

My friend chuckled mischievously. "You don't know that."

She continued brushing, and after a short but lingering

stare I continued applying my makeup. There was limited time before my dates arrived, and we'd always been good at killing two birds with one stone. Plus, Kinsley had a date of her own. She claimed it was someone 'casual', which I knew to be pretty standard for her. But after almost a week catching up with her on the west coast, I suspected she liked this mystery guy more than she let on.

"I still can't believe I'm going out on a date with *three* guys," I bit my lip.

"Why?"

I half-whirled. "Are you serious?"

"If anyone can juggle three men at once its you," Kinsley said casually. "Besides, you're bringing in fifteen *thousand* dollars for Cozy Noses! Do you have any idea what that means for us?"

In fact, I did. Two years ago my friend had abruptly quit veterinary school, taken a defibrillator to a dying animal shelter, and somehow managed to bring it back from the brink of physical and financial collapse. Even now, Cozy Noses was running on fumes. But it was still running. And with each passing month, things were getting a little bit easier.

"You know I'm happy to do it," I said again, letting the warmth of doing a good thing push the nervousness away.

"Besides, is there really anything to complain about?" Kinsley smirked. "You get to go out, have fun, and sit down to a nice dinner with three very generous — not to mention yummy-looking — men." Her smirk widened as she slowly pulled the brush through my hair. "Who knows? Maybe you'll even get your clock cleaned."

My mouth dropped open. "I will NOT get my clock cleaned!"

"And why not?" my friend protested. "*Someone's* gotta brush the cobwebs out of that thing," Kinsley winked. "You're flying back to Long Island tomorrow, anyway. Where's the harm in a last-minute California fling?"

I rolled my eyes, and she laughed some more. Kinsley had been teasing me mercilessly, ever since we arrived back at her place last night. She wouldn't stop asking if I liked any of the guys, or which of them I thought I could hit it off with.

"I don't even know anything about them," I'd told her.

"Well, that tall drink of water is Christian Gardner, a local lawyer and a ruthless one at that," she'd told me. "I can't believe you pulled him! Much less for five thousand dollars."

"And the others?"

My friend had only shrugged.

"I never saw them until last night, but before we left I asked around. Turns out they're contractors, and also friends."

"Friends?" I'd squinted. It seemed strange to me that two friends would try to outbid each other.

"Ex-military, too," Kinsley had nodded. "I think they served together. They run their own outfit now, and build houses all over the Valley. Someone said they'd be bigger if they put the profits back into the company."

"But they don't?"

"Not so much, no," Kinsley had told me. "Apparently they use those profits to build free homes for veterans."

If the guys seemed attractive before, their philanthropy made them damn near perfect, now. Kinsley's explanation certainly solved the mystery of why they'd been so generous. It also left me thinking a lot about them, as I drifted off to sleep.

The sound of my friend's doorbell snapped me back to the present. Kinsley stepped back, dropped the brush, and grinned excitedly.

"Oh my God they're here."

My friend was giddy with excitement, like some kind of proud parent. All of a sudden I felt like a senior on prom night.

"Are you coming or what?"

Kinsley's passion for anything new had always been infectious. Maybe that's why, right after graduation, she ended up at UCLA — clear on the other side of the country.

"What if I'm having a shit time?" I asked suddenly. "Is there some sort of secret code I should text you, or…"

"You put all that negativity out of your head right now," my friend admonished me harshly. Just as quickly, she smiled and kissed me on the cheek. "Now shut up and enjoy your last night in paradise."

She flung the front door open recklessly; a metaphor for Kinsley's life in general. Standing on the other side were two of the men who'd bid on me — the friends and contractors.

And holy shit, they were *gorgeous*.

Both men were tall, topping out at an inch or two over six feet, with smooth, sun-bronzed skin that made it easy to believe they worked outside. Their bodies were strong and lean, their physiques forged from what had to be long years of manual labor. But those years had been good to them. Very, *very* good indeed.

"Hey," the blond said simply. He was staring over Kinsley's shoulder, directly at me. "Autumn, right?"

There was a pickup truck parked out on the street that wasn't there before. Big and blue and near-vintage old, it undoubtedly belonged to them.

"Right," I smiled, noticing that his sexy smirk came with even sexier dimples. "And you are..."

"I'm Shane," he said, flashing an effortless yet still panty-melting grin. Those emerald eyes that had locked on mine from across the auction floor were now right here, in all their glory. It was everything I could do not to get lost in them.

"And this here is Darius."

Shane nodded left, but Darius was already stepping forward to greet me warmly. He slipped past Kinsley and took my hand, his long arms dangling from a pair of impossibly broad shoulders

"Nice to meet you, Autumn."

His strong hands were absolutely enormous. And calloused. And enormous. And did I mention enormous?

"You boys are early," Kinsley stated flatly.

"Damn right we are," said Shane. "We were hoping to get here before he did."

"Who?"

"The other guy," said Darius. "The guy in the suit."

Kinsley had been standing against the open door, her arms behind her. But now she folded them over her chest.

"You mean Christian?"

"The tall guy, yeah," shrugged Shane. "We planned on sneaking you out of here before he showed up. Trust me, our date's going to be a lot more interesting if he's not—"

"Too late."

I smiled at the both of them, then pointed outside. Parked just in front of their truck, a long black sedan was now idling curbside. The vehicle was sleek and dark, with smooth yet wicked curves, and a logo I'd never seen before.

Leaning against it, equally sleek and sexy in his immaculate suit, was my third and final date.

"You were saying?" smiled Christian, crossing his arms.

~ 3 ~

CHRISTIAN

She was strikingly beautiful up close. An absolute vision whose shimmering blonde hair framed a girl-next-door face I could stare at for hours. On top of that she was bitingly sardonic, yet blind to her own unjaded heart. I'd bid on her. I'd won her. I was sitting right across from her...

But on my left and right, I unfortunately had Patrick and Spongebob.

"Really, this is it?" Shane scoffed again. "*This* is place you insisted on picking for dinner?"

He was louder than his friend, but no less disdainful. The two of them, I could tell, had been around each other for a long time. They'd probably settled into some sort of ranked hierarchy, one where Shane still believed he was in command. Either that, or Darius — the more calculating one, in my opinion — had allowed him to think that way.

"And what's wrong with this place?" asked Autumn, before chomping down on her burger again. She was really digging into it, too. A woman after my own heart.

"It's just funny, that's all," Shane shrugged. He jerked a thumb at me. "This guy is fancy. A lawyer in a thousand-dollar suit. He forces us into a four-way date, then insists on picking the restaurant. And of all places, he brings us here?"

"And what's your definition of a good restaurant?" I asked casually.

He looked down at the table for a moment. "One without paper napkins, for starters."

I stifled a laugh. So did Autumn. I couldn't tell if she did it for my benefit, or if she didn't want to give too much away. Her smile was worth it, either way.

"Forget about what he says," Darius chimed in. "These french fries alone are worth the trip."

He held one up to me. I toasted him with nod. Regardless of what anyone thought of the place, all of us had eaten our fill. It made sense that we were famished. We'd been out for hours now, walking the streets of Los Angeles and stopping for drinks, sights, and shows by street performers. The three of us had entertained Autumn's every last touristy wish; from stopping to check out celebrity footprints at the Mann Theater, to finding various stars on the Hollywood Boulevard. We'd even taken her dancing, which outside of weddings or holiday parties was something I never, ever did.

But this woman was worth it. I knew it the moment she'd stepped in front of the auctioneer last night, taking the microphone and taking control. She was smart. Sassy. Heartbreakingly beautiful. Her 'zero fucks given' attitude made her refreshingly raw and real, in all the ways the more plastic people around here could never hope to understand.

And so here I was, driving Ren and Stimpy around town while they sat in the back, flirting with Autumn. Sure, they'd tried bumping me out of our shared date, but it's not like I couldn't blame them. I'd shown up early for exactly the same reason. Ten minutes sooner and I would've stolen her away myself, even if it meant paying off their bids to help out the shelter.

Of course I'd had them thoroughly checked out — that much was a given. Competition aside, they weren't bad guys. Shane Lockhart and Darius Knight had honorable discharges from a pretty serious unit of the United States Army. They'd started their own company from scratch. They gave back to the community. They worked out, ate their vegetables, and took the skin off chicken. I couldn't find a damn thing wrong with them, which was kind of frustrating.

But I knew nothing about *her*.

Looking up Autumn Holloway from Suffolk County, New York might've been easy, but for some reason I resisted the temptation. I wanted to go into this with no knowledge, no history, no preconceived notions. If the feelings that had driven me to do something as uncharacteristic as bid on a charity singles auction were real, it wasn't something I wanted to mess with. I needed our date to be organic. Or at least, as organic as possible when splitting it three ways.

"Excuse me while I powder my nose," Autumn said, sliding backwards. "And by powder my nose, I mean make myself smell a little less like ketchup and mayo."

"Same here," I said quickly, and stood up.

I followed her around the bar and into the narrow hallway where the restrooms were located. Before ducking into the ladies room however, she smiled and turned to face me.

"You used to come here as a kid, didn't you?"

I couldn't hide my shock, much less how impressed I

was.

"How do you know?"

"You've been looking around all night," Autumn replied. "Scanning the place. Seeing things that are no longer there."

I nodded appreciatively. "My parents used to take me and my sister here, when we were young. It was a much different place, back then."

"How so?"

"Well for one, they served free peanuts at every table. And you were allowed — no, encouraged — to throw the shells right on the floor."

Autumn chuckled. "Every little kid's dream."

I nodded. "That other dining room over there was a little arcade area. They had a foosball table and a Battlezone machine. There were a couple of old coin-operated horses, too. My father would give my sister a handful of change, and she'd ride the unicorn until she ran out of quarters."

"So you come here for the nostalgia, then."

"That, plus you won't find a better hamburger in all of LA."

I wanted to tell her so much more; that simple nostalgia didn't even scratch the surface. I came to this restaurant because it was one of the last remaining connections to a happy past. I needed this place to exist, so I could keep a memory alive.

A trio of people came down the corridor, which was already tight. Autumn stepped into me without hesitation to let them pass, pressing parts of her body against mine. It was a level of intimacy we'd already shared in the club, dancing close together. Considering we knew each other for only a few hours, it still felt oddly natural.

"What are the chances of you and I slipping away from Joey and Chandler?" I murmured, inhaling her scent. "There's a side door right there. I already paid the bill."

She laughed, and her laughter was lilting and beautiful. But it was still laughter.

"What's so funny?"

"Joey and Chandler tried the same thing, back at the nightclub."

I raised an eyebrow. "Did they?"

"When you went for drinks, they tried pulling me out the back door."

Although the people in the hall had passed us, I noticed she still hadn't stepped back to her side of the corridor. My head was tilted down, and our faces were dangerously close together now. Our lips, hovering two or three inches from sweet oblivion.

It might as well have been miles.

"I can't just ditch them," she said, her voice cracking a little. "Any more that I could ditch you."

"I get it."

"I mean—"

"No," I said softly. "It's cool. I admire the loyalty to your commitment."

God, she was beautiful. I'd been fascinated by her all night, too. So much in fact, that I hadn't checked my phone even once throughout the evening. I hadn't read a single text-message. I hadn't answered a single email.

Those things alone were huge indications as to how much she'd affected me. Normally I wasn't one for instant connections. But this, I quickly realized, was on a whole different level.

"Wait, what was I saying?" I blinked.

Autumn grinned. "You were telling me how much you admire me."

Her skin was flush and pink, as our eyes searched each other's in the dim light. I could smell vanilla on her skin, now. The whole sensory experience was driving me wild.

"Tonight can't be the end of this," I told her flatly. "I know you're leaving, but I'd love to see you tomorrow."

"Maybe you *will* see me tomorrow," Autumn countered. She held up her phone. "See?"

I squinted at the glowing screen in the darkened hallway. There was a text-message from her friend, Kinsley. Something about getting together, followed by an address.

"There's a Midnight Mischief party, back in the Valley," she said. "A whole bunch of Kinsley's friends, plus some of the people from the fundraiser. She's asking us to swing by."

"What's a Midnight Mischief party?"

Autumn shrugged. "Fuck if I know."

If her New York accent was already sharp, it was a razor when she cursed. I don't know why I liked it, but I did.

"Wanna go? We need to head back toward Encino, anyway."

"Sure."

"And then it'll be after midnight," she smiled. "And so you'll see me tomorrow. Technically."

"Who's seeing *who* tomorrow?"

I didn't even have to turn to know Shane was standing there. Darius too. Their expressions were sour, like someone had just pissed in their beer.

"Making plans without us?" Darius folded his arms.

"Well the original plan was to sneak her out the side door while the two of you finished your fries," I said, without a hint of apology. "Similar to the plan you came up with back at the club, only my plan was better." I jerked a thumb. "I already parked on this side of the building."

"Thinking ahead," smirked Shane.

"Always."

"Almost as if—"

"Sorry," Autumn interjected loudly, "but all three of you are stuck with me for the duration of the night. And each other."

Diplomatically, she positioned herself between us.

"Great," Shane grumbled.

"Now, do either of you know what a Midnight Mischief party is?" she asked.

The guys looked at each other in confusion for a moment, then shook their heads.

"No," they said in unison.

"Perfect," our date winked, before finally ducking into the ladies room. "Then we're all gonna find out together."

~ *4* ~

AUTUMN

The place was beyond stunning, with sharp, contemporary architecture that molded it right into the side of the mountain it was built on. There was plenty of glass, complemented by more glass, complemented by beautifully-designed and expensive-looking furniture. And of course, like every other house on this hill, the back opened up into an unobstructed view of the valley. Stadium seating, for the rich and famous.

"Holy shit."

I breathed the words, more than actually said them. The galaxy of twinkling lights in the valley beneath us were astonishingly beautiful. My trio of dates flanked me as we stepped onto the immaculate back patio, which was little more than a frame of priceless-looking stonework surrounding a glowing blue swimming pool. Standing around it were fifteen or twenty people, sipping drinks. Half of them wearing... get this... *pajamas*.

"Oh my God, you came!"

Kinsley rushed me from the side, nearly knocking me over with her very enthusiastic and unquestionably tipsy hug. She wore only two things: a silky, sexy-looking green kimono, and the slippers that I'd gotten her for Christmas two years ago.

"I'm so happy!" she grinned. She stepped back and let her eyes flit from Christian to Shane to Darius. "Wow. I can't believe you're actually here!"

"Well, you *did* invite us."

"I sure did," Kinsley giggled into her wine glass. "And wait until you—"

"We do seem a bit overdressed, though."

My friend laughed again, then shook her head. "Nonsense. Look over there." She pointed at another couple, who were dressed like we were. "They showed up here from a different party. And there's another guy too — a basketball player, I think. He came in a hoodie, so no one would recognize him. And then there's—"

"Kinsley what *is* this?"

I looked around some more. Most of the guests were wearing pajamas, but many of them were in various states of undress. There were people swimming in the pool, too. Half of them were fully clothed, and the other half were skinny dipping. There was no in between.

It should've been awkward, but somehow it wasn't. The light coming from the pool was soft and subdued, and people were speaking in low but happy tones. Soothing music played from strategically-hidden speakers, so distant you could barely hear it. The whole vibe was very relaxed.

A beautiful woman with a spectacular figure walked by, wearing only a thong. She carried two drinks in each hand, and blew Kinsley a kiss as she passed.

My eyes narrowed. "Is this some sort of…" I struggled for the words. "I mean, is this like…"

"A swinger's party?" Darius blurted bluntly.

Kinsley touched my date's chest and laughed. "No, silly."

"So it's perfectly normal to just show up in practically nothing, or—"

"Maybe I should explain."

The new voice was attached to someone tall, dark, and very sexily bald. Wearing silk boxers and a plain white T-shirt, he slid a long arm very casually around my friend's waist. I knew immediately this was Kinsley's mystery man.

"It's a Midnight Mischief party," the man explained. "The party doesn't start until midnight, and everyone leaves for breakfast at dawn. When you come, you're supposed to be wearing whatever it is that you sleep in." He paused to take a pull from the beer he was holding, then pointed the neck of the bottle our way. "Or in your case, whatever you happen to be wearing at midnight."

I looked around some more. It was starting to make a little more sense.

"Autumn, this is Eric," Kinsley grinned. "Eric, this is Autumn… and Christian, and Shane, and Darius. She's *theirs* for the night, so…"

"No, not theirs," I corrected her.

"Well they *won* you," my friend corrected herself. "Fair and square. And they helped out Cozy Noses immensely," Kinsley winked, "so for the sake of the shelter, I hope you've been showing them a good time tonight."

Shane bumped my hip playfully.

"Yeah," he teased. "Where the hell's our good time?"

I smirked back at them. "I thought you boys were taking *me* out on a date."

"Actually, it wasn't specified," Christian teased back. "The event said 'win a date with a beautiful single.' But it never said who was taking whom out."

I thought he might bump me the way Shane did, this immaculately-dressed lawyer who'd only just loosened his tie. He surprised me by stepping even closer, and setting his hands on my hips.

"I *did* win you, though," he murmured huskily into my ear. "For the night, anyway."

His breath was hot on my neck, either intentionally or unintentionally. It made the little hairs stand up there, and sent shivers rocketing down both sides of my body.

"Anyway, go ahead and walk around," said Eric. "Everyone here is super nice, super chill. Get some drinks, and midnight snacks from the kitchen, and whatever else." He pointed to a bowl on the outdoor bar, filled with colorful packets of something that were unmistakably adult-level gummies. "Enjoy yourselves."

"And before you leave," added Kinsley, "go check out the pool house." She tilted her head toward the rear of the property, where an enormous structure looked almost like a second house. I couldn't help but notice it was the direction from which she came.

"What's in the pool house?" asked Darius.

Kinsley's smile was wider than I'd ever seen it before, and that was saying something. She shrugged coyly.

"Games and stuff."

With that she kissed me on the cheek and led Eric away by the hand. The two of them disappeared into the house, leaving us surrounded by glowing blue strangers.

"So that's the friend you've been visiting?" asked Darius. "The one from back home?"

Kinsley's Long Island accent, which was even thicker than mine, should've been confirmation enough. I nodded anyway.

"We played soccer together and ran track all through high school," I said. "Kinsley bolted out of New York the first chance she got though, and ended up at UCLA. She fell in love with California, and the rest is history."

"It's not too hard to fall for this place," Shane agreed, scratching the back of his head with a tattooed hand. "It's pretty. It's seductive. And it's a *lot* crazier than Montana."

"Montana's just as beautiful, though," I guessed. "No?"

"You bet your ass it is," he confirmed with a grin.

By now it was late, well past midnight. On any other night I would've been running out of gas. But there was something in the air here: an electrical charge that kept the night going. An energy of pure intimacy, fed perhaps by my three delicious-looking dates, and the casual connections we'd developed over the course of the evening.

"You wanna walk around a little?" suggested Darius. "Or..."

"Let's get drinks first," I suggested. "I'm thirsty."

Ten minutes later we were touring the house, weaving our way past small groups of soft-spoken adults in various stages of relaxation and undress.

"Is all of southern California like this?" I chuckled.

"You mean this movie-grade over the top?"

"Yeah."

Shane shrugged. "Depends on where you go. The Valley obviously does things differently."

"The richer you get, the more time you have for stuff like this," Darius added, gesturing around. "Not too many of these people are getting up to drive a bus or run a skid-loader tomorrow morning."

"Or to stand before a judge and litigate," Shane finished, jerking a thumb at Christian. "Like this psycho."

I glanced at the tallest of my three dates; who, as usual, had taken the joke in stride. Christian had undone his tie altogether, along with the top two buttons of his shirt. His double whiskey was nothing more than an empty glass now, dangling from the thick fingers of one big hand.

"I don't have court in the morning," he said. "At least not tomorrow."

My eyes flirted with his. "So you cleared your schedule for me?"

"Sure did."

We finished our tour of the house, exiting the master bedroom which had been occupied by two smiling couples sitting on the bed in pajamas. A pair of French doors spat us onto the back patio again, this time in a different spot.

"Sorry about Kinsley," I said, apologizing to my would-be suitors. "She's flaky, but harmless. Still, I had no idea what kind of party this would be. When she said we should stop by, I just figured—"

"Why don't we check out the pool house?"

The question had come from Christian, surprisingly enough. Glowing blue waves of light and shadow danced across his handsome face, reflected up from pool.

"I'm in," shrugged Shane. "Darius too."

"I am, huh?" asked Darius, glibly.

Without realizing it the guys had formed a little circle, surrounding me on the patio. For maybe the first time in my life, I welcomed the lack of personal space. We'd been together for hours, and I found myself enjoying the intimacy. The heat and closeness of their bodies had become strangely reassuring.

In my peripheral vision, I also noticed we were getting looks from all around.

"We're all in," I declared, pulling them toward the back of the yard. "No stragglers."

~ 5 ~

AUTUMN

Stepping into the strange new world of the pool house, I felt warm and loose. Sexy in my dress. Happily buzzed and oddly relaxed among a whole slew of other emotions, all of which happened to be good.

It occurred to me that this was the last day of my sorely-needed vacation. I'd spent the whole week exactly as I planned: soaking up the sun and reliving past glories with my best friend. Kinsley had always been (and still was) a complete wild child; a bit slutty at times maybe, but always in a sweet and somehow innocent way. If she could've fixed me up with any one of the sun-bronzed California studs she was always bragging about while I was here, I would've certainly gone for it. And if my blind date was even remotely good-looking, there was a fantastic chance I'd already be in bed with him.

Hell, I needed a win. I needed a fling. I was even willing to admit that I needed my clock cleaned.

Instead I was surrounded by three dates and not one. Which unfortunately meant my clock had to stay dirty, at least for now.

I turned to look back at them, even as I kept on walking. Shane's face was painted with a swashbuckler's smile. Between those green eyes and tattoos and bad boy swagger, he was everything I needed right now. Darius looked so good I could eat him alive, but it was even more fun to imagine him eating me. And Christian; well, I could imagine what it would be like to take him into my bed. To spread my legs wide for that big, beautiful frame. To bite my lip as he crawled between my thighs and pushed forward, surging into me for the very first time...

"Ummm... are you coming?"

I blinked back to reality only to find Christian staring at me expectantly. Back at the restaurant, I'd come achingly close to tasting those lips for real. The same went for Darius, actually. Shane too. Our bodies had writhed so closely together while dancing at the nightclub, the desires I sensed were a two-way street.

If only it wasn't my last day here. If only I'd had more time. If only—

"Is she wearing *handcuffs?*"

The question was entirely rhetorical. Of course the woman in the flimsy black negligee was wearing handcuffs, and furry red ones at that. You could plainly see them attached to the metal rung of the shelf just above her, as she smiled back at us.

"What time is it exactly?" she asked, as casually as if we were all standing in an elevator.

"One-seventeen," Christian shot back.

"Oh good," she sighed in relief. "I've only got three minutes left."

Bizarrely we continued forward, to where the

enormous pool house opened up into two distinct areas. One was occupied with a hot tub, wall to wall, and that hot tub was packed with people. The other was exactly as Kinsley had described it would be: filled with people playing games.

Adult games.

"Wow."

I counted over a dozen party-goers in various types of pajamas, from cozy-looking flannel to more daring and sexier outfits, like the woman in handcuffs. There was a man blindfolded in a chair, while two women took turns kissing his neck. They were doing it slowly, silently, trying not giggle or give away who was who, because apparently he was supposed to guess.

Another foursome was gathered around the board of another adult-themed game. We stood and watched a round or two, only to learn it was like a kinky truth or dare, but with dice. On one turn someone dared a pretty redhead to kiss another guy in the room, while her partner watched. After circling the room for a minute she chose someone from another game entirely. Immediately afterward, her partner was dared to kiss a girl from the hot tub, too.

"This is crazy," I murmured, but only half-heartedly. In reality, the casual wantonness of the whole scene had me strangely turned on.

"You ever see anything like this back in New York?" asked Darius.

I shook my head. I hadn't.

"Well I'll tell you one thing," laughed Shane. "Strip poker is dead and buried."

We made it to the back of the room, where the largest group of people were gathered around a small table. There was no game board on it, though. No playing pieces, or colorful dice.

Stacked dead center, in the middle of the table, was an oversized game of Jenga. The wooden tower was already very tall, with several blocks taken from the middle and re-stacked on top.

"Now *this* is something I can actually dominate," Shane grinned.

A young woman with hoop earrings and a half-shirt overheard his declaration. She whirled on him. "You really think so?"

"I *know* so," Shane boasted.

"Then go ahead," she challenged, adding a sly smile. "Take your turn."

The girl stepped back to the sound of whistles and whoops of encouragement, all around. All of a sudden, Shane looked only half-certain.

"Better get on with it," Darius encouraged him. "Can't back out now that they called your bluff."

Shane shrugged, approached the table, and carefully withdrew one of the lower pieces. As he went to put it back on the stack however, another player stopped him with an outstretched hand.

"You've got to do what it says, first."

My date's two blond brows knitted together. "What?"

"Read it."

He did. Those cute blond brows arched upward in surprise.

"Read it *out loud*," the girl with the half-shirt prodded.

34

Shane shrugged, turned, and looked back at us when he spoke.

"Take a body shot."

The crowd whooped again, and the girl immediately reached for the nearest bottle. Everyone watched as she leaned all the way back, earrings dangling, and braced one hand on the wall behind her. With her taut stomach stretched as tight as it could go, she deftly filled her navel with a small pool of crystal clear vodka.

Shane looked back at me questioningly. I smiled and nodded.

"Don't keep a girl waiting," I chuckled. "Go for it."

Shane did the shot with deliberate slowness, licking his way up from the smooth patch of skin just below the girl's alcohol-filled belly button. It was a hot thing to watch, especially with his eyes glued to mine the entire time. For a fleeting moment, I felt a sharp yet delicious pang of jealousy. Almost as if his lips should be kissing their way along my skin, and not hers.

By the time he closed those lips over her belly button and sucked it down, the crowd was already going wild.

"You got off easy," laughed Darius.

The moment was over, and collectively we began to shuffle away. But the man running the game stopped us the way he'd stopped Shane.

"You can't go yet," he pleaded, his eyes suspiciously locked on me. "At the very least *all* of you should play a round."

The four of us looked at each other. Before we could say anything, Shane shoved Darius forward.

"Alright, then."

He extracted the next block and read it aloud: "Lightly run your fingertips across someone's butt."

"I've got this," Darius winked.

He moved in the direction of a cute little blonde, stopped, then looked my way. Teasingly, he cocked his head.

"Go on," I told him. "Fair's fair."

The blonde turned a little and stuck her ass out to accommodate him. But instead of reaching for her, Darius made his way back over to me.

"Do you mind?"

I smiled and turned sideways. His hand started at my hip, the fingers extending ever so slowly from one big hand. Then, tantalizingly, he dragged them downward. The electric feel of his fingertips hovering just barely above the fabric of my dress was absolutely exquisite. I broke out in instant goosebumps, as he went one step further to drag the flat of his palm over one whole side of my ass.

Darius was frowning now, perhaps feeling a sliver of the same jealousy I'd just felt. Which was interesting, all things considered.

Both my dates carefully set their blocks on top of the stack. Christian, who'd kept silent until now, stepped forward confidently. He chose another block, slid it out, and read it to everyone:

"Whisper something dirty in someone's ear."

He looked back at me, and my goosebumps intensified. But not for long, because to my dismay he moved to the other side of the table and bent to whisper in another girl's ear entirely.

What the hell?

The girl was grinning as Christian held his hand to her ear and began whispering. But then, slowly, her smile disappeared. Her eyes took on a far-away look, then went somewhat glassy. She didn't look nervous, or amused, or anything other than a single base emotion:

She was getting turned on.

Christian continued whispering and the girl's eyes finally regained a spark of life. Eventually they flitted to me. She was biting her lip.

"What the fuck is he *doing* to her?" swore Darius.

Eventually he stepped away, leaving her standing there stock still. It was a long time before the girl moved again. When she did, she couldn't stop staring at Christian… or me.

"You're turn, New York."

If I was envious before, I was damn near livid now. Only I wasn't really livid. The jealous part of my brain had tricked me into thinking I was. Especially since Christian's expression was all amusement.

"Fine."

I yanked a block free without even thinking, and read it just as haphazardly:

"Seven minutes in heaven with your current date, or the person you came here with."

The first time didn't register, so I read it twice. Then three times.

"Okay… so who's your date?" the guy who was running the game asked.

For several seconds I just stood there. Like my brain

was broken.

"I ummm… I guess I have *three* dates."

The entire pool house erupted at once, with the 'ooohs' and 'aaahs' drowning out all other conversation. Even the people in the hot tub looked over.

"Three dates, huh?" the host grinned.

"Uh, yeah."

By now it was obvious who my three dates were. Everyone was sizing us up, trying to figure out our deal.

"Well it's not like…"

"Right there," the host pointed over my shoulder. There was a door in the opposite wall. "That closet's the size of a laundry room. It should be big enough."

I turned, and the guys were already grinning. Even Christian's mouth had turned into a smirk.

"Here, let me help you fine people."

The host of the game walked over and cracked the door for us theatrically. He pulled his phone and began tapping the screen. "I'll even set the timer."

Shane shrugged, then stepped inside. Darius too. With the crowd cheering even more loudly, Christian reached back for my hand. I took it mechanically, as the host ushered us forward.

"You sure you don't wanna bail?" Christian murmured into my ear, on the way through the doorway. "We can you know. It's not like we owe these people anything."

For a second I hesitated, wondering exactly how much of a hand Kinsley had in this. Then I squeezed his hand and pulled him inside.

"Screw it," I told him. "It's only seven minutes of standing in a closet. What's the worst that could happen?"

~ *6* ~

AUTUMN

The closet was big and wide and shelved on two sides, filled floor to ceiling with soft-looking towels. We shuffled inside, with me stepping forward between Shane and Darius. Christian filed in behind me, as the door was closed with a click.

"Did anyone have getting locked in a pool house closet on tonight's BINGO card?" I joked awkwardly. "At a Midnight Mischief party? In the middle of fucking nowhere?"

The sound of my voice was muffled by all the fabric surrounding us. I noticed the guys were staring at me, but in a strange new way.

"This is like the weirdest night ever." I chuckled.

Just then the lights went out. The switch, I knew, was on the outside.

"Great," I sighed. "I guess we're—"

A pair of lips closed over mine. It happened so swiftly, so eagerly, it caught me completely off guard. The rest of my sentence was inhaled by a strong, masculine mouth that rotated against mine. The lips were soft, but insistent. The hand that cupped my face was calloused, yet gentle.

In the pitch darkness of total anonymity, I kissed him back.

Whoever it was, I could feel them, smell them, taste the sweetness of his tongue on mine. And there were hands, too. Not just the kisser's hands, but other hands as well. They fell to my hips, my thighs, my ass… but that's only where they started. Because barely a few seconds later, those hands had begun to roam.

Oh my God…

The closet became its own silent world, pitch dark, my quivering body enveloped by the three warm bodies surrounding it. There was no sound but my whimpers. No movement, save for the motion of hands and fingertips and lips that took my breath away.

For a brief moment I considered pulling back, to maybe get my bearings or figure out what was happening. But the moment was fleeting. It surrendered quickly to the heat rising in my belly, as my own questing tongue rolled silently and hotly through the mouth of whoever was standing in front of me.

The kisses were slow. Thunderous. Beautiful in every way. But then someone took my chin, tilted me gently to the other side…

… and *another* pair of lips crashed into mine.

My head was spinning, my whole body trembling with heat and adrenaline. And yet again, whoever it was, I kissed them back. This time I brought my hands up to sift through the hair of whoever was drinking so deeply from my lips, as I sighed softly into their open mouth. My hands brushed two sexily stubbled cheeks…

Darius.

I was sure it was him. I'd been watching that stubble all night, daydreaming about what it might feel like beneath my eager palms. And now I knew. I ran my hands back and forth a few times before burying my fingers deep in that luscious, dark hair. Then I opened my mouth and *really* kissed him, just as another pair of lips closed over my neck…

And then a *third* pair, on the opposite side.

Fuck!

There weren't any words. Nothing could possibly describe the feeling of being held, touched, manhandled; all while being kissed by three men at once. Their mouths were hot against my skin. Their facial hair tickled, yet exhilarated me at the same time. I reached out, grasping desperately, grabbing for whatever I could to hold onto. My hands closed over ripped biceps, triceps, and shoulders. My palms grazed taut, muscular asses dressed in fabric… my fingers grazing a sea of deliciously shredded abs that hid just beneath the surface of a button-down shirt.

Another man kissed me, and this one tilted my chin upward before his lips found mine. I could feel a presence about him, even in the darkness. And he was big. Powerful. So incredibly tall…

Christian.

A long arm slid around my waist. It pulled me inward, crushing me against Christian's hard, gorgeous body. I cradled his face delicately with one hand as our tongues continued their dance. His kisses were absolutely amazing. His jaw was so square and masculine, and uniquely strong.

This… this is the craziest…

My thoughts were incoherent now, as my mind joined my body in complete and total surrender. I kissed Christian until my legs were jelly, and then someone else took his place. I was beyond hot, beyond horny. Burning up all over, as my wet mouth was passed from man to man, kiss to kiss. The heat in my stomach was an unstoppable fire now. A roaring fire that was spreading outward in every direction.

And that's when I felt them; two hands gliding their way down the outside of my thighs. They slipped beneath the hem of my dress, lifting it to my waist. Exposing me to a whole new set of roaming fingertips, traveling upward and inward to where only the slim fabric of my thong stood between my womanhood and the rest of the world.

Of course by now those panties were utterly drenched.

A hand slid tantalizingly over my ass. Another pair slipped upward from behind, cupping my breasts. With every touch I released soft sighs of encouragement. With every new place on my body explored, I melted just a little bit more.

A warm hand slipped through my thigh gap, and a thumb deliberately brushed my mound. I steered into it, whimpering happily as I was kissed even harder. Another arm came from behind, the hand attached to it sliding down the flat of my stomach. A second later I felt the distinct pressure of my thong being pulled to one side.

They were working as a team — all three of them together. I didn't stand a chance. There was no fight left in me.

Not that there ever was to begin with, mind you.

"Ooooohhhhh…"

My sigh was an audible hiss of exquisite pleasure. It came as a finger slipped daringly inside me.

I twisted into it, burying my face in the nearest shoulder. There was more movement, more insistence and pressure. That finger was joined by another, and before long they were dragging slowly in and out of the unquenchable fire between my legs. They plunged deep into my sopping wetness, as I clutched the taut waist of my nearest date and moaned happily into his hard chest.

I was smooth and bare and wholly exposed, as more hands roamed every inch of my body. My dress was lifted even higher, until two bare hands settled over my tits. They withdrew only to be followed by two hot, searching mouths and twisting tongues, causing me to reach out and clutch them against me in absolute ecstasy.

A hand grabbed mine and moved it commandingly between a pair of thick legs. I'd forgotten I'd even had hands! I began rubbing the significant bulge there, my breath catching in my throat as I realized the size and thickness. Instinctively I reached with the other, and found another bulge to play with. This one was a warm knot, all thick and heavy. Still uncoiling like a snake beneath the thin fabric of a pair of dress slacks.

Two fingers pried my mouth open. I sucked them in eagerly. I was moaning, groaning, whimpering like I was lost in heat. Which I was, of course. I was so far gone I'd forgotten about tonight, tomorrow, my flight back home. Kinsley and California and everything else in the universe...

... that is, until the lights blinked back on.

We were blinded by the sudden brightness and scrambling wildly, pushing ourselves backward and apart. I saw Darius busy pulling his zipper up. Shane and Christian — who thank God had helped me pull my dress back down — were straightening themselves while trying to look casual.

"Uhh... hello?"

The host poked his head inside and grinned. His eyes were everywhere.

"All done? Your time's up."

We left the closet single file, in a complete daze, to a round of applause from half the pool house. Even the girl in the fuzzy handcuffs was back. She smiled at me as we walked on by.

"Seven whole minutes, and the three of you still have everything *on?*"

I shrugged sheepishly, as Christian led us awkwardly toward an exit that seemed a million miles away.

"You're a stronger woman than I am," the girl elbowed me and winked.

~ 7 ~

AUTUMN

The drive back from LA felt slow and surreal, like the events of the long evening were nothing more than some convoluted dream. I should've been tired. Mentally and physically exhausted.

Instead, I couldn't stop thinking about *them*.

I was too charged up; too excited after the events in the closet. Wordlessly I glanced from man to man, soaking them in, studying their handsome faces so I could imprint them onto my brain. I wondered if this would be the last time I'd see them. That seemed like a bygone conclusion at the start of the night, but now the very thought of it wracked me with pangs of regret.

Look at them...

They were all so hot, even at one o'clock in the morning. Christian sat in the driver's seat looking casually beautiful, the sleeve of one arm rolled up as it rested comfortably on the steering wheel. My other dates sat on either side of me in the oversized back seat. They looked thoughtful and serene, each staring out his own window into the crystal clear California sky.

Kinsley and her date had quietly left the party, and the rest of us had followed suit. It was far too early for breakfast, and too late to do anything but take me back to my hotel. After all, I had a long flight tomorrow. One that was little more than twelve hours away. I'd touch down in New York, and immediately be re-immersed in my turbulent ocean of problems. California had been a welcome diversion from the issues at hand, but ultimately that's all it was: a distraction. An escape.

In twenty-four hours, I'd have to face everything I'd been putting off. And exactly the way I always had:

All by myself.

As we wound our way back through the San Fernando Valley, I pushed the thoughts from my head. I was still here, still in the present. Still on a date with the three hottest guys I'd ever seen up close, much less danced with, held hands with, been locked in a darkened closet with. Kissing them had been so fucking *amazing*. Touching them — and having them touch me — even more so.

Until it finally ended, this was *still* our date.

With that in mind I became determined to relish every last second of it; from the moment Christian killed the engine, to the awkwardly slow stroll along the sidewalk in front of my hotel. I felt so safe, surrounded by the three of them. So happy. So protected. As we reached the glass doors of my hotel, I didn't want them to leave.

"Come up with me."

The words tumbled easily from my mouth, without my brain even thinking them through. But I undoubtedly meant them. I meant them with all my heart.

"*Up*, up?" Darius repeated hesitantly.

"Yes."

His eyes narrowed. "Who?"

"Who do you think?" I replied glibly. "All of you. Together. With me."

My heart was pounding! It was like I'd stepped out of my own body, and someone else was calling the shots.

Someone wicked.

Someone *wild*.

Darius tried murmuring something, but no words were coming out. Shane looked confused. Even Christian, always so totally composed, appeared out of sorts.

"Look, what almost happened back there?" I whispered urgently. "In the closet?"

I stepped into them now, letting their presence surround me. I could feel the warmth emanating from their hard bodies in the cool night air. I could smell the sweetness of their distinct scents, as one by one, I took their hands and pulled them close.

"I *want* it."

Realization dawned upon them in an instant. They were simultaneously shocked and excited.

"In fact I need it," I urged, "more than you realize. And I *very* much want it to happen."

I stood on my toes and kissed Darius, then Shane, then finally Christian. The kisses were soft. Like goodnight kisses, but with the added extra of a very delicious promise.

"Besides, you boys *did* bid on me," I went on. "You won me. You paid for the night with me."

Wickedly I twirled, giving them a view from all sides. I even pulled the hem of my dress out, for theatrical flair.

"I'm still technically yours, right?" I prodded, pushing a finger in Christian's chest. I grinned shamelessly, squeezing Darius's hand while winking at Shane.

"I think it's only fair that you get your money's worth."

The decision wasn't a decision at all, at least not in anyone's mind. The only delay in action came from their pure, unadulterated shock. I have to admit, I was in shock myself. But I knew if I didn't do this, I would regret it for the rest of my life.

It was Shane who moved first. Placing his hands on my sides, he spun me around and urged me in the direction of the tall hotel's front doors.

"Let's get her up there then," he said thickly, squeezing my hips. "We're wasting time."

AUTUMN

The elevator ride was magical. Christian rushed me the moment the doors closed, pinning me against the mirrored wall. He kissed me so hard I could barely breathe, then spun me into the combined arms of Darius and Shane. They were kissing my lips, my face, my neck; all while touching me everywhere. My dress rode up. My panties came down. Someone helped me step out of them — I don't even know who — and the next thing I knew, a firm hand was cupping me gently, its fingers gliding like butter through the slickness between my legs.

All of this happened in the span of less than a minute. Twelve floors later the doors opened, dumping us into a thankfully empty hallway. I was delirious and drunk with want. Totally breathless, and dripping wet.

"Which way?"

I came to my senses just long enough to point. Somehow I produced the keycard to my room.

"Twelve thirty-one."

I was guided down the carpeted hallway in a haze of lust, dizzy at the idea of what was about to happen. The lock beeped. The door opened. I was carried more than guided into the darkened room by a whole sea of taut, muscular arms.

The bed, thankfully, was a king. I liked to flop. I liked my space too, which was why I'd declined Kinsley's invitation to stay at her apartment.

Thank fucking God.

My eyes hadn't adjusted, so the darkness of the room made it hard to tell who was where. A pair of hands gripped my hips again, and a body came up behind me. Two pairs of lips closed over my neck, one on either side, reminding me sharply of our fun back in the closet.

"Get this thing off her, already."

The voice, belonging to Christian, was hot and husky against my ear. Two pairs of hands grabbed my wrists and pulled my arms high overhead. A third pair lifted my borrowed dress up, over, and off. A moment later it was nothing more than a crumpled shadow on the hotel room's carpet.

Kinsley would approve, I thought absently.

I was bra-less and exposed. Utterly and completely naked, in a room with three strange men… all of whom had been given full permission to sexually destroy me.

"Right here."

One of them patted the bed. Someone else pushed me forward, bending me over, driving the upper half of my body across the mattress. The feel of the cool sheets against the warmth of my exposed skin was amazing. But not as amazing as the mouth that closed over my sex.

Holy FUCK.

A hot tongue drove into me, causing me to screw the comforter into two tightly-clenched fists. Two big hands settled over my ass, spreading me open, as my mystery lover proceeded to devour me from behind.

It was hot. Dirty. Absolutely incredible. There was nothing to do but squirm backward into the warm, wet mouth that was eating me so expertly, so thoroughly, as my ears registered the sound of clothing dropping to the floor all around the big bed.

"Enough. Our turn."

Strong arms lifted me effortlessly and turned me over, leaving me spread eagle on my back in the center of the bed. The mattress shook as two bodies dropped down on either side of me. I barely had time to whimper as a mouth closed over mine, kissing me deeply. Thick fingers stroked my cheek gently, coaxing me to loll my head in the opposite direction and kiss that way as well.

Back and forth they traded my mouth, as my eyes adjusted to the dim light.

Christian. Darius.

They worked together, drinking their fill of me. Kissing me over and over until tears of happiness streamed down both sides of my face, as a third pair of arms deftly lifted my legs over two rock-hard shoulders.

Oh my God, YES.

The bed shifted again, and something thick and warm was prodding my now molten entrance. When I looked up I saw Shane's magnificent body hovering over mine.

His chest and arms were gloriously naked, chiseled and

perfect, like the marble statue of some Roman god. His eyes gleamed as he stared down at me questioningly. I nodded in assent, biting my lip.

"Do it."

Ecstasy washed over me as he surged forward, driving himself deep, filling me all the way to the hilt with his incredible thickness. He stayed there for a moment, just buried inside me. Our eyes searched each other's in the shadowy darkness, as together we savored the feel of being so deeply and intimately connected.

Then, with his two big arms wrapped snugly around my naked thighs, he began pumping away.

The feeling was indescribable. Getting deeply and beautifully fucked by some buff California fling was a fun little fantasy I'd played with, ever since arranging this trip. But to do it while being kissed, nuzzled, and held by two *other* sizzling hot guys? That wasn't even the wheelhouse of reality. It was something I hadn't imagined in even my wildest, most far-flung dreams, mostly because it was too unrealistic. Too far beyond the scope of believability, that even on the loneliest of nights with only my own fingers buried inside me, it destroyed the thin facade of what was even possible.

And yet here I was, shamelessly giving myself to three men at once. I was about to fuck them. Suck them. Take them as lovers, irrevocably and forever, one by one by one.

Something warm and bulbous pushed past my lips, and that something was Christian. He was kneeling beside me now, knees spread wide, feeding me the manhood he'd slung down between those muscular thighs. I opened my mouth and swallowed him deep, thrilled with the idea of being penetrated from both ends at once. Now *that* was something I'd fantasized about! And as amazing as the fantasy was, the reality of the act itself blew the fantasy right out of the fucking water.

MMMmmmmmmmm…

I went absolutely crazy, sucking and writhing and grinding away. On my left was Christian. To my right, Darius. He'd taken Christian's lead and assumed the same basic position, providing me with another toy in the form of his long, rock-hard shaft. I reached out for leverage, and gripped them both by the base. Then I began blowing them in turn, rolling my head left and right. Switching back and forth between two very distinctly amazing cocks, as Shane never let up in his own quest to make me come.

At first the rhythm of being trapped between them was warm and soothing, almost cathartic. In time however, the pleasure I was giving these men came back to me tenfold. I began bucking and thrashing and screwing my eyes shut. Focusing on the unique pleasure of being so thoroughly *used*, while working eagerly with my hands and mouth to make sure everyone had their fair share of attention.

The heat, the stimuli, the fulfillment of such a hot, twisted fantasy; in the end, it was all too much. I came in an explosion of euphoria around Shane's ever-thrusting member, physically crying out with the sheer rapture of finally letting go. Somewhere in the back of my mind I could feel myself contracting around him, again and again, while still gripping Christian and Darius. I climaxed so hard it was borderline frightening, and that's when a firm hand clamped itself over my screaming, heaving mouth.

"Shhhhh!"

Darius chuckled evilly as his lips brushed my ear.

"Keep it down, or they're gonna throw us out of here!"

He removed his palm but kept his fingers there, probably because I was sucking and chewing them. My mouth was so wet, so hungry and eager for whatever came next.

"Awww, *FUCK!*"

My body protested briefly as Shane withdrew, and a moment later I felt a hot rain splashing down against my skin. He came in thick spurts, shooting his seed everywhere. It fell across my neck, my breasts, all over my quivering stomach. And the beautiful sight of his hand gliding up and down, milking himself dry, was something I'd never, ever forget. Not in a thousand years.

"Seriously?" I heard Darius say.

Shane looked euphoric, but disappointed. Happily drained, but also let down.

"I— I couldn't stop," he murmured breathlessly. "It was just too fucking hot. Watching her, I mean. With the two of you. It's... it's just..."

Christian was shaking his head. Shane growled at him.

"Oh yeah? Let's see how long *you* last in there," he breathed heavily.

He stepped back and I scissored my legs together, letting the palm of one hand wander downward. The others watched as I dragged my fingertips slowly through the warm pools on my belly. Then, mesmerized, they looked up at each other.

God. I couldn't wait to fuck them.

"Is that it?" I teased, letting my thighs fall slowly, sensuously open. I purred like a cat as I nodded in Shane's direction. "Or are one of you willing to prove him wrong?"

~ *9* ~

DARIUS

She was perfect, right from the jump: smart, sassy, funny as hell. Of course, being blonde and gorgeous didn't hurt either. But it was the confident way she carried herself on the auction stage that made me realize I had to win her, no matter what the cost.

Unfortunately for me, Shane had the exact same idea.

Bidding her up had been nothing more than a very expensive extension of our long, competitive dick-measuring contest. I should've won her. I *did* win her. But somehow, as with so many other things throughout my life, I'd had to share her with Shane.

And apparently, some strange local lawyer as well.

I'd convinced myself it was fine, especially since Shane and I had come to an agreement. We would date her together and let the best man win. We'd take her out, show her a good time, and let *her* decide which of us she might like to see again, when the night finally ended.

The fact that she lived in New York only seemed like a

minor inconvenience. As far as Shane and I were concerned, we'd overcome much bigger obstacles. Then again, there was the presence of the hotshot lawyer to consider. He'd kept up with us throughout the night; talking, flirting, even beating us to the punch when it came to moving on her in that pitch black closet. He was a wrench in the works, the fly in the ointment.

The John McClane to our Nakatomi.

And now here he was, pushing his way between her thighs. Burying himself to the hilt in the golden valley between those smooth, beautiful legs, as she gasped and cried and looked up at me pleadingly.

"Darius…"

I held her pretty face in my hands, as her striking blue eyes searched mine. They were glazed with heat. Swimming with lust.

"Kiss m—"

My lips crashed into hers, and Autumn drank from them like she was dying of thirst. Her tongue drove hotly into my mouth, swirling, searching, gliding alongside mine. Her hands shot upward, sifting into my hair. Seconds later she was pulling me tightly against her, kissing me so hard, I actually saw stars.

Unfuckingbelievable…

It was one thing to let the best man win. But in this case, there was no best man. There was only Shane and myself, and now this newcomer, Christian; who we'd only barely heard about before tonight. A guy who seemed both capable and resourceful, but also mysteriously proficient at rolling with the situation as it progressed throughout the night.

And yet somehow, I was sharing a *woman* with him.

I might even have been jealous, if I'd stopped to think about it. Right now though, I was too busy kissing and loving this gorgeous, breathless blonde. Little more than twenty-four hours ago she was nobody to me. A complete and total stranger.

But now, all of a sudden, she was everything.

I held her as she bucked and grinded, screwing her hips back against the lawyer, taking everything that he had to give her. Their fucking was hard, yet somehow intimate. Totally primal. At one point she pulled him down to kiss him too, pausing to whisper something that could only be hot and dirty into his ear. Then, without missing a beat, she grabbed my face and went right back to kissing me.

Holy shit.

This went on and on, with me extending my arms to brace her body against his mercilessly deep thrusts. She was totally in heat, now. Trapped hopelessly like prey between two ferocious hunters. Eventually Autumn broke our kiss, whimpering loudly, and I watched her expression turn absolutely rapturous. I was staring directly into her eyes as Christian rammed himself home one final time, screwed his body tightly between her legs, and let out a long hiss of ecstasy.

Then he grunted through clenched teeth and unloaded inside her.

I was shocked, dismayed, incredibly turned on. Never had I watched two people have sex, much less stare into the eyes of a beautiful woman as she climaxed around someone else. There was a moment of intense connectivity between the three of us; a soul-to-soul coupling of our minds, our bodies, our everything, as this gorgeous creature lying between us did nothing but breathe and writhe and ride out wave after orgasmic wave of pure, aberrant pleasure.

Then I was staring at Christian, wondering what the fuck he was thinking. I frowned at him.

"What the—"

"She told me to," he breathed, hands still gripping her perfectly-sculpted thighs. His own hips were still moving, still grinding around inside her. "She begged me to, in fact."

I looked down and Autumn nodded. Her smile was wicked and wild.

"There are *lots* of things I want you boys to do to me tonight," she whispered, pushing me onto my back. I went willingly, sighing as she threw one smooth thigh over my body and mounted me, embedding me to the hilt in the molten folds of her warmth and wetness.

Autumn squeezed me from within, and my eyes rolled back into my head.

"And I'm not going to stop until we've done them *all.*"

~ *10* ~

AUTUMN

I slept like a baby the whole flight home. Six and half hours of dreamless, blissful nothingness, during which my brain was turned totally and completely off.

Too bad the flight ended in the chaos of JFK airport... followed by a three-hour slow roll down the Long Island Expressway. On a normal day, this sort of ride should've taken less than half of that. With summer coming however, normal days went out the window. Entire caravans of weary city-dwellers clogged the arteries of Long Island's roadways, making their way to the north and south forks, to wine country, or to their second homes out in the infamous Hamptons.

Which in theory, should eventually be good for *me*.

At the moment, the ride sucked. The ride *always* sucked. This time though, I had the memories of last night to keep me company. They didn't qualify me for the HOV lane by any means, but they kept me happily preoccupied as I replayed them over and over in my sex-soaked, sleep-deprived mind.

Holy shit, Autumn.

Holy shit didn't cover even a fraction of it.

My last night in California had been epic beyond my wildest dreams, courtesy of Shane, Darius, and Christian. I still reeled from the things they did to me in that hotel room. Terrible things. Magnificent things. On the bed, on the floor, on the desk, up against the wall. Outside on the balcony, bent over the railing for anyone and everyone who just so happened to be up at three in the morning to see. The boys ravished me over and over, even in the shower, where they took turns washing me and cleaning me up only to carry me back to the bed and make me dirty all over again.

So dirty. So *filthy*.

And it all felt so incredibly fucking amazing.

It wasn't all them either, because I certainly did things to them. I did things *for* them. Things I hadn't done with a man in so very, very long. And things I hadn't done ever, as well.

I was greedy with them, pushing them down and taking my pleasures wherever and whenever I wanted them. I served them together, from my knees. They served me individually, or together, at times even three at once.

The memories alone had me twisting in my seat.

The whole thing was wild, beyond any fantasy I could ever hope to have. For those dark, silent hours in the dead of night I became someone else entirely, loving and embracing the freedom it gave me to be anyone else in the world other than Autumn Holloway.

Though they took me together, my lovers were very different as well. Darius and Shane worked in tandem, playing off each other, each somehow knowing what the other was thinking without any words. I wondered at times if they'd even done this before. Their military training as a team was more than apparent. I was the happy, sex-dazed beneficiary of the closeness of their bond.

And then there was Christian, the brooding lawyer. Tall. Powerful. Masculine as fuck. This wasn't something he'd ever done before, not even in the darkest recesses of his brilliant, calculating mind. But I could tell he reveled in it. Like everything the man chose to do, he immersed himself in it, and became one with the task at hand. And for last night at least, that task was *me*.

I replayed every one of these things as the Expressway finally ended, and I made my way further east on smaller and more scenic roads. My body — among other things — was still sore. The boys were hitting me in all kinds of places, including some I didn't even know I had. My hands hurt from gripping the sheets. My throat was raw from moaning around them, or screaming into an open hand while they took turns being inside of me.

I'd been reckless, too. Birth control pills aside, it wasn't like me to give myself over so fully and completely; and to total strangers, to boot. But these didn't seem like ordinary men, and this wasn't an ordinary situation. There was a level of emotional comfort and familiarity I couldn't put my finger on. A level of safety and intimacy that took every one of my normal guards down, allowing me to have them in ways normally reserved for long-time lovers and boyfriends.

And shit, let's be honest. I hadn't been properly laid in a long, long time.

I yawned as I made my way down the last few side streets, then turned into a long dirt driveway that was both familiar and foreign to me. I passed row after row of poorly-trimmed grapevines. An entire vineyard set wildly against the now moonlit landscape, after a whole day had escaped me through travel.

And all of it, as of last year, inexplicably mine.

It was one thing to learn of the passing of your estranged uncle, but quite another to find out he'd left you an entire abandoned winery. Never mind that I didn't really know my father's only brother. Like me, he had no family, no legacy, no heirs. No choices left but to bequeath his unrealized dream to a niece he never knew, before shuffling off his mortal coil, and laughing his way into the next world.

I'd taken the leap without thinking, selling off my parents' business — the last true link I had to them — in order to make this place work. I'd poured my heart into reversing years of decay here, trying to get the place operational again. I'd spent my life savings, and in a frighteningly short time, I'd gone into a mountain of debt.

And I'd done all of this without knowing a single thing about wine, except how to drink it.

I pulled up to the tremendous main lodge; a converted barn with sky-flung ceilings supported by a lattice of impressively thick rafters. At the moment, the place served as my home. And one day, hopefully soon, those big oaken doors would open into a tasting room and merchandise shop.

But it wasn't the doors I focused on, as I wearily killed the engine. It wasn't the sudden silence that crept over everything either, save for the whispering of grape leaves as the wind blew down the long, seemingly endless rows.

No, the problem was much more sinister than that. Especially in the darkness.

There seemed to be a light on upstairs.

~ *11* ~

AUTUMN

A chill slowly made its way through me, as I tilted my chin upward. There was no doubt about it, there was definitely a light from within. A glowing yellow square, in the second floor window.

Exactly in the room I was using for my bedroom.

I sat numbly in my car, wracking my brain as the hot engine ticked loudly against the cool spring evening. Had I left the light on when I left? It was entirely possible. I had a million things going through my mind at the time, and I'd packed fairly quickly. That was my MO, unfortunately. Some things I could plan for meticulously, especially in business. But when it came to taking care of myself, I tended to leave things to the last minute.

I looked again. The light was still on. Probably had been for a week, now.

"Dumbass."

I chided myself out loud, mostly because it was reassuring to have another voice around. Even if it was my own.

With that I got out, grabbing my carry-on bag and leaving the majority of my luggage for tomorrow. I wanted my sweatpants, and the TV on, and a roaring fire to warm me up. And although it was late, according to Eastern Standard Time anyway, I wanted a big cup of coffee, too.

I went to unlock the big door, but it wasn't locked. I went to push it open, but it wasn't latched.

What the fuck is going o—

An animal suddenly darted past me, scaring me out of my mind! I cursed and swore as it slipped through my legs, then bounded onto a chair, scurried across the table, and disappeared through an archway leading to the next room.

A surge of adrenaline kicked my heart into double time before my mind recognized the animal as a cat. It was a big gray one, too, exactly like the feline from *Pet Semetary*, whose name currently escaped me.

"The cat," I breathed, reassuring myself. "Okay. It's only the cat."

There was only one problem with that statement:

I didn't have a cat.

My legs propelled me forward mechanically, as the warmer air coaxed me inside. The big foyer I'd been using as a makeshift kitchen was still empty, and so was the darkness beyond. I began flipping on lights — or at least the ones that still worked — illuminating areas one by one. Everything was as I'd left it. Nothing seemed out of place. Except...

Groceries?

I took a half step backward. Sitting on the counter were various boxes of cereal, rice, and instant potatoes. There were cans of corn, and beans, and crushed tomatoes. One of them was even open, and my can-opener rested nearby.

"H—HELLO?"

I called out instinctually, without even thinking. It was a dumb move. A movie move. If someone was still here, I'd just made them completely aware of my presence. It could be a squatter, or a burglar, or even worse. I was dealing with someone sadistic enough to buy Captain Crunch's *All Crunchberries* cereal, and in the family size box too.

"Ah, you're here!"

A man's voice echoed distantly, followed by the sound of footfalls on the staircase, making their way downward. I could tell immediately those footfalls were too loud, too chaotic for just one person. Which meant—

FUCK.

I backed into the doorway, and the cool air hit me from behind again. And that's when two identical figures appeared, standing side by side. The men had the same sandy hair, the same heavily-lidded, hazel eyes. They were undoubtedly twins, and complete strangers. But they were also somehow... familiar.

"Autumn?"

I tilted my head, while fumbling for the keys I'd put back in my pocket. I didn't immediately answer. My mind too busy calculating the distance to my car, and how quickly I could jump in and lock myself inside.

"W—Who the fuck are you?" I managed. "What are you doing here?"

The guy on the left looked a lot less serious than the guy on the right. He also had a spoon in his hand. Maybe even some milk on his face.

"We've been waiting for you," the other guy answered in a southern drawl.

Anger took the place of fear. Not entirely, but enough that my hands were suddenly clenched into fists.

"You're in my *house!*" I spat angrily. "What did you think? That you could just—"

"*Our* house," the first guy replied. Scratching under a birthmark on the side of his face, he gave a noncommittal shrug. "Soon enough, anyway."

My brows fell together in rage and confusion. My fists kept clenching and unclenching.

"Autumn, it's *us*," the guy with the spoon said. His voice was softer, and a little more amiable. "Emmitt and Edward."

Emmitt. Edward.

Nothing registered.

"She's pretending she doesn't know?" the first guy scoffed. "Seriously?"

Very slowly, I shook my head. "Know what?"

The strange twins stared back at me for a beat. Eventually they shrugged, glanced at each other, and laughed.

"We're your *cousins.*"

~ 12 ~

CHRISTIAN

It was exactly twenty-two steps from my bed to the shower. I spent nine minutes beneath the four overhead jets, spraying down a constant temperature of one-hundred and eleven-degrees, before exiting to shave in front of my frameless, no-fog, LED backlit mirror.

And through it all, I could only think about *her*.

I was dressed and in the kitchen four minutes later. My breakfast consisted of half a grapefruit and one egg on whole grain toast, washed down with guava juice and black coffee. I spent eleven minutes answering emails. Another three on text-messages. For a moment I considered catching up on the news cycle, but with today's news cycle being an ever-increasing stream of mindless bullshit, I saved those six minutes for something far more important:

An even deeper dive into Autumn Holloway.

Since the events of two nights ago, I'd been totally consumed by this woman. Her body, her face, the smell of her hair… these things echoed in my memory and reverberated in the hallows of my mind. She was beautiful for sure, but it was her intellect I admired most. Her strength, her drive, her optimism about the future in the face of odds that were stacked against her. She was ambitious, yet grounded. Entrepreneurial, but unwilling to let go of even the smallest iota of control.

Just. Like. Me.

Every single one of her mannerisms made her attractive to me, from her charmingly sardonic smile, to her no-bullshit, New York attitude. She was saucy. Sassy. Able to parry any verbal attack and skillfully riposte, without a moment's hesitation.

And on top of all that, she fucked like a demon.

The events of two nights ago had been nothing short of legendary. They didn't just live in my memory, they'd kicked the doors to my mind open and demanded front row seats to anything and everything else I might be trying to do with my brain. The briefs I'd been trying to file still sat on my desk. My physical inbox was untouched, and undisturbed.

But damn, I could still taste her lips against mine. I had only to blink, and I could feel the curve of her hips clenched tightly in my hands. I'd done things to this woman I hadn't done with established, long-term girlfriends, and in front of an audience too. Sharing her with Beavis and Butthead had been inexplicably hot, and I was still low-key struggling with how much it turned me on.

By now, my co-winners of the charity auction had undoubtedly retreated back under whichever rock they'd crawled out from. Beyond the very heated memory of our team efforts, they were meaningless now.

The only thing that mattered was *her*.

I blinked as the phone suddenly rang, breaking me from my trance. Nine minutes had gone by, almost ten. I picked it up and swiped quickly, knowing full well my associate's tone would be an impatient and irritated one.

"Good morning, Jacqueline! I'm sorry I haven't—"

"Oh, thank God you picked up. I need your help!"

The voice at the other end of the phone wasn't impatient, or irritated, or anything other than frantic. And it definitely wasn't Jacqueline.

It was *her.*

"I came home late last night and these two guys were in my house — well, not really my house but the winery — which right now I'm using as my house, but—"

"What guys?" I jumped in quickly.

"They said they were my cousins, Emmitt and Edward," Autumn reset, before rambling anew. "They drove up from Georgia and they had their stuff moved in, and they said the place was theirs, and they were going to fight for it, and I should leave right away because I had only forty-eight hours to get out, but then—"

"Where are they now, Autumn?"

"I— I don't know. They left. I started screaming and yelling and threw them the fuck out."

"Good."

"But they're definitely coming back," she went on. "They left a whole bunch of their stuff here. I'm ready to drag it outside and burn it in the fucking fire pit, that's how angry I am."

"Don't do that," I advised strongly.

There was frustrated pause on the other end of the line, as I could sense her internal conflict. "A—Alright."

"Now, go on."

"Well they were here in the middle of the fucking night!" she blurted. "Scared the shit out of me. They moved in last week while I was down there in California, with you guys, and now they have all this stuff here, and there's even a damn cat. And they claim to be contesting the will, they said. Something about undue influence or lack of formality. Do you know what those things mean?"

"Yes, I know what those things mean." Reaching across my desk, I picked up a pen.

"And then—"

"Autumn, relax," I interrupted. "I'm going to help you, but you need to slow down."

She must've been holding in a deep breath, because it came out as a long sigh of relief. "Okay."

"Now, start from the beginning. Are these men really your cousins?"

"I... I think so. Probably, yeah."

"Why probably?"

"Because they look a *lot* like my uncle Jeff," she admitted. "He's the one who left me this place. The winery, I mean. About a year ago."

My hand moved fluidly, jotting things down. It was a habit I still had; writing. Most attorneys I knew put everything through a keyboard these days.

"What about the rest of your family?" I asked. "Is there anyone else who could corroborate—"

71

"No family," she said simply.

"Parents, grandparents, siblings…"

"My parents died almost four years ago. Avalanche. Austria."

My hand holding the pen went suddenly limp. "Autumn, I'm sorry."

"Don't be," she admonished. "They were hardly around. They traveled the world together, and left me the family business as soon as they could sign it into my name. XXXtreme Sports, with three 'x's. Creative name, right?"

"I—I guess."

"Except that it came up dead last in the phone book, way back when they started the place. And now that the internet's here, the three leading X's ensure any search for the company name gets buried beneath an *avalanche* of porn sites."

A moment of silence ensued. I said nothing.

"Do you see what I did there?"

"Yeah," I smirked inwardly. "I sure do."

"Anyway, I have no parents, no grandparents, no siblings," she went on. "No aunts, no uncles, no cousins. Not until last night, anyway."

"And you're running *two* businesses?" I squinted.

"I'm running zero businesses," Autumn shot back. "I sold XXXtreme Sports last year, when I inherited the winery. We used to sell skis, snowboards, rock-climbing stuff. Everything extreme. The place did well for a long time, especially during the extreme sports boom in the 90's, but eventually the internet killed us. Did you know you could buy a kayak off Amazon now?"

"Ummm… sure?"

"A fucking *kayak*, Christian. They deliver it right to your house, for free."

"I get it."

"Anyway, I ran the place for a few years after they were gone. Sold it while it was hemorrhaging money, to some guy who turned it into a skate shop. He poured a mini-skate park behind it, and it attracts all kinds of kids now. I guess that's one thing the internet can't provide you with."

"No, I guess not," I agreed. "Now tell me how you got the winery."

Autumn sighed wearily. "My father's brother Jeff passed away last year. They were estranged. *Very* estranged. So much that I only met the guy three or four times during my childhood." She paused to take another breath. "Anyway, he had no family either, as far as I knew. I didn't even know he'd passed away until a lawyer called me."

"And he left you a winery."

"He left me a *defunct* winery," she corrected. "Overgrown, unkempt, falling apart. Hasn't been active in years. Apparently it was his dream to fix it up, the way people fix up old cars after a mid-life crisis. Only this crisis is 45 acres, and it's not like I can just order parts on the internet."

I scribbled some more, then tapped my pen against my lips.

"Can I ask you something?"

"Shoot."

"Why didn't you just sell it?"

Autumn sighed again, this time more heavily than ever.

"Because I had this dumb romantic notion I could fix it up and make it into something beautiful," she said. "I did hundreds of hours of research. I spent every last dime I had, including the money I got for selling my parents' shop."

"I see."

"It's spring now, and I'm racing to trim everything out before the bud break, because once flowering begins I'm screwed. I secured a few loans. I spent the winter fixing up the lodge and clearing out the cellar. I've got enough casks for about thirty to forty-percent of my expected yield, and I have buyers lined up for the excess grapes. Provided I get a decent enough fruit set, that is."

None of this was a surprise to me. Someone with Autumn's mindset would figure these things out quickly and efficiently, and she wouldn't hesitate to act on them. She could've inherited an F-18 Hornet last year, and by now she'd know how to execute a perfect carrier landing.

"Send me the names of these so-called 'cousins' of yours," I told her. "Along with everything else you know about them. Your uncle Jeff, too."

"Okay," she said, sounding relieved. "Will do."

"I want you to change your locks immediately," I told her. "Move their stuff if it's in your way, but otherwise don't touch it. In the meantime, I'll look up local enforcement codes. That's going to dictate our next move."

"Do you need my address?"

"I already have your address," I said, probably a little too quickly. There was an awkward pause. "I, umm…"

"Internet-stalked me?"

Sitting up straighter, I shrugged. "Yes."

She laughed. "Ditto."

Her laughter was cute, and sexy, and set me instantly reeling with memories of our night together. It was utterly ridiculous, this loss of control. But I could feel my pulse picking up speed, regardless.

"Christian?"

"Yes?"

"What do I do if they come back?"

I felt my jaw go tight.

Fuck.

I could see her in my mind's eye, as clearly as if she were sitting right in front of me, instead of three thousand miles away. The thought of her all alone and vulnerable in some old barn was driving me crazy.

"Christian?"

She'd called *me*. She could've called anyone else in the world, but she'd reached out to me first.

No parents.

I let the pen drop from my hand. The notes I'd scrawled seemed suddenly insignificant. So did my inbox. So did everything else on my desk.

No grandparents, no siblings, no aunts or uncles.

For years Autumn Holloway had nobody else to rely on but herself. Maybe that's what made her strong. It's what set her so far apart from everyone else, that I had to have her. I knew this very clearly, now. As much as I knew anything else.

"Do you trust me?" I finally asked.

Her answer came without a moment's hesitation.

"Yes," she said simply. "I do."

"Good," I told her. "Then change those locks, sit tight, and let me handle things."

~ 13 ~

SHANE

She was in my head, my heart, and so many of my other, more strategic places. Since waking wrapped tightly around her naked, slumbering body, I couldn't get the girl from New York out of my mind.

And as far as I was concerned, that was just fine.

We'd brought in coffee and offered her breakfast, looking to spend every last minute we could with her on her last day here. Of course, we all knew she was temporary. Like a beautiful snowflake, we could possess her for but a brief, glorious moment. Even so, I'd be lying if I didn't admit that each of us was hoping for one more taste of what we'd had the night before.

Instead Autumn had finished her coffee, smiled slyly, then walked us to her hotel room door. There, one by one, she kissed us softly, deeply, longingly. In what seemed like a forever goodbye.

BZZZT!

I didn't feel the phone the first few times it rang, but

that's to be expected. Jackhammers tend to vibrate a lot harder than the rectangle of warm metal in my left front pocket. Your body even vibrates long after you've powered them down and walked away. Like now, for instance.

"I'm taking five!"

I had to shout across the construction site in order for Darius to hear me. He nodded back from just inside the old office building, where he'd been running the demolition hammer to take up a horrendously-set tile floor. Between the two of us, and the rest of our crew, we'd been raising hell with the neighbors for most of the day.

"Take over for ya, boss?"

I nodded as Matteo approached, and I passed him my gloves. The big foreman's smile was goofier than usual as he squinted into the sun.

"Take it slow," I pointed at the stonework, "and don't go past the chalkline. If we take up any more of the patio than we're supposed to, they're gonna make us pour them a whole new one."

His smile didn't budge a millimeter as he followed my arm downward. "Got it."

I took my phone out on the fourth or fifth ring. When I realized who it was, I scrambled to answer it.

"Dad?"

My mother's voice greeted me on the other end of a line that was somewhat choppy, as usual. All the way from the mountains of Montana, such a connection wasn't that uncommon.

"Honey, it's me. I'm calling because dad wants to talk to you."

My heart simultaneously soared and sank at the same time. "Sure, of course! Is... is he..."

"He's okay," she said apologetically. I could hear the melancholy in her voice. "He's not having the best day, I'm afraid. But it's not the worst day either."

I nodded in complete understanding, while my eyes scanned for the nearest hill. Elevation helped sometimes. It all depended upon the satellites.

"If you could talk to him," my mother said needlessly. "Cheer him up. But mostly, *reassure* him."

"Of course, of course," I breathed, climbing straight up an almost sheer embankment to reach higher ground. I wanted to get the signal right. I needed it clear.

"Shane..." my mom said hesitantly. "Just so you know, he's a little confused."

"That's alright. Put him on."

The sun was beaming down now, bathing the entire construction site in its golden light. It was coming along beautifully. We were ahead of schedule, as far as I could tell.

Still, nothing could untie the knot in my stomach.

"H—HELLO?"

Tears welled up, filling my eyes. I couldn't help it.

"Hey, dad!"

Silence followed. Way too many seconds of it.

"Who's this?"

"Dad, it's me. Shane."

"Shane..." he repeated slowly. "Shane?"

"Your son."

The stretches of silence seemed longer, week by week, month by month. The lump in my throat was getting bigger each time, too.

"Oh, hey son. How are you?"

"I'm great dad. How are you doing?"

His voice was mechanical. Still in the uncertain phase.

"I want to go fishing."

"Fishing would be fantastic," I agreed.

"Do you want to go fishing?" he asked excitedly.

"I wish I could dad," I swallowed hard. "But I'm in California, remember?"

More silence. More uncertainty.

"Are you sure?"

"Yes, dad. Don't you remember?" I prodded gently. "I moved here a few years ago."

"You did?"

"Yes, dad."

"Wow, that's great, Jason!" he said genuinely. "You'll love California. Especially—"

"Dad, I'm Shane," I corrected him. "Jason is still in Kalispell with you and mom. Mark too. They stayed, but I left for the Army."

"Oh."

Pulling the safety glasses from my head, I mopped the sweat from my brow. "It was a long time ago," I tried to grin. "Sometimes I forget myself."

"Yeah," my father agreed. "I know what you mean."

"So it's—"

"Shane," my dad interrupted suddenly. This was the part where something changed. Sometimes he came around. Sometimes he didn't.

"Shane..."

He sounded somewhat aggravated now, even disappointed in himself. I wanted to reach through the phone and hug him as hard as I fucking could. The fact that I couldn't broke my heart.

"I'm sorry Shane," he said, more clearly. "I get it now. I just... I was just... you know."

"It's cool dad," I assured him. "Don't worry about it. How have you been?"

"Alright I guess," he sighed, adding a chuckle. "You know me. I'm just a dinosaur, looking for a tar pit."

"Yeah, well they got some of those over here," I smiled into the sun.

"Do they? You'll have to show me when your mom and I come out and visit."

"That better be soon, old man," I challenged him jovially. "I miss your grumpy ass."

"Well take better aim next time," he joked. "I'm not exactly hard to hit."

The tears felt wonderful now, as I squeezed my eyes and let them roll down my cheeks. His voice, his laughter, his razor-sharp wit. It was all back, at least for now. And I knew I needed to cherish every second of it.

"Dad, I think maybe I'll head out there," I told him. "Sooner rather than later."

"Really?"

The knot in my stomach was gone. Only warmth remained.

"Definitely. Gimme a few weeks, maybe a month to wrap some things up here. But yeah, I'm due to come home. I miss the hell out of you and mom. And besides, *someone* needs to teach Mark and Jason how to fish."

He laughed again, and now I could hear the excitement in the thickness of that big, hairy throat. There was hope in his laughter. There was love.

"Hot *damn*, I want to go fishing," my father swore.

~ 14 ~

AUTUMN

The vines of my vineyard were bleeding.

Well, not really *bleeding* bleeding, but more like seeping a clear mixture of water, organic acids, hormones, minerals, and sugars. And this was a good thing, apparently. It signaled the start of a long growth cycle that would, ultimately, give me grapes.

And mash. And wine. And tons upon metric shit-tons of work.

Eventually.

I walked the rows at dawn as I'd taken to doing in past weeks, sipping from a worn ceramic mug. The steam from my morning coffee drifted slowly upward, teasing my nostrils. I inhaled its earthy fragrance, as I toasted the crisp blue sky.

"Fuckin' A."

Things were looking good, maybe even better than I dared to hope. All the trim work I'd done over the winter was finally paying off, and the far-flung rows of ancient vines were no longer an overgrown, untamed mess. A few buds were even forming on some of the more mature plants. Within weeks they'd be flowering into spiky-looking green clusters that would eventually be grapes.

"Who's got the green thumb now, mom. Hmmm?"

Once again, I raised my mug to the sky. My mother had always poked fun at the little plant I'd brought home from a school field trip, and subsequently grown in my childhood bedroom. Although it was more of a good-natured ribbing, I always figured she was just jealous. She'd never been able to keep anything green alive, not even the simple do-it-yourself Chia Pet herb garden my father and I put under the tree for her one Christmas.

"Red over that way," I pointed, sweeping my arm over a large swath of vines. "And white all the way back there," I pointed. "You preferred martinis, of course. But I'm not growing martinis this year."

An image of my mother floated to mind. Very vividly I could see her angular face, framed by those bright blue eyes I'd been lucky enough to inherit. Her sardonic smile, which was never more than a half-smirk, was permanently etched in my brain.

My father was a lot less sarcastic, but no less self-invested in his and his wife's own happiness. That part was sweet, I guess. The two of them were unquestionably made for each other, even if they weren't cut out to be parents. Raising a child tended to limit the number of times you could go mountain climbing, or cliff diving, or helicopter skiing in a given year, although my mom and dad still did all those things anyway.

In that respect, I was a happy accident. A formula-guzzling, diaper-trashing anchor that grounded them for a while, as they built XXXtreme Sports into a thriving, self-sufficient business. And when I was barely old enough to push the key into the lock of that place? They put me in charge of it. They taught me how to open and close and ring people out, while they planned every thrill-seeking getaway they possibly could.

Even the one that ultimately got them killed.

I never really got all the details, and I didn't want them. As it turned out, avalanches in the Austrian alps weren't all that uncommon, and that year had already logged record snowfall. Deep down, I knew there was a recklessness involved on their part, too. My parents were thrill-seekers as well as extreme sports enthusiasts. No matter what they were doing, they were always pushing the envelope.

I mourned them, but the true tragedy at the time was the death of my family. I was the accident my parents would never make again, so of course I had no siblings. There were no grandparents to commiserate with, no aunts or uncles with shoulders to cry on. My parents' funeral was attended solely by their friends and customers, and only a few of mine. Kinsley got me cataclysmically drunk. I woke up more than a day later and everything was over. Even the messes were cleaned up. Everyone was gone.

And that was it, the end of my lineage. I was the last one left. The end of the line. The—

What in the world?

I heard voices ahead in the next row, talking in low tones. As my feet propelled me forward, I could even glimpse faces between the rapidly budding leaves.

"Ummm… excuse me?"

The voices that floated in were calm and casual. Dead smack in the middle of my vineyard, two perfect strangers

85

were carrying on an everyday conversation.

"EXCUSE ME," I cried loudly, ducking under a series of twisted branches to reach the next row. "This is—"

I froze, mid-sentence. The men standing in front of me, face to face, weren't strangers at all.

"Hey cuz."

Emmitt's mouth was already curled into a twisted smirk. He shot me a sideways glance that bordered on total annoyance before pointing calmly back to the clipboard Edward was holding.

"Everything from this point on is be cut back," he said coolly, "starting at this row right here. That should keep the harvest a lot more manageable, and also make enough room for—"

"Cut *back?*" I swore loudly. "Cut BACK?"

"More or less, yes," he shrugged. "I don't know what the hell you've been doing here, but we'll take it from—"

"GET OUT!" I shouted.

Edward appeared instantly rattled, and in that moment I saw a distinct physical difference between the two of them. He frowned as he lowered the clipboard.

"But—"

"Get the fuck out of—"

"Our vineyard?" Emmitt finished, cutting me off.

They both pivoted, turning to face me. The sun was behind them, shining directly into my eyes.

"This place was left to me," I told them. "I moved in here a year ago. I poured every last dime of my savings into it."

"So?"

"So I sold off my business," I growled, "and my childhood home. This place is all I have now. This place *is* my home."

"Unfortunately that's not true," Emmitt continued coldly. "And it never was."

Edward tapped the clipboard nervously against his leg. "This was our father Jeff Holloway's place," he said, his voice sounding every bit as identical to his brother's. "It's our birthright. We're here to claim it."

I scoffed. "Your birthright?"

"Yes."

"Then why didn't he leave it to you when he passed away?" I challenged. "Why did the executor of his estate call *me?*"

Edward sifted a finger through his sandy hair and scratched. Apparently he didn't have an answer.

"Now," I said loudly, shattering the silence, "get off my property before I—"

Emmitt took several aggressive steps in my direction. In no time we were toe to toe, face to face.

"Or you'll *what?*" he sneered threateningly.

His hand closed over my wrist. It happened quickly; too fast for me to even be afraid. I tried pulling away but his fingers only tightened around me. Pain flared. But the anger was worse.

"Now," Emmitt snarled. "You listen to me..."

His scent was strong; all heat and sweat and something else that reminded me of dirty motor oil. His breath was sour against my nostrils. Or maybe it was his teeth. Or maybe it was everything, all at once.

Either way, my hand was already balled into a fist. I could hit him in the nose, and possibly break it. That would be painful, but the pain would be temporary. I could throw hard for his temple, and try to knock him out. Or hit him right in the eye socket, and maybe—

My mind was still running through my options when Emmitt was suddenly and violently shoved backward. He let go of my wrist, stumbled a few steps, and then fell, his arms pinwheeling wildly in a desperate bid to regain his balance. His efforts failed miserably. He ended up flat on his ass, covered in mud from the weeping roots of a nearby row of vines. The look in his eyes was murderous.

"Who the *fuck* are *you?*" Edward roared.

Emmitt scrambled to his feet, his hate-filled eyes locked on something over my shoulder. I whirled to find Christian standing behind me, immaculately dressed in a suit and tie. His alligator shoes were covered in thick, reddish-brown mud. My mouth hung open in shock.

Calmly and without fanfare, the lawyer slipped a phone from his inside jacket pocket and started dialing.

"W—What are you doing?" asked Emmitt.

"Calling the police. Having you trespassed."

"Trespassed?"

Ignoring the twins, he turned to address me. "You've been living here, correct?"

I was so stunned, it took me a moment to answer.

"Yes. Of course."

"Then you have residency."

"Umm... us too." Emmitt finished brushing his legs off, then slung the mud from his hands. He pointed at himself and his brother. "We live here also."

"Good," said Christian. He was still dialing. "Then you'll be able to provide proof of that when the police get here."

"We have stuff inside the house," said Edward.

"And your names are on the utility bills?" Christian countered.

"Well... no." All of a sudden he looked unsure. "But that doesn't matter."

Christian's smile savagely placating. "Doesn't it?" He turned his full attention back to the phone. "Hi, Suffolk County sheriff's office, please."

Edward glanced at Emmitt. It wasn't a good look.

"Was that assault?" Christian asked me casually, tilting the phone away. He looked down to where I was rubbing my wrist. "That looked like assault for sure. I suppose we can let the police decide when they get here."

"Emmitt," Edward stammered. "S—Should we—"

The muddier of the twins cut his brother off with an angry glare. They were big, but Christian was bigger. There were two of them, but Christian had the element of surprise. The lawyer's sudden appearance and authoritativeness had made them uncertain. Enough so that it delayed any thought of retribution.

Eventually their shoulders sank.

"Assholes," Emmitt spat, as he stomped off. "This isn't *nearly* over."

It took a moment, but Edward eventually followed. We watched as they continued marching down the row, in the direction of the main road. Only when they were finally out of sight, did Christian slip his phone back in his pocket.

"Don't take this the wrong way," he grumbled apologetically, "but your cousins are real dicks."

~ 15 ~

AUTUMN

I slid a fresh mug of coffee across the table, deftly enough that the liquid didn't slosh over the side. It would've been impressive enough to take note of, if I weren't still in shock. Christian took the handle and raised it appreciatively.

"So they *are* my cousins?"

The big lawyer from California — and most incredibly, my lover — nodded.

"They're your full biological cousins, yes. Emmitt and Edward Kent."

"Kent?"

"They took their mother's maiden name," Christian went on. "Erica Kent gave birth to them a little over twenty-five years ago, in Blue Ridge, Georgia. And they're all still there."

I slid into the chair across from him, but not before shooing the cat away. The big gray had taken to following me around the house, although cautiously at first. After several unsuccessful attempts at chasing it away, I finally let it.

"I... I don't know who that is."

"I didn't expect you would. You said your uncle was estranged."

I sipped my coffee and nodded. "He and my father had a huge fight over something when I was very young. I never knew what it was, but after that, I never saw him again." I shrugged. "I barely saw him anyway."

"Well you must've made *some* impression on him," Christian reasoned, spinning his finger in a circle. "If he left you all of this."

I followed his gaze slowly around the old barn, scanning from wall to wall, rafter to rafter. The place was admittedly impressive. Architecturally beautiful. Even if it was covered in dust and filthy as hell.

My attention was drawn back to the table with a soft flop, as Christian dropped an overly-thick file on the table. He slid it toward me with strong, well-manicured fingers. It occurred to me that they were same fingers that had touched me in *all* kinds of places.

"That's everything I could find out about your uncle," he declared.

I reached for the file and paused. "Plain manila folder?" I teased. "Do you lawyers buy these things in bulk?"

"They hand them out in law school," he countered without missing a beat. "They deliver them by forklift on pallets."

I was trying to get him to smile. I'd never felt happier to see someone in my life than when Christian showed up this morning. Just having him here made me feel safe and secure.

Hefting the folder in one hand, I dropped it back to

the table with a thud. "This is about a thousand times more than I ever knew about him." I swore.

The lawyer took a pull of his coffee. "Want the rundown?"

"Yes, please."

He nodded. "Jeff Holloway was a lot of things both before and after he became your uncle. He was a carpenter, a plumber's apprentice, a stone mason. After losing two fingers in a machine shop, he started his own telemarketing company. When that failed, he taught himself to program, and wrote software for three different dot-com startups during the late 90's tech boom."

I blinked. "Well... shit."

"And those are just the ones I could find," Christian nodded. "He was a genuine jack-of-all-trades, your uncle. A true renaissance man. He was a thrill-seeker too, like your father, but it was something he grew out of fairly early in life."

I sipped my coffee, silently wondering how long my parents would've stuck around had they grown out of the thrill-seeking stuff themselves. Christian paused, perhaps gauging my reaction.

"He *did* love skydiving though," Christian added. "Your uncle logged over six-hundred solo jumps that we could find record of."

"We?"

"Me and my team, yes."

A team. Of course he'd have a team. Only a team could fill a folder like the one on my table right now.

Bet you Christian could do it himself, though.

"Anyway, one of the startups was assimilating another company in 1996. Jeff Holloway spent three weeks down in Blue Ridge Georgia, moving the servers and data centers over. Erika Kent was one of project managers tasked to work alongside him, and, well…"

"They boned."

"Yes," Christian finally smiled. "At least once that we know of."

He flopped open the file and separated a portion that had been paper-clipped together. I saw the names Emmitt and Edward, highlighted in yellow.

"So he sired my dear cousins down there," I spat disdainfully, "and just flew the coop? Left poor Erika to raise twin boys on her own?"

He shook his head. "It wasn't like that at all."

"No?"

"Just the opposite, actually. Jeff Holloway must've tried to make it work, because he rented a house in Blue Ridge for more than a year. There are filings of him suing for both custody *and* paternity rights in Fannin County. The court records down there aren't that great, unfortunately. But we do know he sued for visitation and got some. He paid child support voluntarily."

"So what happened?"

"As far as we can tell, Erika kept the kids from him as much as possible. She moved them around a lot, and denied visitation often. Police reports were filed, but ultimately the courts weren't very sympathetic. She was a treasured local as far as they were concerned, and he was some out-of-town, Silicone Valley hot-shot. Jeff Holloway moved back to California when the kids were still toddlers, but never stopped paying child support. Eventually he ended up where he originally started, back here in New York."

"So his kids were estranged too," I realized. "Just like his brother."

"Yes," Christian agreed. "But apparently not for lack of trying. Your uncle went down there a few times, over the course of many years. But never for very long."

My guest sat back and relaxed his shoulders, staring at me over the rim of his mug. I couldn't believe how fast he'd managed to gather all this info. Or how quickly he'd caught a flight down here. He'd dropped everything in his busy life for me. He'd set it all aside, instantly. Unconditionally.

And all of it, without me even asking.

"Could you take that tie off, already?" I mused, wanting him to be comfortable.

"No."

My face scrunched into a frown. "Why not? It's not like you're going to court today, in the middle of my vineyard."

"Because you're going to take it off for me."

His voice was strong, his tone assertive. But those piercing brown eyes were as warm as ever.

My body threw a shiver of excitement as I stood up and walked over to him.

"I am, huh?"

His eyes followed mine, now. Unwaveringly.

"Yes," he said, huskily.

I slid into his lap, straddling him right on the worn kitchen chair as Christian's hands settled over my hips. First I undid the knot, staring deep into his eyes. Enjoying the feel of his hands on my body again, as I pulled the smooth silk through its loop and let it hang, loosely, around his neck.

Christian sat wordlessly I undid the top button of his shirt, then the second, and even a third. I began kissing his neck, his jaw, his gorgeously stubbled face. He tasted and smelled like everything delicious in the world. I let his hands explore a little, tickling my sides as my lips hovered just above his. His every breath was my breath. The distance between us so small, so insignificant, it was almost infinitesimal.

But when he finally went to kiss me, I leaned teasingly away.

He seemed confused at first, but only for a split-second. Even so, the look of shattered confidence was absolutely adorable. I squeezed my hero tightly against me, burying my tits in his face as I slid my lips right up against one warm, sexily-shaped ear.

"Thanks for coming out here and rescuing me," I whispered hotly, before biting the lobe gently between my teeth.

The lawyer let out a slow, uncharacteristic sigh. Directly beneath me I felt him relax, while other parts of his body stiffened with desire.

"You actually think I rescued you?" he huffed. "Really?"

Those hands slid abruptly up my body to settle against my cheeks, where he cupped my face, tightly. For an achingly long moment he just held me there, gazing into my eyes. The look was powerful. The ball of heat building in the pit of my stomach, even more so.

"If anything, I rescued *him*," Christian murmured against my lips. "I saw the look in your eye. All I did was save your cousin from getting his teeth knocked out."

I couldn't take it anymore. I had to kiss him! But now, somehow, *he* was in control. He was running the show, at least for now, and I was merely a spectator, desperate for more.

"And of course I came out here," he breathed, scooping me effortlessly into his arms as he stood up. "Since the other night, you're all I think about."

He was standing tall now, holding my body easily against his broad chest. Our lips were still brushing. Our eyes, still locked at a soul-to-soul level.

"Do you have a bed in this place?" Christian grunted.

My arms were draped around his impossibly strong neck. "Yeah. Something like that."

"Better tell me where it is soon," he breathed into my mouth. "Or we're doing this on the floor."

~ 16 ~

AUTUMN

Once the kissing started, it never stopped. It continued all throughout; slowly, frenzily, from the moment our lips touched for the first time to the last breath we shared, chests heaving. When it finally broke we remained inches away, just staring at each other in the morning silence. Christian was still buried so deeply inside me, I wondered if we'd somehow become one.

He'd undressed me slowly while kissing me everywhere, then devoured me mercilessly until my toes curled, my legs shook, and my fingernails were scratching the back of his thick neck. He was absolutely ravenous. Relentless in his quest. I gasped in awe and wonder as his sexy stubble tickled the insides of my tender thighs, ultimately rolling my hands into his hair as I gushed shamelessly, into his gorgeous, talented mouth.

I was ready for him then, spreading my legs so quickly and eagerly I could only imagine what he thought. I expected him to ravage me. To pound me into the oblivion I'd dreamed about the entire flight home. Instead, he slid gloriously inside me and pinned his whole body tightly against mine. Still kissing, never stopping, he made love to me slowly, again and again. I squealed with delight as he screwed me deep into the rickety old bed, which was making all sorts of noises. The light streaming in through the upper windows silhouetted every bump, every curve, every pumping, churning muscle of his perfectly sculpted body.

I would come twice more before his body went rigid, and those beautiful brown eyes glazed over. And we were still kissing as he throbbed and pulsed and emptied himself inside me. Still gasping into each other's wet, eager mouths, as he filled my swollen, happy entrance to overflowing with his warm, wonderful seed.

I don't remember falling asleep, but I remember curling up against his warm chest as those two big arms folded over me. It felt like being back in the womb. All heat and safety and soothing darkness, as his body closed off the now-offensive mounting daylight.

Sleep came hard for me, and somehow I woke up alone. I bolted upright to find Christian standing at the window, looking out over the magnificence of the vineyard. He wore only his boxers. He had fresh coffee, too.

"Morning…" I sighed, bunching the covers around my nakedness as I sat up.

"Afternoon, actually," he replied. He swung an arm back smoothly, without turning around. "Here."

He was offering me another steaming cup of coffee, this one in my favorite mug. On it, a green dinosaur was drinking his own cup of coffee. Beneath him were the very wise and deliberate words: Don't be a Cuntasaurus.

"Thanks," I said, blushing as I took it. "I, uh… umm…"

"Go on," said Christian with a chuckle. "I can't *wait* to hear this one."

"Kinsley and I used to send funny shit back and forth across the country to each other," I explained, looking for clothing. "Back when she first moved to UCLA."

None of my own clothes were nearby, so I settled on his nearby T-shirt. Pulling it over my body felt comfortingly natural. It came all the way down to my thighs.

"What kind of stuff did you send her?" he asked absently.

My mind began sifting through a very vulgar, obscene portfolio.

"You don't wanna know."

I still couldn't believe he was here. Even now, as he stood in my favorite spot in the house, gazing out over the same splendor that made me fall in love with this place. Stepping lightly, I moved to stand behind him. My hands moved forward all on their own, eager to touch his body again.

"And this whole thing is yours?" he breathed. "All of it?"

My fingers grazed upward along his broad back. "Every plant. Every vine. Every soon-to-be-grape."

Christian sipped his coffee and grunted. "And you have to harvest it all. Pulp it down to juice."

"Yes."

"What's your plan, take your shoes off and stomp them barefoot?"

"If I have to, I will."

He chuckled as my free hand slid around him. "Oh, I

know you will."

My open palm lingered on his taut, rippled stomach. It was so sexy, so powerful. I'd been mesmerized by those muscles, earlier. They contracted so incredibly hard, right when he came.

"Looks like a hell of a lot of work," Christian sighed. He stretched one arm backward, to pull me against him. I shivered as his hand settled over my ass. "Still... this is nice."

"What's nice?"

"Your place," he specified. "Your life. Waking up to this every day."

"And what's your place like?"

He laughed as he turned into me. It was a cynical laugh, though.

"My place..."

"Yes."

His eyes crawled briefly up my body, before finally seeking mine. With me already staring at him, they didn't have to go far.

"My house is a contemporary cliff-side mansion, in the Hollywood Hills. Open atrium. Infinity pool. Six-thousand, eight-hundred square feet of marble, stone, and glass. And concrete. And glass." Slowly, he shook his head. "So much fucking glass."

I blinked in confusion. "But—"

"'Sophisticated', they called it in the listing," he laughed. "It came with a state-of-the-art gym, complete with smart features and real-time trainers on call. There's a sauna, a steam room, and a wine cellar in the cavernous basement. The entirety of which, by the way, is carved directly into the mountain itself."

Looking into his eyes I could picture it all. It should've been amazing, every last bit. Somehow, it wasn't.

"Every morning at precisely the same time, my six-thousand dollar espresso maker automatically delivers a cup of piping hot coffee. The specific gravity is always one-point zero seven. The serving temperature is exactly one-hundred thirty-nine degrees."

"Jeeze," I swore.

"Exactly," Christian nodded. "The only surprise is whether it's Turkish Dibek or Hacienda La Esmeralda. Or sometimes Kona. Because every so often, you just need to go Hawaiian."

"Of course," I shrugged.

The tall lawyer looked back through the window again, over the sun-kissed landscape. His expression was suddenly far away.

"Know what I see from my window?" he asked rhetorically. "The valley. It's all yucca and sand and scrub oaks, dotted here and there with other mansions, like mine. It's nothing like this," he gestured. "Not at all."

"So you don't like it?" I asked.

"No," he stiffened beneath me, after a slight pause. "I guess I don't."

A loud bang turned both our heads. As we looked at each other, it grew louder.

Someone was pounding on the front door.

Christian sprang into action immediately. His eyes

swept the room, and a moment later he was leaning over the bed. As I watched, he tore one of the wooden crosspieces free from the headboard. It was about the length of a baseball bat, only thicker.

"Stay here," he growled.

"Yeah," I swore. "Fuck that."

I was out of the room before he was, and together we padded down the stairs. The banging noises grew louder. There were muffled shouts, too.

I moved to look out the window, but an enormous arm swept me backwards.

"At least stay behind me."

Before I could do anything the door on the right exploded violently open. Splinters of oak went everywhere.

"AUTUMN!"

Unbelievably, I saw Darius in the doorway, his arms raised in a fighting stance. Shane stood right beside him. Their eyes fell to me, standing there in nothing but a T-shirt. They shifted to Christian, standing only his boxer-briefs, his weapon still raised.

For a long moment, the four of us stood staring at each other in the awkward silence.

"You've gotta be fucking kidding me," Shane swore.

~ 17 ~

AUTUMN

Awkward didn't even begin to describe the scenario. Still standing there shirtless and pantsless, Christian raised the broken bed post and pointed it at the others.

"How the hell are *they* here?" he demanded.

I shrugged sheepishly. "Well... I called them."

He blinked back at me in disbelief. "You called *them?*" he cried in exasperation. "Rocky and Bullwinkle?"

Shane turned his head curiously. "Who the hell are Rocky and Bull—"

"I called everyone!" I cut in. "I mean, when this whole thing went down I was rattled. I didn't have anyone else to turn to. The three of you were still fresh on my mind, so..."

Suddenly I felt very foolish. I looked down at my feet. "Is that a bad thing?"

The guys stared at each other. All three of them.

"No," Darius said quickly. "No, of course not."

"Especially considering the circumstances," Shane added.

Christian didn't look convinced. He lowered the makeshift weapon, however.

"Look, I needed help and advice," I replied. "A sounding board, maybe. I didn't expect any of you to actually come."

"Sure looks like *someone* came," Shane frowned, scanning Christian up and down.

I sighed in frustration. "That's not what I meant."

"So why break the door down?" Christian demanded. "What the hell was that all about?"

"We knocked first," Shane shrugged. "Then we banged. We saw her car outside, and a strange black one parked behind it, and no one was answering the door. So we thought... well..."

The tension went out of Christian's shoulders. He nodded.

"Yeah. Okay."

"Sorry not sorry though," added Darius with a smirk. "If we interrupted anything, I mean. And we'll fix the door, of course. But first, where are these thieves you called us about? The ones who broke in here?"

"They're not thieves," I corrected him. "Not yet, anyway. But they're trying to steal this place out from under me, because it belonged to their father."

Darius looked concerned as he nodded toward Christian. "Can they do that?"

"I'm not sure yet," the lawyer answered truthfully. "

Depends on the strength of their claim. They can contest her ownership based on their bloodline, that I do know. And they *are* her cousins. I'm betting they're going to be persistent assholes about it, too. They're up here from Georgia, and they've got nothing to lose."

He ushered them inside, then closed the broken door behind them as I shot up the stairs to find some clothing. When I came back down fully dressed, they were all seated around the kitchen table. I threw Christian his T-shirt, silently sad to see those muscles go. He set the broken piece of my headboard on the table and wriggled into it.

"Sorry about your bed," Christian lamented.

I shrugged. "That's okay. It was old and rickety, and I hated it."

Not to mention we almost fucked it to pieces, I thought to myself.

"Besides, one or both of those assholes were probably sleeping in it while I was gone." I shuddered involuntarily. "Just the thought of that skeeves me out."

I sat back for a bit, while Christian caught the others up on everything that had happened since I got home. Darius was concerned, but like Christian he tended to view things from the logical end of the emotional spectrum. Shane on the other hand, was absolutely furious. He wanted to go out immediately and find these men — my cousins, or whoever they were — and do things to them that would get us all in trouble.

It was totally wild though, that they were here. That all three of these men had taken my safety seriously enough to drop everything and come clear across the country. All for me.

"And I *told* you she's not staying here," I heard Darius

saying. "It's not safe."

"Whoa whoa whoa whoa..." I butted in quickly. "And who authorized you to make decisions for me?"

His mouth twisted into a frown, as he stared back at me with those Italian eyes.

"There's no way in hell I'm leaving this place," I said firmly. "I've got too much trim work to do before summer! Then I've got fertilizer bills, tax bills, contracts for product fulfillment. I have to keep an eye on soil conditions, weather conditions, irrigation in case of flooding..." I threw up my hands. "And now there's the motherfucking spotted lantern fly to watch out for—"

"Spotted *lantern* fly?" asked Darius.

"Look it up!" I practically shouted. "And now, on top of everything else, I've got Lilo and Stitch coming up from Georgia, actively trying to screw me out of this place?" I spat and shook my head. "Nope. No fucking way. Ain't gonna happen."

At the mention of Lilo and Stitch I saw Christian smile. He was rubbing off on me. I would've smiled along with him, if things weren't so dire.

"Besides," I finished, "if I left this place for any length of time, those assholes would only come back and take it over."

Begrudgingly, Christian nodded. "She's right. If they're going for residency, they could throw her stuff out and move right back in. The eviction laws in New York are weird as hell. For some stupid reason, they always favor the squatter."

"Well she's not staying here alone," said Shane. "Not a chance in hell."

"No, she's not," Christian agreed. "That's for sure."

"Good," said Darius. "It's settled then. We take turns here each night, watch over the place. At least until—"

"Or you could just all stay here until we get this sorted out."

Once more, they swiveled their heads to look my way. It happened in such perfect unison it was actually adorable.

"Really, there's plenty of space," I explained. "All of the rooms upstairs are empty, except mine. No beds or anything, but you could have your pick. This place is absolutely enormous."

"Seriously?"

"Of course! It's not like I don't *know* you," I winked. "Besides, I could really use the company."

My stomach knotted as I finished talking, perhaps reminding me of what happened the last time we were all together. Did I think things would just be casual all of a sudden? Or was I secretly hoping that they weren't?

"Alright then," Shane nodded. "Beds or no beds, you've got a deal."

"I'd offer one of you boys the couch, but I don't even have one yet. This place came with a second-hand chair that's strangely comfortable, so I've just sort of been rolling with it. But it's not exactly—"

"Don't worry about it," Christian said abruptly. "I'll make some calls. Get it all sorted out."

My face scrunched in confusion. "Get what sorted out?"

"I owe you a bed, for one," he nodded. "And this

broken door—"

"*Well* be taking care of the broken door," Shane jumped in. "After all, it's what we do."

Christian seemed appeased by this. "Fine."

"And in the meantime, lunch!" The sexy blond smacked his lips before leaning back and rubbing his hands together. "Is there an In-N-Out around here, or..."

"In-N-Out?" I laughed. "Seriously?"

"Hell yeah I'm serious," Shane shot back, looking wounded. "We took the red eye out here last night. An hour into the flight they served us a hockey puck disguised as a breakfast sandwich." His lip curled. "It was inedible!"

"And yet you ate it," Darius laughed.

"What was I supposed to do!" cried Shane. "I was wasting away at thirty-five thousand feet."

"You ate mine also," added Darius, "now that I think about it."

It was funny, watching the two friends banter. They'd been doing this forever. It was part of who they were.

"Nevertheless," I cut in, "we don't have In-N-Out Burger here. Not a single one in the entire state."

My words were sacrilege, apparently. All three men's mouths dropped open in shock.

"One of you grab your keys though," I told them. "You're in luck."

Shane tilted his head. "What sort of luck?"

"You're in New York now," I added proudly. "I'm taking you all out for real, actual pizza."

~ *18* ~

DARIUS

"Yeah, sure. Double-check the purchase order and put it through. We'll be back in a few days."

The loud clacking of keys was the only sound at the other end of the phone. Javier's model-F internal spring keyboard was an IBM antique. We'd offered to buy a new one of his choice, or even provide him a laptop, like the rest of the crew. For some odd reason, our foreman insisted on sticking with his old machine.

"Got it. Everything's green again."

Maybe it wasn't *that* odd a reason, actually. The older I got, the more I was realizing I liked things exactly the way they were.

"Thanks Javier."

He was a good foreman, and an even better contractor considering his vast experience in the field. Javier had been hammering nails through plywood since before Shane and I were even born. He loved his new role as a facilitator, though.

"And hey," I said, looking at the time. "Shouldn't you

be picking up your grandson by now?"

"Another hour," Javier answered, still typing.

"But—"

"Time difference, jefe. Remember?"

He'd been our first hire, just after Shane and I had gotten out of the Army. The construction boom that had originally brought me to LA was apparently back, and in full swing, too. All the more reason men like Javier were diamonds in the rough.

"Well tell him to score another goal for me," I instructed our foreman. "I know he's got playoffs this weekend. And I want a celebration dance, this time."

"What kind?"

"I dunno, maybe a triple fist-pump or something."

Javier laughed proudly. "He does that every goal, anyway."

"Fine then," I relented. "Tell him to drop to his knees and play air guitar. Show him how to move his arm in a big windmill, and I want at least two or three power chords. Got that?"

"You're crazy, jefe."

"Yeah, what else is new?" I joked. "Record it for me, Javier. Record it, or it didn't happen."

I hung up and made my way back inside the cute little Italian restaurant. Michelangelo was everything it looked like from the outside and more. The scent was intoxicating. The food was ridiculous.

"Shit, did you let him eat *all* the calamari?" I lamented, giving Shane a dirty look. "I told you to save me some."

"Relax," my partner laughed. "I ordered more."

Autumn held the tablecloth away from my chair, smiling at me as I sat down. She looked amazing in a pair of pre-ripped jeans and a cute blue top. Her face was pink and flush, apparently from laughter.

"So what's this asshole going on about now?" I prodded.

"Nothing but good things," she answered. Her pretty eyes scanned me strangely, now. As if seeing me in a new and different light.

"I was just telling them about Kosovo," Shane said merrily. "And how you almost got turned into Swiss cheese."

"I *did* get turned into Swiss cheese."

"Oh, I know," Shane agreed, popping another piece of fried squid into his mouth. "I was the medic who patched you up."

Christian was staring at me too, now. The lawyer had eaten exactly one slice of pizza, so neatly that his cloth napkin was still virgin white on both sides. Restraint-wise, I don't see how he could've stopped at one. Hands down, it was the best pizza I'd ever had.

"Six holes in your back, right?" asked Shane.

"Seven."

He rolled his eyes. "You're such a martyr."

"Hey, you're the one who brought up the story," I pointed out. "Might as well get it right."

I caught his eye, and silently conveyed for him to cool it. Almost imperceptibly, Shane nodded his assent. We'd been through a lot together, and there were limits to the things we shared. Each of us had seen victory, triumph, glory in combat. But we'd also seen abject failure. Devastating loss. Together we witnessed horrors that we knew never to speak of again.

As comrades-in-arms, we'd been through things that forged us inseparably together. Things that made us brothers, in every sense of the word.

Our sarcasm and good-natured banter were merely masks we wore voluntarily, to hide those deeper levels of emotion.

"Anyway, it was a whole lot of sewing," Shane concluded. "One guy with an AK, lying in ambush for days at a time. He ruined everyone's night."

"And he left me a souvenir," I added, patting myself on the back. "Bullet fragment embedded in bone."

Autumn's beautiful eyes widened. "It's still in there?"

"Up against the sixth rib, just behind the scapula," Shane acknowledged. Casually, he dragged a piece of bread through a plate of oil and spices on the table. "Too close to the heart to mess with it."

Christian and Autumn exchanged a look, just as the second order of calamari arrived. They had questions, of course. Generally, everyone did. But like most people, they knew when such a story was over. Just as Shane and I had turned the page on that part of our lives, and begun an all-new story of our own.

"So what's the plan?" I asked, helping myself to the lion's share of the crispy, golden goodness. "We just wait for them to show up again, or—"

"We find out where they are, where they're staying," Shane jumped in. "This far out on the Long Island, there can't be too many places."

"You'd be surprised," said Autumn.

"It's definitely worth a shot," Christian theorized. "And I've got some people looking already. It may take a little time, though. I think we spooked them today."

Time. It was one of the luxuries Shane and I didn't necessarily have. We had projects to manage, and deadlines to meet. There was a foreclosure auction we'd be missing too, whether we liked it or not.

Still, it's not like there was an alternative. We couldn't leave Autumn to fend for herself, especially considering how bold her so-called cousins had been. And I wasn't about to leave her with the lawyer either.

That one's for much different reasons, though.

The admission was silent, but no less bitter. Yes, he'd gotten here before us. And yes, he'd 'connected' with her first. I didn't know what I expected, really, or how things would go. All I knew is that whatever we'd started back in California was still wholly unfinished.

And Shane felt the same way.

Christian's phone buzzed. Glancing down at it, he stood up and dropped his napkin to the table.

"I need to run," he said. "They're here for me already."

"Run?" I blinked. "Run where?"

"Affiliate office," he said dismissively, as if the term actually meant something. "I'm meeting some colleagues prepped to brief me on New York Property law."

Autumn looked relieved. "Good. If you need anything—"

"I will."

He disappeared from the table with a flourish, leaving a storm of twenty-dollar bills in his wake. When I looked up again, he was gone. The whole thing was amazing, really.

"Jeeze," I breathed. "He's like a DC superhero."

"Vortex, the Mystical Lawyer!" laughed Shane.

"The Litigator!" Autumn chimed in.

I tried to think of a funny name, but my brain was just too tired. We'd come a long way, Shane and I, from one coast to the other. We'd been up a long time.

"So what's next?" I yawned

"That's easy," said Autumn. "Food shopping."

"Food shopping?"

"Well up until now it's been just me, so I have nothing in the fridge. But right now, with four times as many people staying over…"

"Ah," Shane agreed. "Food shopping."

"Exactly."

"You got a Big 5 or a Walmart around here?" asked Shane. "Sounds like we'll need sleeping bags, too. Maybe a few pillows…"

"Now *that* we have," said Autumn.

"I wouldn't mind some extra snacks either," he added.

"Of course you wouldn't," I chuckled.

"Chips. Cookies. Ice cream. Maybe even those quarts with the hard chocolate shell on top. You know, the ones that you have to smash through with a spoon, or—"

"And we still need to fix your door," I pointed out. "So we'll stop at a hardware store too, if you have those."

"Pretty sure we have those," Autumn smirked.

It was a lot of fun, helping her. Being here for her when she needed us.

Flirting with her.

All of it, really. I barely knew this woman, but somehow I found myself wanting to solve Autumn Holloway's every problem. I wanted Shane and I to fix things for her. To get her life quickly back on track.

Just not *too* quickly, at least.

~ *19* ~

AUTUMN

We returned well after dusk with a car full of groceries, to a house glowing with light. No fewer than three delivery trucks were rolling away as we pulled in. No more than a half-dozen strange workers made their exit as we walked in, all of them wearing jumpsuits or uniforms of some kind.

"Thanks again."

Christian stood in the doorway, shaking the last man's hand. His tie was off, and his hands were dirty. Apparently he'd been helping do... something.

"What the—"

Upon entering, I stopped dead in my tracks. The kitchen lights were fixed, and so were the ones in the living area. Everything was brighter and better lit, but no less cozy.

"Is that a *couch?*"

I ran to the big leather sectional, dropping the bags that still dangled from both my tired hands. It looked so perfect I wanted to hug it. I wanted to hug *him.*

"Sorry, but I had my assistant pick from whatever they had in stock," he explained. "If you don't like it, it can always go back. But for now at least—"

"I love it!" I said, throwing my arms around him. "But you didn't have to. You didn't need to…"

"Are you kidding?" he chuckled. "The room was empty, the television way too small for the space." He shook his head. "If we're going to stay here, we may as well be comfortable."

My eyes shot upward. My jaw dropped down.

"You replaced my TV, too?!"

"Well, you still have the old one," Christian shrugged. "I just had it moved into one of the other rooms. I had beds brought up there too, including a replacement for yours."

My face registered pure shock, now. I was overwhelmed. It was too much at once.

"This place is amazing, by the way," he went on. "Do you have any idea of the history of this winery?"

I whirled at the sound of Darius and Shane, who'd just finished dumping their bags onto the table. Their eyes scanned the couch, the TV, and then instantly the front door. Thankfully, it was the one thing Christian hadn't touched. It was still broken.

"You got any tools?"

Numbly, I pointed to a cabinet.

"We bought new ones," Darius went on, "but dopey here forgot the wood glue." He tilted his chin in Shane's direction. "I guess we could make do with the 2-part epoxy for now, but what we really need to do is match the oak and cut out a replacement plug."

"Uhhh… sure."

He could've suggested tearing the house down and rebuilding it around the existing doorknob, my reaction would've been the same. I watched in disbelief as the three men went about fixing the door, putting away the groceries, and starting a fire. Christian and Shane brought in four loads of wood. Darius installed the door lock as well as a heavy-duty deadbolt that locked from the inside.

I had to admit, it felt so good to just not be alone. The whole place was brighter, warmer, cheerier — filled with laughter and conversation. It was everything I'd been missing for the past year.

Longer than that, I realized numbly.

Even the cat emerged, leaping onto the thick leather back of the new couch and settling in comfortably. He knew exactly what I knew; that for now at least, the place was no longer merely a dimly-lit abandoned winery. For the first time since I got here, it felt like a home.

"C'mere, cat."

If it was going to stick around, the animal would eventually need a name. While at the grocery store with the boys, I also broke down and decided it needed to eat and drink.

The cat watched me curiously as I pulled open a can of fish-flavored cat food and emptied it onto a paper plate. By the time I was filling the plastic water dish I'd just picked up, it had already leapt down and was eating ravenously.

"Church." Darius chuckled, pointing downward. "Doesn't it look like that cat from the Stephen King movie—"

"That's it!" I declared, snapping my fingers. "That's the name! Church!"

Together we watched the big gray devour its dinner and lick the plate clean. It positioned itself with its back to the cabinets though, so it could keep an eye on us while it ate.

"So are you going to call him that?" asked Darius.

"Should I?"

"I dunno," he warned. "The cat in that movie was evil. It ate people, didn't it?"

I shook my head. "I don't think so, but it definitely wasn't good. It tripped someone down the stairs, maybe. It's been a while since I—"

"Pssst! Felony!"

Darius bent at the knees, and slowly placed one hand on the floor. Extending the other, he offered one of the treats I'd bought, from a nearby foil pouch.

The cat ran right up and took it straight from his fingers.

"Felony, huh?" I chuckled.

"Didn't he break in here, along with your cousins?" Darius asked.

"I guess he did."

"Well there you go."

Very gently, he reached out to pet the cat as it ate. Somehow it let him. He gave it a second treat, then pulled me into a corner of the kitchen as the others fed the fire.

"Autumn..." he said gently. "Are you okay?"

Darius held me warmly by both shoulders. It was the first time we'd been physically close since California. The proximity of his body brought up all kinds of fond memories.

Slowly I nodded.

"Christian said the twins put their hands on you."

"Only one of them," I acknowledged. "Emmitt, I think."

I looked down reflexively at my bruised wrist, and Darius's eyes burned with a sudden anger. I smiled and patted his hand.

"It's okay," I told him. "They barely even—"

"It's *not* okay," he cut in sharply. "And we're going to fix this. One way or the other."

Those eyes flashed again, but this time I saw something else there. It was something dangerous. Something deadly.

"When we're finished with these cousins of yours, they're going to wish they never left Georgia," Darius growled. "And if they're not smart, they might never get back there, either."

It wasn't an idle threat — I knew that immediately. When it came to a man like Darius, his words weren't bravado.

"Until then," he said, edging just a little bit closer, "you're safe with us."

With that he placed his hand on my face, and kissed me tenderly.

Mmmmm...

The kiss was soft and hard at the same time. Tender and sweet, with the sexiest hint of raw, unchecked passion just behind that cool facade. I opened my mouth to kiss him back, and for a brief moment our tongues said hello again. The kiss ended just as abruptly as it began, leaving me hot and breathless and wanting more.

"I know this is a lot," I said, my voice practically a whisper. "I know you and Shane are busy, and I pulled you away from important things." As my eyes sought his, they were filled with gratitude. "But I'm really glad you're here."

He pulled me against him, this time cradling my face against his chest. Between the voices in the next room and the crackle of the fire, I felt truly happy. Safe. Fulfilled.

"Autumn…" Darius said, one hand moving up to stroke my hair.

"Right now, nothing is as important as *you*."

~ 20 ~

AUTUMN

I lay awake well after midnight, cozied up in an all-new bed with strange new sheets and blankets. Christian had similar beds delivered to three of the upstairs rooms, but had arranged for a king-sized mattress right here in the master. As a result, none of my existing linens fit. Not that I wasn't throwing them out, anyway.

Still, he was just so… so…

Presumptuous?

No, that wasn't the word. Christian just acted. He was a man ruled by logic, and compelled to finish as many tasks as possible in any given day. As a result, he just *did* things. Sometimes without regard for whether or not he should get outside input.

Still, I was grateful for all he'd done. We'd enjoyed the fire, ate some food, even watched some TV. I'd gone up to take a baptismally-hot shower, and come down to find the guys still lounging around, talking softly. It was incredibly strange to hear voices in the house, but the sound was music to my ears. By then, the guys were showing signs of exhaustion, though. I could see it in their eyes. They'd traveled far, they'd done a lot.

And all of it, for me.

I was still thinking about them when a gentle knock was followed by the sound of my bedroom door opening.

"H—Hello?"

I called out in a voice sleepier than I actually was.

"Hey. It's me."

I sat up as the door closed quietly, yet not all the way. Shane was standing there completely shirtless, the moonlight illuminating his tattoos in a way that gave them a beautiful purple hue.

"There's something wrong with my bed," he said quietly.

"What?"

"You're not in it."

I couldn't help but chuckle "Cute."

"I know, right? And I can't sleep. So…"

My eyes traveled with his body as he made his way to the edge of the bed. He wasn't just muscular, I realized. He was fiercely strong. I envisioned those sculpted arms, fighting through whatever nightmare campaigns he and Darius survived. Those thickly-coiled thighs, pumping hard. Marching their way across deserts and fields and—

"Shane…" I breathed softly, as he reached for me. "I —"

"You're coming to bed with me."

I didn't resist as he lifted me up. Then, without warning, he slung me right over one hard, broad shoulder. A supportive hand went to my ass, thick fingers spreading wide. They steadied me tightly against his body, as he padded back toward the hallway.

Holy FUCK…

The way he'd just *taken* me was so hot, so sexy. Such a fucking turn-on. As my sleep shirt rode up over my mostly-naked ass, the idea of what was about to happen had me soaking my thong.

This is crazy.

I'd fulfilled a dark, dirty, fantasy, but now that fantasy had followed me home. All of a sudden I had a house full of incredible lovers, each one hotter than the last. All of whom had taken me in ways that few men ever had.

And all of whom had taken me *together*, too.

I'd gone from fucking Christian to kissing Darius without batting an eyelash. And now Shane had carried me half-naked out of my bedroom. Just thrown me over his shoulder like some barbarian's prize, only to do God-knows-what with me.

Oh, please. You know exactly what.

We crossed the hall and pushed into his room, where I expected him to drop me unceremoniously onto the bed. Instead he fell backward, pulling me on top of him. Our bodies molded together. Our lips locked in a fiery, smoldering kiss.

He didn't even close the door!

That was the crazy part, really. The idea that these men had already had me, and therefore doors meant absolutely nothing. They could take me alone, together, wherever and whenever they wanted. My dry spell wasn't just over, it had been spectacularly ended. My sex life had gone from zero to five-hundred miles a fucking hour, and I wasn't about to utter a single word of complaint.

If only Kinsley could see the mess she'd created.

"This…" Shane murmured hotly into my mouth. A hand slid possessively between my thighs, eliciting a whimper as he cupped me. "This is *mine*."

By now my panties were drenched like I'd gone swimming in them. Shane rolled them off me like a bathing suit with his tattooed hands, and I never broke eye contact as I lifted my hips to oblige him.

"I was coming back for this no matter what," he whispered, as his mouth dropped between my outstretched thighs. He kissed the inside of one, then turned and did the other.

"You were, huh?" I teased.

My hands sifted his hair as he nodded, then planted a third kiss right on my button. The feel of his lips brushing my clit jolted me like an electric shock.

"There was never any doubt."

His tongue dove. My eyes crossed. I rolled my fingers into Shane's thick blond hair, pulling him deeper, screwing my hips downward as I craned my chin toward the ceiling. At the same time, he wrapped two powerful arms around the outside of my thighs and pulled.

Oh my fucking God…

I lolled back on the new pillow of this strange new bed, in this strange new room. None of it made any sense.

None of it had to. All I cared about was getting off; sighing in ecstasy against the hot mouth that was driving me absolutely insane. I wanted Shane as deep inside me as possible. I wanted to explode against that beautiful face, screaming against that thrashing tongue as I came and came and came some more.

And when I drenched us both, as I inevitably would, I wanted him to stay locked tightly against me. I wanted to drown this man, screw his face, and scream his name. I wanted him to drink every last drop of me, all the way down. And when he was done, I wanted to kiss myself off his gorgeously stubbled face.

One mind-erasing orgasm later, I got my wish.

I was still reeling from climaxing so hard, still kissing those wet, beautiful lips when Shane once again pulled me on top of him. His boxers were comically tented outward. Beneath the thin fabric lay a *massive* hard-on, just begging to be free.

"Your turn."

Shane grunted as he pulled them off, and together we looked down. The man was gifted, that much was obvious. He had one of those dicks that started out thick and then thinned a little before getting fat again, just beneath the head. And this one got *really* fat. So fat that I could already feel it buried inside me, and the feeling was seriously fucking amazing.

"*Fuck*, Shane."

I grabbed it and pulled it toward my eager lips, but Shane had other ideas. Instead he fell backward onto the bed again, pulling me right alongside him. He twisted me sideways, spooned right against my trembling legs, and entered me from behind…

Hhhhhhooooolllly shit.

127

One thick forearm went around my waist, pulling me tight. And then we were FUCKING. Bucking and screwing and banging against each other, as we wasted no time getting right into it.

"Shane…"

His new bed came without a headboard, and I was thankful for that. As it was, we were rocking the frame against the wall. Pounding it rhythmically against the plaster with every gloriously deep thrust, as my soft, round ass perfectly concaved itself into his body.

I could feel the strength of his fingers; splayed against my belly. The flexing and unflexing of his wonderfully ripped abdominals, surging beneath me. Shane drilled me deeply, comfortably, kissing every inch of my exposed neck as I reached back to cradle his face against mine. One hand moved up to cup and knead my breast. I clasped it tightly against me, gasping for air as he continued to rock my world.

I was sighing, moaning, breathing his name as he fucked me. And all throughout, Shane was speaking unspeakable things in my ear. They were dirty things. Incredible things. Things that made me want them so badly, so guiltily, that soon I was squeezing myself tightly around him again.

My rapture was exquisite in its totality. I was sleepy, euphoric, sated; all at once. We rocked for what seemed like forever, as my mind swam slowly through a warm ocean of sweet, delicious dopamine. And all throughout: the kissing, the touching, the flexing of my quivering thighs as he pounded me even harder. I was saying his name. Crying it into the stillness of this once-empty room, which was now absurdly filled with heat and passion and the combined scents of our sex.

I didn't realize I'd gotten too loud, I only knew there

was a hand over my mouth. Shane's palm was thick and warm and turning me on. I bit down it, snaking my tongue through his fingers. Those fingers went into my mouth as I whimpered and moaned around them, all while grinding and screwing and ——

"I knew it."

My eyes flew open. Standing in the open doorway, Darius had both hands on either side of the jamb

"I fucking *knew* it."

We froze for a moment, our bodies still lying side by side. Shane was still spooning me, still buried inside me. His fingers were still in my mouth.

And then, almost simultaneously, we began fucking each other again.

Darius paused, shook his head, then placed his hands on hips. His eyes followed our every movement.

My stomach did a barrel roll as he began peeling his shirt off.

~ 21 ~

AUTUMN

I'd never had jelly-legs before. I certainly had them now as I stumbled across the hall, holding onto both walls for support. My thighs were impossibly tight, my legs, trembling like mad. The near complete disconnect between my brain and my feet was disconcerting. I could barely walk.

"Need some help?"

The voice was low and maybe even a little sarcastic. It wasn't Shane's because I'd put Shane to bed shortly after he and his friend finished fucking me half to death. They'd held me down, and taken turns on me. And then they'd used me together.

"You can't even get back to your own bedroom, can you?"

The voice didn't belong to Darius either, because I'd just left his room. But not before another half-hour of breaking in *his* bed. I'd climaxed so many times I'd lost count.

"Alright, c'mon."

Two arms scooped me against a warm chest,

mercifully ending my struggle. I snaked my arms around Christian's corded neck and sighed.

"Thank you."

It was all I could say. It was all he required. The big lawyer looked down on me somewhat mischievously, then carried me into the bedroom.

His bedroom.

What the actual fuck, Autumn...

Before California, I'd gone almost a year without sex. And without good sex? Even longer than that. Sure, I had a couple of friends-with-benefits; a leftover ex, plus a guy or two I'd hooked up with. But it was never satisfying. The way things went, it always seemed like they were getting most of the benefits. And for that disappointing reason alone, I'd pretty much stopped making those calls altogether.

But now? Now I'd taken a rocket-launcher to the doors of my self-imposed celibacy. And I'd blown those doors clean off.

The room was dark and cool, and the door clicked as Christian closed it behind us. I held onto him for support as he laid me gently into his bed. Absurdly, it was an exact duplicate of the other two I'd just left, right down to the pillows and linens.

"Are you mad?"

I murmured the words sleepily as he stared down at me. I scanned his expression for even the slightest hint of disappointment.

"At you? Hell no." Smiling gently, he jerked his head toward the hallway. "And it's not like Batman and Robin did anything I wouldn't have done."

The bed creaked beneath his weight as he slid in beside me, and pulled the blankets over us both. Almost immediately we became a face-to-face tangle of arms and legs and hands and feet.

Christian and I stared at each other for a while, nose to nose, as our eyes adjusted to the darkness. Eventually, he planted a single kiss on my lips.

"Tell me something," he murmured softly.

"Sure. Anything."

"Tell me about your parents."

My parents. It was a common question, of course. It's not every day someone loses both parents at once, and this wasn't a car accident or a plane crash, this was a fucking *avalanche*. As such, the story was a lot more interesting. But it was no less hard to tell, whenever people asked.

And they always, *always* asked.

Still, Christian knew all this already. He'd admittedly done research on me. He knew exactly when and where I'd lost my mother and father, and he knew the circumstances surrounding the accident. He wasn't asking what happened to my family, he was asking *about* them. Cozied up beneath the growing warmth of his blankets and sheets, that meant everything to me.

"Please don't think I'm pressing you," he added in a whisper. "If you don't want to—"

"You know how some people should never have kids?" I interrupted.

Christian nodded on his pillow. His stubble was thick, this late at night. It made his face even rougher and more masculine than it already was.

132

"Well, my parents were like that. I think I was probably an accident. They would never admit it, of course. But when I was born I sort of cramped their style."

"Having kids tends to do that," he agreed.

"True, but some parents are ready for it. They want it, or they embrace it once it happens. My parents... well, I think they *endured* it more than anything else."

I paused, and his eyes searched mine. There was empathy there, but no pity.

"So you don't think they loved you?"

"Oh they loved me," I admitted, "but in their own way. My parents first love was each other, and their second love was travel. I never saw them fight. Not even once. They loved each other so much it was almost sickening, which might be why I was sort of relieved when they finally took off."

Thinking back, I could remember the exact day. The very hour, minute, and second they deemed me 'old enough' to look after myself.

"When they were around they always included me, of course," I went on. "And like I said, they loved me in their own way. But it was more of a pride thing. Teaching me to ski at two and a half years old. Snowboarding a year later. They dragged me from slope to slope with them, but were even more thrilled when I could stay home and take over the shop. It meant they could finally start taking off again, all over the world."

"And how old were you?"

"Fifteen. Barely."

Christian's mouth curled up on one side. "And you had the house to yourself?"

"Sure did."

"As a teenager, that must've been fun."

"You'd think so," I sighed, "but I had to go to school, I had soccer practice, and I had grades to keep up. And of course, the shop. We had a part-timer covering for the early shift, but I'd spend practically every evening there, closing the place out."

Christian shifted his great body beneath the blankets. Our bare legs scissored together in ways that were so intimate, so personal, it was like we'd done this a thousand times. I couldn't remember the last time I'd felt this comfortable with someone.

"It's not fair that they did that, you know."

Somewhere under the sheets, his hand found mine.

"You were still a kid. That wasn't right."

I bit my lip and nodded. "I know, but I forgive them for it. After all, they were generally good parents. They were always positive, they were encouraging..."

"They also weren't there."

He squeezed my fingers. I shrugged and smiled.

"I have to admit, I was a little shocked when they took off. At first I laughed at how little they needed me, but eventually realized they only needed each other. My heart hurt like hell when they were gone, though. They were all I had, as far as family." I tried to chuckle, but couldn't. "Shit, I don't even think I know what that word means."

The hand squeezing my fingers moved upward to caress the side of my face. I closed my eyes, enjoying the feel. There was such tenderness behind his cool facade. A serene gentleness; behind his strength.

"Family," Christian breathed, "is something I'm still struggling with myself."

I swallowed, letting my eyes flutter open. "You said you had a sister, didn't you?"

"Anna," he nodded.

"Are you close?"

His expression went somewhat grim. "We should be a lot closer," he said guiltily. "It's my fault that we aren't."

"And what about your parents? Do you—"

The finger against my lips was gentle, but it did the trick. Still staring into my eyes, Christian exhaled a long, deep breath. He reached out tenderly, to tuck an errant lock of hair back behind my ear.

"Another time," he said softly.

I didn't have to nod, or agree, or say anything else. No words were needed between us. There were only actions, emotions, feelings. An ocean of what I took to be shared experiences, that we'd been sailing on for perhaps most of our lives.

Leaning forward, I kissed him softly, right on his pretty-boy mouth. I did it again, then a third time, and then suddenly I just couldn't stop.

Christian responded by coming alive, his arms flexing powerfully, pulling my body into his. Our clothing was gone. His shaft was a heavy piston, pinned snugly between us as he rolled me onto my back

It was nothing for him to nudge my thighs apart, and drive it home.

~ 22 ~

AUTUMN

Darius was the first one down the stairs. I plied him with coffee as he slid into his chair, then went back to folding the eggs.

"Morning, sunshine."

I looked up to find Shane, yawning as he stretched his arms toward the vaulted ceiling. Christian was right behind him, somehow already showered and dressed. Beneath their cheery facades, all three men still looked somewhat exhausted. And with good reason.

"How do you like your bacon?" I asked, spinning back to the stove.

All three liked it chewy. Which was good, because crispy bacon kinda sucked.

The biscuits I found in the fridge came out of the new toaster oven I'd also discovered this morning, and I put them on the table next to the butter. There were sausage links too, and hash browns I'd made from scratch. I'd had quite a busy morning. That tended to happen when you were so excited you could barely sleep, and started slamming coffee around four-thirty am.

"Did you all have fun last night?" I asked casually.

The looks around the table were awkward. The men glanced at each other, then down at their plates, no one really sure what to say.

"Did everybody have a good time?"

Still no answer. Not that I expected one.

"Great!" I said cheerily, as I slid the last of the food onto the table. I removed the cover from a platter of lukewarm pancakes with a flourish. "Now let's get a few things straight, before I'm crippled."

Their eyes had been collectively following the plume of fragrant steam coming off the pancakes. But now those eyes were on me.

"After what happened last night, you'd think I'd be telling the three of you to cool it," I began. "That I'm going to say things like 'this is wrong' or 'we can't keep doing this' or some other protest along those lines."

I fell into my chair, and began scooping eggs onto each of their plates. When I was finished, I slid whatever was left onto my own.

"Actually, I'm here to tell you just the opposite."

Piercing the fluffiest part of the eggs, I popped some into my mouth. After chewing a few times, I pointed my fork at them.

"We can have all the fun you want, but you boys are gonna have to pace yourselves," I told them. "Because otherwise, I'm going to be walking crooked."

Their comical looks of dismay were so funny, so perfect, I wished I could take a picture. Instead, I snapped one mentally in my mind.

"You're not... ummm..."

"Mad?" I ventured. "Upset?"

Darius nodded. "I guess so, yeah."

"At what?" I shrugged, reaching for the syrup. "We're all adults, here, right? We all knew what we were getting into right from the night of the auction. And it's not like we're doing anything we haven't already done back in California." I glanced at Shane and added a sly wink. "Well, except that *one* thing, but who's really keeping score?"

Shane's handsome mouth curled into a grin as I finished pouring the syrup. I handed it off to Darius, who took it out of reflex more than anything else.

"Look, last night was pretty fucking amazing," I said matter-of-factly. "What girl wouldn't love it? And to tell you the truth, I need this. Hell, I've been needing it for a long time, I just didn't know it."

"This..." Christian said numbly. He twirled a finger at all three of them in turn. "You want—"

"Yes," I confirmed, cutting into my pancakes. "And why shouldn't I?"

He didn't have an answer. Eventually the lawyer shrugged his big shoulders.

"You boys flew all the way out here to help me," I went on. "You dropped everything. You gave up your lives. And it wasn't just one of you that did this, it was all three. You need to know how much I appreciate that."

I finished cutting my pancakes. Setting the fork and

knife down, I folded my hands beneath my chin.

"It's only fair you let me *show* you," I grinned.

I might've looked cool and confident, but my internal temperature must've been a thousand degrees! I'd clasped my hands together only to keep them from trembling. My heart was a secret jackhammer, thundering away deep in my chest.

"So you're saying we can just *have* you," Shane folded his arms. "All of us."

"Oh yes."

"Anytime we want you" added Darius.

I nodded. "Anytime."

"And *anywhere* we want you," Christian spoke up.

"Sure," I grinned evilly. "In your bed, on the floor, up against the wall. You can have me right on this table if you want me," I added sweetly, tapping it with my fingernail. "I'm going to finish breakfast first, though."

I picked up my fork again, trying to fight back the growing wetness between my legs. This was crazy! Totally reckless and absurd! And yet...

And yet I couldn't stop thinking about fucking all three of them, and being pinned between their hard bodies. Crossing the hallway in the dead of night, on legs that trembled. Hopping from bed to bed to bed.

I needed more of Shane's wonderful cock, of Darius's incredible kisses. Of Christian's slow, deep lovemaking, stroking my face with the backs of his fingers as he drilled me into sweet oblivion. And most of all, I wanted them *together*, doing me at once. Sharing me. Tag-teaming me. Spitroasting me hotly from both ends, just as they'd done last night.

I wanted all three of these men to use my body until they were pulsing and throbbing inside me, flooding my womb. I wanted to sigh happily as they shoved each other out of the way, so the next one could take his turn.

There were no limits to my depravity, apparently. No boundaries to how badly I wanted to be used by them.

I wanted to be their own personal toy.

The sound of a chair scraping the floor shocked me back to the moment at hand, and suddenly I was being pulled to my feet and deeply, soulfully kissed. Darius's lips moved slowly, rotating against mine. They took my breath away, but not for long as I was soon passed into Shane's firm, unyielding arms.

Ohhhhh…

His friend kissed me with just as much heat and fire, holding me with a fierceness and possessiveness that was both exhilarating and a tiny bit frightening. Reluctantly he gave me over to Christian, who kissed me so hotly my legs physically buckled.

He was still holding me up as my gaze drifted over his shoulder and out the window. Still reeling from the heat, half in a dream-state, Shane's voice seemed very distant and far away.

"You *sure* you want to do this?" he was asking with a smirk. "Because I'm not sure we'll be able to hold back very much. Especially when you're walking around with—"

"No…"

My voice silenced him immediately. But it wasn't Shane I was talking to.

"Oh my God, NO!"

I extracted myself from Christian's arms and ran to the big window. Horror gripped me. Both hands went to my mouth, as my eyes confirmed what my heart already knew to be true.

From end to end, the entire first row of my vineyard had been cut down.

~ 23 ~

CHRISTIAN

A tear rolled down Autumn's face as she sifted through the piles of greenery at our feet. Clipped-off tops of the grape trees lay everywhere. Tiny buds there only just emerging, that would now never grow.

"Fuckers!"

They'd done it to the frontmost row, too; the one closest to the window. They could've chosen anywhere else in the vineyard, a place that would've been more secretive and less risky. But this was meant to be spiteful. They'd wanted to send a message.

"I'll kill them both!"

We let her rage for a while, but it's not like we could've stopped her. Autumn swore like a drunken sailor as she stomped up and down the long row of neatly, but savagely-clipped shrubs. She touched jagged tips them one by one, as if she could somehow bring them back.

"They did all this with clippers and hand-saws," Shane growled, shaking his head. "It must've taken them hours."

Autumn whirled. "And we didn't *hear* them?"

"I guess we were busy," he shrugged, albeit a bit guiltily. "Or maybe it was afterward, when we all slept like the dead."

She didn't look happy, but she accepted his answer. It was the truth, of course. Whether any of us liked it or not.

"They were quiet this time," said Darius. "But next time they wont care. They could come back here with Sawzalls and cut down half the field before we could get out and stop them."

Autumn looked suddenly fear. "What the hell's a Sawzall?"

"Never mind," Shane stepped in. He shot his friend a scathing look. "That's not going to happen."

I wished I could be as sure as he was, but I wasn't. It sounded like a bunch of false hope. Autumn clung to it temporarily anyway, in lieu of anything better.

"Why would they *do* this?" she eventually pleaded. "Why destroy the place if you're trying to take possession of it?"

"Because maybe they don't want the winery at all," Darius offered. "Do you have any idea of the price of real estate out here? If I were them, I'd subdivide it and sell off the land. Builders around here would slit each other's throats for the chance to—"

"That's not possible," I interjected.

Both contractors turned to look at me, ready to bludgeon me with their expert opinions. I headed them off.

"Most of the farms on the north and south fork are protected parcels. Like this one, they're zoned for agricultural use only. You can't build on them."

Shane raised a blond eyebrow. "You checked?"

"Yes."

Darius nodded and scratched at the back of his neck. "Well, shit. Maybe they don't know that."

"I wouldn't expect them to," I agreed. "We're not dealing with the sharpest knives in the drawer." I shrugged and turned toward Autumn. "It's not going to stop them, though. Especially if they think it'll drive you away."

"Burning this place to the ground wouldn't drive me away," she barked back at me. "I'd sleep on the still-warm ashes."

The look in her eyes convinced me she absolutely would. Autumn stormed off defiantly, to double-check the rest of the vineyard. Although we'd already gone down the rows and columns together, I couldn't blame her.

"Cameras," Darius declared. "We're gonna need cameras."

"And where would you put them?" I looked back at him placatingly. "Up near the house? Out by the entrance?"

He shot me a dirty look. "Both, I guess."

"Would you install them in each row? Every column? Where would the power come from? Are you going to run extension cords, or—"

"If we have to, yes," growled Shane. He took a couple of steps toward me. "What is it with you? I thought you were on our side?"

"I am," I shrugged. "I'm just the only one being realistic."

"Realistic?"

"You're not going to be able to cover an entire vineyard with 4k cameras," I reasoned. "And they *would* have to be 4k if you wanted to get an actual picture you could rely on. Not to mention high-definition night vision. The expense alone would be ludicrous."

"Even so…"

"And who's going through hundreds of hours of footage every morning?" I piled on. "You? Me? The four of us?" I shook my head. "It's not going to happen. She has a business to run."

We watched together as Autumn wandered back into view on the other side of the vineyard. She was on a slight rise, looking down. Perhaps mentally sifting through all the work she had ahead of her, in the near future.

"Look, cameras are good if you want to learn who's committing a crime, but we already know who the culprits are," I told them. "Even if we had proof, do you think we could just run to the police and show them the footage? Spend all our time getting people to look at our recordings, and then wait several months, possibly years, for 'justice'?"

The pill was a bitter one. But they both swallowed it.

"Fine," Darius relented. "What do *you* suggest?"

"We find these assholes, rather than wait for their next bullshit move. We take this fight to their turf, where it'll actually make a difference."

Shane whistled low, and slapped his friend in the chest. "I told you this guy was alright."

"Until then, we drop cameras out near the road and up by the house," I said. "Good equipment, too. Motion sensors that only turn on when something's happening. That way we can monitor it real-time, and hope for the best."

The two men were side by side now, nodding appreciatively. They wanted the same things I did.

"Most important of all though," I pointed into the distance, "we need to keep her safe. We don't let her out of our sight. Not even when she goes into town."

"*Especially* when she goes into town," said Darius.

"Yeah," Shane agreed. "Who knows what they'll do next?"

She was walking one of the rows now, arms outstretched, touching the plants on either side of her. There was something about her dedication to this place that moved me. Yes, I wanted to help her, to hold her, to make her safe. But I also wanted to be the part of something bigger. I found myself wanting the same things she did.

"So we agree?" I asked aloud. "We're all in this together, for as long as it takes?"

Shane folded his arms across his chest. Darius nodded.

"Looks that way, law man."

I'd been frustrated and even disappointed to see them, especially when they first got here. But now, I was slowly coming around to the idea that these weren't ordinary men. Shane Lockhart had served as a scout and forward reconnaissance observer, while Darius Knight spent six years as an Army medic for the same 2nd Cavalry Regiment. They'd gone deep into enemy territory together, and been called in with fire teams to hold impossible positions. Usually, while vastly outnumbered.

The two of them had been through a hell of lot together, according to the files I'd been provided. They had skills that could help keep Autumn safe, and from what I could see, they cared about her, too. Maybe every bit as much as I did.

And for that, I was grateful for their presence.

~ 24 ~

AUTUMN

"And that was really the name of the shop? Extreme Sports with three 'X's in front?"

"Yup."

Guiding us through a right-hand turn, Darius chuckled merrily. "Didn't you parents realize that in an internet search—"

"We'd look like a porn site?"

"Yeah. That."

I shook another round of M&M's into my palm. "No, definitely not. The internet was still in its infancy, and my parents were the furthest thing from computer people. Besides, everything had a 'www' in front of it back then."

I popped the candies into my mouth and used my tongue to push them into my cheeks. It was something I'd done since I was a little girl. I enjoyed letting them all melt into a delicious chocolate mush, rather than crunching down on them.

"Still, you'd be shocked at how many people came in

looking for dirty movies, lingerie, vibrating dildos…"

"Did you have any vibrating dildos?" Darius asked slyly.

"None that I was sharing, no."

He smiled, and his perfect white teeth glowed against those full, kissable lips. Memories of those lips danced in my head. They made my stomach flutter.

"I still don't understand why you'd limit yourselves to extreme sports though," said Darius. "Rather than carrying stuff for every sport."

He was wearing his tight black shirt again — the one that rode up high on his arms. Darius was driving with one of those arms out the window, and every flex of his biceps and triceps distracted me.

"Do you remember the big X-rush when we were kids?" I asked, recovering my train of thought. "X-Games, Snowboarding, Shaun White?"

"Yes, actually. I used to love when they flipped the snowmobiles off ramps and stuff."

"Well my parents cashed in on all that, back when it was huge," I explained. "They got the jump on things. The shop made a whole pile of money in those early years; enough to keep them on an almost-permanent vacation later on."

He brought his arm inside the vehicle momentarily and slicked his hair back before returning it outside. The sunlight kissed his tan skin like an experienced lover.

"Your parents sound sooo radical," he joked.

I nodded. "They sure thought they were. Throughout my childhood, they threw every one of their hobbies at me, too. None of them really stuck, though."

"My parents only threw insults and shoes at us," Darius said with a smile.

"Shoes?"

"It's an Italian thing, I think," he explained. "Whenever we did something wrong, my mother could slip out of a shoe and whip it down the hallway faster than my siblings and I could ever run. The best you could hope for was that she missed." He winced, remembering. "But misses were rare."

I couldn't hide my smile. "Did it hurt?"

"Oh, fuck yeah," he asserted. "Even the slippers were deadly. Once she got Gemma square in the ear, and it bled for an hour. After that, she only threw at the boys."

I blinked in incredulity. "How many of you were there?"

"Six. Well, seven including my cousin who came to live with us when he was twelve." He turned to look at me. "See, my uncle went to jail for a while. And my aunt was... well..."

"Don't worry about it," I assured him. "You don't have to explain it."

"Nah, it's alright." Darius cleared his throat. "My aunt sort of had a mental breakdown, and she went away for a few months. By the time she got back she could barely take care of herself, much less a kid."

"That sucks."

"Yeah, but she was always around, and we always included her. Plus it was nice, growing up with my cousin."

Darius grinned and I smiled back at him, glad for the semi-happy ending. It was good to have the windows down. The wind felt great in my hair.

Look at him, I couldn't help but think to myself. *He's so fucking sexy.*

Darius continued driving us to our mystery destination, and I continued letting my mind happily wander. The three of them had been here for a week, as of yesterday. In that time, the boys had fully taken me up on my offer. Both day and night, they'd used me anywhere and everywhere. And in every possible way.

Instead of pacing themselves though, they'd only amped the sexual energy up. And rather than slow them down, I found myself encouraging them to go even harder. The scope of my own libido was the one unknown in this whole sordid equation, and it was also the one thing I hadn't counted on. It turned out that the more I got, the more I wanted. And the more I wanted, the more I *took.*

It got to the point of absolute craziness, where I was jumping them whenever I got the urge. Like right now, for instance. Darius's chest and arms looked so good in that shirt, it reminded me of how much better they'd look without it. I could undo my seatbelt right now and start climbing all over him. I could be kissing his neck, squeezing those arms. Rubbing that warm, shifting knot between his legs, until it grew so thick and hard he'd have to pull over and fuck me.

I'd had a whole week of unbelievable sex, but also a week of companionship. I had people to wake up to. People to feed, and eat alongside, and laugh with at the end of the day. The boys helped me enormously with my daily chores, and as a result the whole winery was flourishing. They'd cleaned the place out and begun fixing it up. They'd even started on the enormous main bar my uncle had apparently planned and gotten permits for. The blueprints had been filed with the town. They'd gone down and gotten them, without me even asking.

Every day I woke up in a strange new bed that was becoming less and less strange, next to one or more lovers that were growing more familiar. Christian disappeared for the better part of each day, meeting up with associates and lawyers and only God knew who else. He'd found the petition to challenge my uncle's will, filed recently by my would-be cousins. He was also busy working on a countersuit that he hoped would scare them right back to Georgia.

Shane and Darius spent all day doing what they were apparently born to do: fixing things with their bare hands. Sometimes those things even included me, and we rutted happily throughout the day. I felt slightly guilty Christian wasn't getting any afternoon fun, so I tried making it up to him at night. I'd slip into his bed at all different hours, and bring him alive in my mouth. I loved getting him all nice and hard before climbing on top and straddling him; riding that thick shaft slowly up and down to a sleepy, satisfied orgasm.

At night one of us usually cooked something, because we were too tired to go out. We'd light a fire, then lounge around on the big leather sectional, watching television while trading foot-rubs. I usually got rubbed in some more strategic places as well, but whatever happened beneath the blankets stayed beneath the blankets.

So far we hadn't encountered Emmitt or Edward again, which was both a good and a bad thing. Because while setting up cameras might've scared them temporarily away, it also meant we couldn't find or confront them. If they were still here on Long Island, they were apparently well-hidden, and the handful of favors Christian cashed in to find them hadn't turned up anything so far.

Still, the nights passed uneventfully — at least beyond the confines of my four cozy walls. There were no more incidents in the winery. Nothing else in the way of sabotage.

Every moment I had with the boys was serene and magical, with nothing to distract us from focusing on the winery... as well as each other.

Darius, Shane, and Christian called their companies back in California often enough, but they also trusted the people running them. I knew they couldn't stay here forever though, as much as I wanted them to. It was hard to imagine going back to an empty house, or climbing into a cold, lonely bed each night. I'd been spoiled. Pampered. Maybe even totally fucking ruined, all by—

"Ah, here we go," Darius announced happily.

The car turned again, this time into a large gravel parking lot, then rolled to a stop. A pleasant, woody scent filled my nostrils, both familiar and nostalgic.

"Why are we at a lumberyard?"

"It's a milling yard, really," Darius replied. He hopped out, ran around to my side, and opened the door for me. Chivalry might be on life support, but it apparently wasn't dead.

"What are we doing here, though?"

He pointed, and to my surprise I saw Shane standing with another man. They were on the display side of the yard, dwarfed by a long row of thick wooden planks that I recognized as oak, pine, mahogany...

"If we're going to finish the bar in your tasting room," he said simply. "You'll need to pick slabs."

~ 25 ~

AUTUMN

The vines were blooming, at least in this part of the vineyard. Not with pretty flowers, but with bright green buds that would eventually be grapes.

They smelled no less amazing than actual flowers, however.

I was far from the house, deep into the lush green rows and columns. The vine map I'd inherited with the place listed the names and regions that each column of vines had originally come from. Some bloomed early, some late. Some needed moderately dry soil, while others needed three times the normal amount of water.

The entire operation was overwhelming, when you looked it at as a whole. But once you broke it down section by section, you started to see a method to the original designer's madness.

I bent low to check the next portion of the micro-irrigation system. Something was clogging one of the drip lines, because from a certain point onward, this particular column of shrubs was getting very little water. The frustrating part was that I'd just had the system overhauled a few weeks ago. Yet despite multiple calls, they couldn't get someone out to look at it again until 'the end of the week'.

Way off in the distance, the sound of an electric saw screamed again. Darius and Shane had been woodworking for most of the day. I would've gone to see what they were up to, but a few days ago they'd put up a thick plastic curtain across the front of the tasting room. Whatever they were building in there, they wanted to surprise me.

For anyone else, that would've been cute and exciting. In reality, it only made me anxious. There were very few things I didn't like to take charge of; a habit that very often acted as a double-edged sword.

I just loved the fact that I was finally willing to give up control.

My hands slid downward, hefting the irrigation line, checking its weight. I wasn't exactly sure what I was looking for. But I knew that if I didn't manage to—

"Ohhhhhh!"

I jumped as a corded arm slid around my waist from behind. I recognized its thickness, its possessiveness, as an oversized hand pulled me tightly against a hard, familiar body.

"Jesus, Christian…" I breathed in relief, reaching back for him. "You scared me!"

Christian came and went as he pleased, so none of us ever knew when he was bound to show up. This morning for example, he'd left before any of us were even up. And now here he was, deep in the vineyard. Sneaking up behind me, as I bent over the rows.

His warm mouth closed sensuously over one side of

my neck. The kisses he planted there were hot lightning, rocketing through me.

"I— I didn't know you were back."

His hands slid over both globes of my ass, then shot commandingly forward. I was wearing my oldest pair of jeans, ripped in several places along the thighs and back. The ones with the button-fly in front, that was always way too tight.

As his eager fingers were finding out right now.

"Fuck," he grunted in frustration.

He kissed me harder, more furiously, as I grinded backward and into him. His dick was beyond hard. He must've been worked up for quite a while now, because even through his slacks he felt outright massive.

"Here…" I reached down, closing my hands over his. "Let me help—"

Before I could do anything, Christian's fingers found the holes in the back of my jeans. He pulled upward and outward, tearing them to shreds. Grunting hotly, he ripped them even more, creating a giant hole that exposed my entire, thong-covered ass.

HOLY—

The sheer violence coupled with the sound of fabric rending made me instantly wet. As the cooler air kissed my bare ass, I stood there trembling, my shredded jeans hanging down by my knees in tatters. Our eyes moved in tandem to glance back at my tiny, white lace panties.

"You can rip those too," I said breathlessly.

"Yeah?"

"Yeah. Fuck it."

I shivered as thick fingers brushed my mound, followed by a firm tug and a loud SNAP. I wasn't just wet now, I was totally drenched.

Holy fucking shit.

Christian's hands closed so brutally over my hips that I practically melted. He stepped out of his slacks, pressed his naked thighs against mine, and pushed straight into me.

MY GOD...

He felt huge. Swollen. Absolutely enormous. His hands screwed into my flesh. His fingers dug just deep enough that I let out a shuddering, whimpering gasp.

"Fuck me."

I didn't need to tell him anything of the sort. Christian bent me forward at the waist, waiting only until I had both hands firmly grasping the thickest part of the vine in front of me. Then he pulled all the way out... and came crashing back into me.

"FUCK!"

I squeezed my eyes shut and bit my lip, but nothing could take me out of this moment. Christian pistoned in and out of me, railing me hard, burying his beautifully-thick manhood so deep I could feel it against my tender womb. His hands went to my shoulders, and then into my hair. Pulling it back, arching my chin toward the sky, he drove into me faster and faster, screwing me with a vengeance that had my crying out in a mixture of fear and happiness.

Ohmyfuckkkk—

There was nothing I could do but screw back at him, as he fucked me deeply and savagely from behind. This wasn't doggie-style, it was way more animalistic. This wasn't simply screwing or fucking, it was something on a whole different level. Something raw and unrefined and totally primal.

I was gripping the vine so tightly I wondered if I might snap it in two. But I didn't care. I was egging him on, screaming for joy. The harder he pulled my hair the harder I screwed my ass back against those iron-like thighs, taking him even deeper. Urging him to use me in exactly the way he'd probably been imagining for most of the day.

He fucked me so hard we fell to our knees, then onto our sides. And through it all, Christian never left me. He kept pounding me as I slumped backward against him, fucking me sideways, lifting one leg so he could scissor me deeply, as I craned my neck to look at him. And then we were kissing, while staring into each other's eyes. Rolling and grinding and fucking like animals in the wet grass, as the shreds of my ruined jeans danced against my smooth, bare thighs.

The scene was beautifully perfect. Sexy as fuck. And just when I couldn't take another second without climaxing around him, Christian grabbed my face so I couldn't look away. He stared into me... *through* me. My lips parted in breathless shock as he took me to all new heights of pure emotional connection, staring into my soul as I spasmed euphorically around his thrusting, surging body.

And then just as I was coming down, he finally lost it. I saw all measure of control in his expression drop away. His lip curled, his eyes unfocused, and his whole body went rigid.

I had to admit, it made me feel strangely powerful for those initial few seconds.

"Come..." I smiled, tracing his face with my finger.

Christian pulled out at the last possible moment, shooting the first two spurts all over both my holes. He continued spraying them hotly, gripping his shaft to smear it all around. Everything was so wet and wild, so crazy and sticky and warm. And then all of a sudden... he pushed.

There was a flash of pain, followed immediately by an intense heat and sinful pleasure. Pointing himself directly between my asscheeks, he'd slid right in.

All the way in.

My eyes flared. My mouth dropped open. Christian's lips curled into a satisfied grin as he continued throbbing and pulsing, finishing out the rest of his orgasm while buried balls-deep in my ass.

It was the hottest, dirtiest thing I'd ever seen. But it was also the most incredible.

His body remained molded to mine for what seemed like a very long time, as together we rode out every last ounce of pleasure between us. Eventually, our breathing slowed. Christian extracted himself from me, and pushed his way back to his feet.

"This is my new favorite part of the vineyard," he said, pulling up his pants.

I was lying there in the grass in literal tatters, my jeans and panties shredded beyond all hope. Down below, I was throbbing all over. Christian's seed was leaking from my most sacred of places, and running down the insides of my two trembling thighs.

"Meet up at the house when you can," he called over his shoulder, as he buckled his belt. "I've got news."

~ 26 ~

SHANE

"So they're renting a house, a little ways from here. Airbnb. It's about five miles east, near the inlet."

The lawyer pointed to a map on the digital tablet in front of us. He pinch-zoomed onto a specific street, but with everything so flat, the streets all looked the same to me.

"How do you know?" Darius demanded.

"Because I trust my sources," said Christian. "And my sources tell me—"

"Yes, but how do your *sources* know?"

The lawyer threw me an annoyed look. I only shrugged.

"Fine, I've got people monitoring and downloading the video feeds from the cameras we set up," he said. "One reported back to me that the same gray Chevy Silverado was seen slowing down as it passed the winery on three separate occasions." He reached into a folder and pulled something out. "On one of those occasions, someone leaned out the window in an attempt to examine the cameras."

We all watched as he spun a blown-up photo across the table. The monotone, night vision print was sharp enough that Edward was clearly visible.

"How many people do you have working for you," Darius swore.

"Enough."

He shook his head. "Who the hell *are* you? Super Lawyer?"

"The truck had Georgia plates," Christian went on without missing a beat. "They were followed to this address, right here."

I picked up the photo for a moment, then put it down. It was pretty fucking conclusive.

"Well shit," I swore. "Why didn't you just show us this in the first place?"

The lawyer paused before shifting his gaze guiltily to Autumn.

"I didn't want to frighten her."

Our host didn't appear amused. She looked a bit frazzled, though, or rather, bedraggled. She'd been out in the rows all day, working on the vines. For some odd reason she had grass in her hair, and all over her shirt.

Curiously, she'd also changed into sweatpants.

"You didn't want to *frighten* me?" Autumn demanded.

"Yes, well—"

"These assholes break into my house, trying to take over my place," she swore furiously. "They cut down part of my vineyard. They slept in my bed. They even saddled me with a cat…"

She swiped an arm in the direction of the nearby counter. The cat was just sitting there, swatting its tail.

"And somehow you still want to protect my *feelings?*"

Christian glanced down for an awkward moment, then glanced to us for help. The look in our eyes told him there wouldn't be any.

"Listen, this lone wolf bullshit is over," I told him. If you're not going to share your intel, none of this is going to work. We're in this together, remember? All four of us."

"Yeah," he sighed finally. "Okay."

"So what else?"

"I'm working on getting them a permanent tail," he said. "For now, I had an air tag dropped on their truck. It's a tracking device that works on a blue-tooth connec—"

"We *know* how it works," Darius cut in sharply. "We've done field reconnaissance with everything from this primitive shit to live satellite feeds accurate to within less than a foot."

"Not to mention in resolutions that would make you dizzy," I added.

Christian nodded, apparently unimpressed. He punched a few more buttons on the tablet and the tracking app came up. The target dot on the map corresponded with a place I knew well.

"They're at JFK airport."

"Yes," he agreed. "Or at least, their truck is."

"Maybe they're flying home?" Autumn offered hopefully.

"But they drove up here," Darius noted. "Maybe they're flying back temporarily. Taking care of something."

"If the truck stays where it is, we'll know in a few hours," Christian agreed.

"Speaking of taking care of something…"

I forced the words out with a heavy heart. The decision had been weighing on me all day, but I'd finally made it.

"I need to go home for a few days," I said, turning toward Darius. "Not California either, but *home* home. Back to Montana."

The look in my friend's eyes was instant understanding. He nodded curtly.

"I won't be long," I added. "A few days at most."

"Of course," Darius said without hesitation. "Is… is dad—"

"He's okay," I jumped in. "I just need to see him. More than that though, I need to see my mother. She's been through hell, and she could use a shoulder."

She had my two brothers' shoulders, of course. Shane knew this more than anyone. But sometimes you just needed a shoulder that wasn't always there. Someone new yet still familiar, to step in and break the monotony of a recurringly bad situation.

Autumn knew about my father's illness too; we'd stayed up late talking about it on more than one occasion. She'd been kind and compassionate. An incredible listener. It felt insanely good too, finally unburdening myself to someone other than Darius. But it felt even better to lie in her lap with her hands gently sifting through my hair, laughing at my stories of childhood as we half-watched old movies. I told her damn near all my best Montana tales, but the greatest ones included fun times with my father. Back before this insidious sickness

163

began to take him away from us, piece by piece.

"Shane…"

She was beside me now, laying a soft hand on my shoulder. I covered it with mine.

"It's okay," I assured with a smile. "I'll be back in a few days."

"It's just that I…" I could see her struggling. "I wish I could go with you."

"So do I," I admitted. I reached out, touching her face. "My mother would love you. But there's too much work to still do here. This place needs you."

Autumn sighed. Sullenly, she looked down at her feet.

"These dorks need you too," I chuckled, jerking my thumb back and forth between them. "Can you imagine how much they'd bitch about it if I whisked you off for a few days?"

Darius rolled his eyes at me. Christian on the other hand, appeared nonplussed.

"Besides, I'm not going right now. Tonight, Darius and I have other plans."

My friend looked confused, but only for a moment. Then his eyes lit up.

"You mean—"

I pointed down at the digital map and tapped my finger.

"What better time to hit this place than when these assholes aren't there?"

AUTUMN

"I'm telling you I should've gone with them," Christian said for the fifth or sixth time. "They're going to do something stupid. Something that'll get them in trouble."

The fire crackled, spitting an ember against the protective mesh screen. Sitting cross-legged before it, he didn't even flinch.

"And I'm telling you they know exactly what they're doing," I said, handing him a new glass of whiskey. "They served together for a long time, Darius and Shane. They have years of combat experience. You know all this already, better than I do."

I plopped down beside him, sinking into the cozy nest of pillows and blankets I'd arranged before the fireplace. Christian brought the whiskey to his lips and downed half of it without flinching. He didn't look any more relaxed, however.

"Look, I know you like to be in control," I told him. "Of all people, I understand this. But let them handle things for tonight," I urged. "If you'd gone with them, you'd only be in their way."

I shrugged and took a sip of my wine. The fire felt pleasantly warm on the side of my face.

"Besides, then I'd be all alone. And you don't want me alone, do you?"

I smiled and toasted him. Begrudgingly, he toasted me back.

The fact that I would've been alone was the only thing that prevented Christian from insisting on going. That, plus the solemn promise that Darius and Shane would video-conference us in the second they got to their destination.

That call had taken place about an hour ago. The house my cousins had been renting was already dark. We watched them park across from it for a while, to ensure the coast was clear, then move with military precision through the yard and around the back.

Once there, they'd broken in. It was grimly satisfying, knowing the shoe was on the other foot for once, but Shane had merely picked the lock and let themselves inside rather harmlessly. The idea of course was not to blow our cover, or let them know we'd found them out. But part of me really wanted Shane to smash their door to smithereens.

. The inside of the house was surprisingly well-kept. My cousins were using all four of the bedrooms for some reason, and none of those beds were made. There were pizza boxes and Chinese food containers in the garbage, beer in the fridge, and all manner of snacks stocked in the cabinets. But that's all there was. No clues, no weapons, no indication as to what their next move was. There was nothing else.

I wasn't sure what we expected, really. I didn't know much about Emmitt or Edward, but they didn't seem like planning ahead types of guys. They were unlikely to draw up detailed plans for the siege of my vineyard, much less leave them splayed across their kitchen table.

From there, a decision was made to track their truck. It was still in the short-term parking at JFK. They could've taken a flight, maybe. Or they could still be sitting in it for all we knew.

"We're going to the airport," Darius had said simply, and much to Christian's dismay. "We'll let you know what we find."

That left me, Christian, and Felony the cat, who'd taken over the back of the couch again. The wine and whiskey were going down easily. We'd turned the TV off because it was a distraction.

The pillows and blankets were something I'd set up earlier; sort of a hint that I wanted to sleep with all three of them at the same time. Bed-hopping was sexy, but tonight I wanted to fuck myself into oblivion and just sprawl. I wanted to cuddle sleepily against three hard bodies. Drift off, surrounded by a pile of fire-warmed muscle and man-flesh.

God, I was getting greedy.

Right now, we were sitting beside each other, quietly staring into the fire. I left Christian to bask in his own thoughts. For a long time, neither of us said anything.

"We're a lot more alike than you realize," he eventually murmured. "You and I."

"Oh yeah?" I teased. "You traded an extreme sporting goods business for a ramshackle winery?"

"No," he admitted. "But my parents probably shouldn't have had kids either."

I knew from experience it was a hard admission. So I sat silently, waiting for more.

"My parents hardly paid attention to us," said Christian. "As a result, the house always felt cold. It drove my sister and I closer together, because they could sometimes go entire days without interacting with us. And whenever they did, they would always blink in surprise."

"Almost like they were noticing you for the first time," I whispered.

Christian whirled to look at me. "*Exactly* like that," he swore. "Yes."

I nodded and cleared my throat.

"I'll bet that made you independent."

"It did," he agreed. "It didn't stop me from wanting to impress them, though."

"No," I laughed bitterly. "It never does."

"At first I thought my father wanted me to be a lawyer so I could follow in his footsteps," he continued. "But now I realize he didn't care what I did. Law school was an easy way to get me out of his hair. It left him more time to focus on *his* true love. And his only true love was work."

"Even so, he *has* to be proud of you," I countered. "And I'm sure he cares—"

"*Cared*," he corrected me. "My parents are both dead, Autumn. One from cancer, the other from a broken heart. Happened within six months of each other. They never even got to retire."

The resulting silence was deafening. I slid closer to him, until we were side by side. Still staring into the fire, I laid my hand gently on his knee.

"You're not going to say you're sorry, are you?" he asked.

"Nope."

"Good. Then you understand."

I squeezed him beneath my palm. "More than most people on the planet, yes."

Christian sighed and nodded appreciatively. He swirled the remaining whiskey around a few times, then took another pull from his glass.

"We were shell-shocked when it happened, my sister and I. Anna took it the hardest, of course. She still lives in our childhood home, all these years later."

"You said you wanted to be closer than you are now."

"I do."

"So what happened?"

"I took on the burden of raising her by myself, even though she was practically an adult," he explained. "And in doing so I destroyed her independence. I provided anything she needed, rather than let her get those things for herself. And for years I kept driving her suitors away. I sabotaged anyone who got close to her."

"Big brothers sometimes do that," I shrugged.

"Yes, but not in the manner that I did," Christian admitted. "I was... I was—"

"A total dick?"

"Among other things, yeah," said Christian. "I'm finally coming around, though. Anna's engaged now. The guy's really nice, too. He treats her right."

"So... happy ending?"

"For her maybe. But when it comes to me..."

He finished his whiskey, then stared down forlornly into the glass for a moment before setting it aside.

"Do you know why I was at that charity auction, bidding on a date?" he asked.

"Well, I *have* wondered," I admitted. "It doesn't exactly seem like something that's up your alley."

"No, it's not," replied Christian. "But a few weeks ago I had an epiphany. I realized that professionally, I'm on track to do everything my father did, and ten times more. But in getting there, I've completely sacrificed any chance at enjoying a personal life."

He shook his head slowly, somberly. The invisible weight on his shoulders was crushing.

"I want a life, outside of the courtroom. I want a *family*.

"I made a promise to myself that I'd start dating again. Because if I told you the last time I'd been out on an actual date, you'd laugh your ass off."

Silently I imagined the conversation Christian must've had with himself. The one that brought us to where we are now.

"So I was... practice?"

My lover shrugged. "Originally, sure. The whole premise seemed innocent enough. A date, but without any real pressure. I figured I could start out slow, dip my feet back in."

"Slow?" I chuckled. "So much for that."

"Yeah, well..."

I nodded out the window, back toward the vineyard. "And I'm pretty sure you dipped more than just your feet in, earlier today."

He stared at me for a moment, before smirking back.

"Not saying I didn't enjoy it, mind you," I added. "Just saying I was a little shocked when—"

Christian pulled me into him, his full lips kissing away the rest of my sentence. He kissed me slowly, tenderly but there was more behind it than simple lust this time. I could sense something much deeper behind our obvious mutual attraction. Something stronger. Something… significant.

Uh-oh.

But as he dragged me down into the warm, wonderful world of the pillows and blankets, it suddenly hit me:

It was something I felt in the pit my *own* stomach, as well.

~ 28 ~

CHRISTIAN

"Christian…"

It was my mind that stirred first. It fought through a haze of sleep, of pleasure, of deep-seeded emotion.

"Christian, wake up."

Very slowly, my body followed. Everything was way too warm, way too comfortable. My eyes fluttered open, and I found myself exactly where I wanted to be: still wrapped around Autumn from behind.

We'd talked, kissed, cuddled, then talked some more. Eventually we'd drifted off to sleep, staring lazily into each other's eyes. I remember her shifting sideways so she could spoon into me, and as my arms folded around her it felt like the most serene thing in the whole fucking world.

"CHRISTIAN!"

She twisted away from me, and I bolted upright. The room was dim. The fire was nothing but glowing embers. In my foggy state, I had zero conception of how much time had passed.

"There's someone *here.*"

There was fear in her voice. I could hear it in the way it faltered.

"How do you—"

I stopped talking instantly as a muffled bang came from somewhere in the direction of the kitchen. It was followed by a second, similar noise as I leapt to my feet.

"Stay here," I hissed.

Autumn shot me a dirty look and shook her head. She handed me one of the fireplace pokers. I noticed she was holding the other.

Alright fine, I mouthed silently in the near darkness. I put a shushing finger over my lips. *Let's go.*

We were clothed, thankfully. I could've easily made love to her in front of the fire, but just falling asleep wrapped around her was an amazing consolation prize. Extending an arm, I kept her behind me as we crept silently toward the kitchen. I peeked around the corner...

The room was empty.

Or rather, it was *almost* empty. The godforsaken cat was sitting there in the middle of the floor, staring back at us, casually licking its paw.

Autumn moved forward, pressing herself tightly against my body. I could feel her shivering in the scant clothing she had on: a T-shirt and a tiny pair of silk sleep shorts.

"Do you think it was the—"

Another noise jerked both our heads upward. This one was even louder, and totally unmistakable:

The sound of footsteps crossing the upstairs hallway.

Autumn left me momentarily as she padded to the window and back. I leaned down to accommodate her, as she pressed her lips against my ear.

"It isn't Shane or Darius," she hissed, in a voice so low I could barely hear. "Their car isn't back yet."

Fuck.

Silently I cursed myself for falling asleep at all. What the fuck was I thinking? How the hell could I let this happen, while the others were out, and I was responsible for—

BANG!

We both jumped at the loudest sound yet. The noise was so loud, so obnoxious, it sounded like someone had knocked over a grandfather clock!

"Stay *here!*" I hissed again, this time putting my hands on her shoulders.

In that moment the moonlight shifted across her face, and Autumn shot me a wounded look. Even in anger, half-terrified, she looked heartbreakingly beautiful.

I didn't look back as I ran to the base of the staircase.

Fuck fuck fuck fuck...

I was such an asshole, both now and before. Yes, I should've safeguarded us both until the others got back, but her body had been so warm, so soft and fragrant. It felt so amazing against me, it put my right to sleep. But as I drifted off...

Something important and perhaps wonderful had happened. But also, something that bothered me greatly.

You told her she was 'practice', remember?

Damn. Yes, unfortunately I had. And in doing so, I'd

inadvertently belittled the connection we'd made. I'd diminished the fact that I'd gone out of my mind with happiness just to place the winning bid that first night. I'd turned the whole thing into something as insignificant as me 'practicing' dating on her, so I could get back on the horse again.

And shit... it wasn't really like that at all.

The fact was, I hadn't considered Autumn's own feelings, and that was shitty. Was she practicing too? Or was she catching feelings the way I was?

B—BANG.

A similar series of noises floated downward, as I crept silently up the stairs. There wasn't time for it now, but I needed to tell her the truth. It wasn't fair that I'd only considered my own needs. This woman very likely had three times the confusion I was feeling right now. It had to be overwhelming for her. And we hadn't even—

I froze as something flew into the hallway. It came tumbling through the wide open master bedroom door before crashing into the opposite wall.

I rushed past the now-shattered antique hope chest and burst into the room. The bed was on its side. The dresser was on its face, its drawers upended, its contents scattered across the wide-paneled floor.

The man staring back at me looked just as shocked as I was. It wasn't Emmitt. It wasn't Edward.

No, this was someone entirely fucking different.

The man was dark-haired and beady eyed — an ugly stranger if there ever was one. He was way shorter than average, too. But what he lacked in height he made up for in sheer aggressiveness.

"You're here?"

He seemed to know me, but without expecting me. His confusion passed quickly though. His hands clenched tightly into fists, as his face curled into a snarl.

"Good. Even better, then."

His southern drawl was unmistakable. I made a mental note of it in the split-second before he flung himself at me, roaring as he did. I didn't see the knife until almost too late. I wouldn't have seen it at all, except for the blue flash it gave off as the steel blade passed the moonlit window.

I dodged at the last possible second. I felt a flash of pain in my side as he flew by, and then I was spinning... whirling...

And bringing the hooked end of the fireplace poker down on his exposed back.

The man screamed, his arms flailing as he went flying into the wall behind me. Then he bounced, so hard that his neck snapped back with a loud SNAP.

I wondered if I'd killed him as he crumpled to the floor.

"BROOKS!"

I whirled again, and there was a giant standing in the doorway. This man was the opposite of his counterpart; taller than me, short blond hair, and wide as a linebacker. He took a second to stare down at his fallen comrade, his mouth hanging open in confusion and dismay. Almost like an ape.

"What the—"

Attacking him first seemed the only reasonable answer.

I feigned low, then punched him square in the face as

hard as I could. My hand connected solidly with his jaw. It was like punching a granite statue.

FUCK!

I felt the crunch of my knuckles as they collapsed in on my fingers. Pain flared again. Much worse than the stinging in my side.

He's too big. He's too—

Something else hit me, hard, this time in the back of the head. There was a quick flash of light, too bright and silvery to be anything good, and then I was falling forward, dazed and dizzy. Trying desperately to put my arms out to break my fall...

Then the gray fog closed in from all directions, taking away my sight.

And to my horror my arms were no longer working.

~ 29 ~

AUTUMN

The sounds coming from my bedroom were horrific. Screams. Shouts. Voices.

I'd been creeping my way up the staircase, but now I ran full tilt from landing to the open door. Fuck staying put. Fuck covering in the living room, while others fought my battles for me.

No. No more sitting back as things were decided all around me.

Now I was *pissed.*

I leapt over the broken hope chest — an abandoned gift from the winery itself — and landed in a room that didn't resemble my bedroom at all. Everything was broken, everything was overturned. A stranger lay face-down against one of the walls, his head twisted at a very odd angle. Buried in his back, I saw the poker I'd handed to Christian.

Oh shit.

Christian himself was lying there too, face down, not far from the doorway. The man standing over him had greasy black hair pinned back in a ponytail. I didn't recognize him. He had striking features, though.

Before I could do or say anything, he whirled on me.

"You…"

His smile revealed two jagged rows of crooked teeth, top and bottom. He might've been handsome, otherwise. As it was, it made him look like a shark.

"Step away from him!" I snarled loudly. Gripping the heavier of the two fireplace pokers with both hands, I hefted it menacingly over my shoulder.

"Oh for fuck's sake," the man ordered me. "Put that thing down."

His tone was infuriatingly condescending. As if he were talking to a small child.

"Put that thing down and you won't get hurt." He smirked evilly. Then, looking me up and down, he added: "Maybe."

It was all I needed to hear.

I flung myself at him, screaming like a banshee, so loudly and ferociously his hands moved reflexively to his ears. It gave me an edge. A split second of time during which his hands weren't in front of his body…

Rather than slash him with the poker I reversed course and slammed the butt end of it into his stomach. It was the last thing he expected. The intruder caught the blow dead center, right in the solar plexus, gasping in shock as I knocked every ounce of wind from his lungs.

Then I reversed the poker again, slamming the business end upwards and into his chin.

179

The result was horrific. I'd given Christian the log-poker itself, because it was longer, while I'd taken the heavier, two-armed wood-gripping tool. The steel teeth at the end of the tool tore into the man's face, raking themselves upward along his entire cheek and tearing it wide open.

He screamed as a bright scarlet gash bloomed across one half of his face, from chin to ear.

I stood over him for a moment, my fury turning to shock as he lay there gasping, desperately trying to reboot his lungs. Which was bad, because fury — plus the element of surprise — was all I really had.

That's when a groan reached my ears, drawing my attention back where it belonged.

"Christian!"

I rushed to him. He was trying to get up over and over again, but failing miserably.

"Christian, stay down."

The back of his head was bleeding. It was all over his neck, his shirt, his hands.

"Davis!"

Insanely, a *third* man slid into view, running up from the hallway. He was tall, blond, and absolutely enormous.

"We need to go *now!*"

The new giant braced both hands against the doorway and looked inside. By his expression, I could tell he wasn't happy with what he saw.

"Let's go, they're coming!" he urged again. "The others, they're—"

He saw me, stopped talking, and took a step inside. I

braced myself for whatever he might do, but he strode right past me and picked up the guy who'd been crumpled against the wall.

"Davis, now!"

Without another word, the big blond threw the first guy limply over his shoulder. Then, stepping back into the hallway, he disappeared back the way he came.

By now, the man I'd struck — obviously, Davis — had finally regained his breath. He rose to his feet, still clutching his ruined face, and shot me a murderous look. For a second or two, I began scrabbling around for the poker again.

Then he, too, rushed into the hallway, and disappeared.

Thank GOD.

Christian had stopped moving altogether. I was cradling his head in my lap, while holding a bunched up T-shirt against the back of his head. Absurdly, I couldn't remember if it was from the clean pile or the dirty one. I didn't think it mattered really, but—"

"AUTUMN!"

Shane's frantic voice was music to my ears. I shouted back to him:

"Over HERE!"

The sound of footfalls on the staircase was followed by him flying into the ruined bedroom. His eyes darted everywhere, assessing the chaos of the situation.

"It's just me," I said quickly. "But Christian... he's hurt."

Shane dumped the bed back onto its four legs with a flip of his two big arms. He centered the mattress and together we lifted Christian onto it.

"What the hell happened to him?"

"I don't know. But there were others. Three of them! And they—"

"I know. Darius is on them now."

He looked pained and helpless, like he should be out there helping his brother-in-arms. But I also knew his priority had been to find me first, and while I was in danger he would never leave my side.

"Are you hurt?"

His hands glided over me quickly, checking me with the expert fingers of a combat medic. They lingered on my blood-splattered hands.

"I'm fine," I told him. "It's not my blood."

The relief on his face was palpable. "And you said there are *three* of them?"

"Two, really," I replied. "One of them was already knocked out when I got here. And another one is all fucked up, because I hit him with that."

I pointed to the heavy, wrought-iron fireplace tool. Shane's expression was shock and awe.

"You hit him with *that?*

"In the face, yes."

He grinned. "Fuckin' A."

Christian stirred, then sat up abruptly, coughing. He tried to get to his feet, but Shane placed a hand on his chest to stop him.

"Easy there, big guy."

"Where—"

"They ran off," I said, reaching out to sooth him. I rubbed one hand up and down his back. "Shane's here now. Darius ran after them."

"If anyone's catching them," Shane asserted, "it's going to be Darius."

We gave him a moment. Christian blinked a few times, his expression returning to normal.

"I got blindsided," he groaned, rubbing his head. "There must've been two of them."

"Three, actually."

He coughed, wincing. "Damn. I'm sorry, Autumn."

"Don't be," Shane told him. "She did just fine."

He went through a series of medical checks, which included holding a finger before Christian's eyes and telling him to follow it. After a few seconds of playing along, the lawyer swatted the finger away.

"Did you see who they were?"

I shook my head. "No, I've never seen them before in my life. They weren't my cousins, though."

"Your cousins ditched their truck back at JFK," said Shane. "Only it wasn't their truck. Turns out it was stolen, back in Georgia."

"So what were they doing at the airport?" I mused. "Flying back?"

At that moment Darius stepped in from the hallway, all covered in sweat. He pushed through the disaster that was once my bedroom, then strode to the window.

"You want my guess?" he asked.

All three of us nodded, numbly, as he pointed downward.

"They were flying those assholes *in*."

~ 30 ~

EDWARD

"And I'm telling you, he needs a hospital!"

I watched grimly as Brooks tried to get up again. He barely made it to his feet, took two faltering steps, then crumpled back to the kitchen floor like a sack of potatoes.

"Get up," Emmitt snarled.

There was fear in our friend's eyes. It had been there ever since he finally came to, in the back of the car. Whatever had hit him, had hit him hard. I only wished I'd been there to help him.

"I— I can't feel my—"

"Then get him up," my brother ordered, pointing at me and Connor. "We need to leave. They've already been here, and they're coming back."

A fresh round of terror settled over me. It didn't sit well with the already bad taste in my mouth.

"They've been *here?*" I asked, incredulously.

"Yes."

"How do you know?"

"Because the curtains on the back door are different," my brother grumbled. He looked at them again. "Way different than when we left."

I didn't doubt him for a second. Emmitt knew these things. Throughout our childhood and beyond, my twin had an annoying knack for noticing every last detail, no matter where we were or what we were doing. It even came in handy sometimes.

Most times though, he only sounded like a dick.

"You told us they were out," Davis sneered. The mass of gauze he was holding against his face was already soaked with blood again. "You told us they wouldn't be there."

"And they *weren't* there," Emmitt barked back at him. "Their car was gone. The house was dark."

"At least two of them were there," Davis coughed. "The tall one you said was a lawyer. And the girl."

The girl. Our *cousin*. It hadn't sit well with me to begin with, what we were doing to her. After all, we didn't even know her. We hadn't even tried to talk to her.

"He sure didn't fight like a lawyer," barked Davis, dabbing at his face. He nodded toward Brooks. "Ask him."

Brooks couldn't care less about our conversation, and that's because he was too busy trying to walk again. Every time he stood up, his legs shook like a newborn doe. I could see him focusing on them now, mentally willing them to work. His fear was slowly turning to terror as he realized the injury might not be physical, but more of an actual disconnect with his brain.

"You fucked us," Davis was growling at Emmitt.

"You brought us all the way up here to do your dirty work, and you couldn't even—"

"No one told you to ransack the house!" Emmitt shouted him down. "You were there for a specific reason! Not to rob the place like some common thief!'"

"I didn't rob the plac—"

"Connor says you tore the bedroom apart!" Emmitt spat. "Drawers, mattress, everything. That wasn't part of the plan."

Davis shot Connor a dangerous glance of betrayal. Looking miserable, Connor only shrugged.

"Look, we came up here... because... we owed you," stammered Brooks. His face was streaked with tears, now. Every word that came out was grunted through a haze of pain. "But we're finished. *I'm* finished."

Brooks turned at me pleadingly. "Take me to the hospital."

I stood up. My brother's icy glare almost sat me right back down.

"Take me, Edward," Brooks pleaded. I'll tell them.... it was a car accident. I'll tell them I fell... off a fucking ladder... or maybe—"

"Fine."

Emmitt's voice was pregnant with disgust. I couldn't believe it. Normally, my brother never gave up.

"Go!" Emmitt shouted impatiently. "Do what he says. Drop him off in the front of the hospital if that's what he wants," he bared his teeth at Brooks. "But after that, you're on your own."

Connor stepped forward, and together we helped Brooks to his feet. It had seemed like a such a good idea, getting them involved. Bringing the three of them up from Blue Ridge, to do all the things we couldn't legally do.

Not that you're doing everything legally, anyway.

The thoughts were useless, so I pushed them aside. The cameras recently set up at the winery had thrown a wrench into things for us. This was supposed to be a workaround.

Instead, it turned right into a huge clusterfuck.

"I'm going too," announced Davis.

My brother tensed up all over. His head tilted sideways, like a cobra about to strike.

"And *where* the fuck do you think you're going?"

"To the hospital," Davis said defiantly. "To get my face stitched up."

Emmitt shook his head. "Forget it. I'll stitch your face up."

"The fuck you will."

My brother took a step closer, rising up to his full height. Davis was by no means short, but in the shadow of Emmitt he seemed almost insignificant.

"I stitched up your leg when you tore it open crossing that fallen log, remember?"

"Yeah, and I have a scar from my knee all the way to my hip," said Davis. "We were fifteen."

"Sixteen," I countered.

"Whatever man," he rolled his eyes at me. He stared at Emmitt. He even pressed a finger into my brother's chest.

"But this is my *face*. So no fucking thanks."

Connor and I glanced at each other, both of us waiting for Emmitt to snap our friend's finger clean off. For some reason, it never happened.

Instead, my brother stepped uncharacteristically aside. He even opened the door for us.

"You fucking cowards."

Somehow I felt better outside, bathed in the blue moonlight. Connor and I loaded Brooks into the back seat of the nearest vehicle, while Davis headed for the driver's seat. But Emmitt shook his head.

"No way," he scowled, heading him off. "You two are taking the shitmobile."

The pair of trucks we'd stolen from the airport parking garage were like night and day. They were both older models, unlikely to have tracking, but one pickup was significantly more beat up than the other.

I saw Davis *almost* argue, but he was smart enough to pick his battles. We'd been down many roads together, and he knew which ones were dead-ends.

Eventually the two of them drove off, leaving us standing before the house we'd been living in for the past several weeks. At this hour, everything was deathly quiet. My mood was quickly turning to shit.

"Head back inside" said Emmitt, forking his fingers at me and Connor. "Grab only the things we need and—"

"No."

My brother looked confused for a moment. Almost as if he'd heard me wrong.

"What did you say?"

"I said no. I'm done being ordered around."

It was the first time I'd stood up to him in years — maybe even since we were teens. I thought it would be awkward, and even frightening. Instead, if felt strangely good.

"You're the one who told them to drive straight over there," I insinuated. "You're the one who fucked this up."

He crossed his arms. "I did, huh?"

"You sure as fuck did," I snapped. "Did you see Brooks? His neck is probably broken. A concussion at minimum." I laughed acidly. "And Davis? Holy shit. He's gonna need twenty stitches right up the side of his face. All because you couldn't formulate an actual plan. All because you couldn't wait."

Emmitt's smug expression hadn't changed one bit. But Connor's mouth had dropped all the way open. He looked absolutely terrified.

"We were supposed to take what was ours," I said. "Just scare her away. Instead we're terrorizing this poor girl, and everything she owns. Kicking in the door of her house—"

"OUR house," Emmitt snapped.

"—and cutting down her crops," I continued. "And now you called *Davis*, in? He's here for other reasons and you know it."

The wind picked up, urging me forward. Reminding me that we needed to get out of here, and fast.

"I'm going in there," I pointed back to the house, "and grabbing what's mine. And then Connor and I are going to the nearest motel. I'm tired."

My brother's look was cold and calculating. "Are you done?"

"Yeah, I'm done," I grumbled. "Come with us or don't come. I don't care."

Emmitt's eyes bored into my back like two lasers as I turned and stormed off.

"But if you want your stuff, you get it yourself."

~ *31* ~

AUTUMN

"You're too young to understand this, but it all goes so fast, Autumn. Too damn fast."

My father was holding my hand as he said the words. I must've been ten. We were at Adventureland, standing beneath the Hurricane. I could still taste the cotton candy on my chin. Still feel the stickiness as I clenched and unclenched my little fist.

"Seems like just the other day your mother and I were dancing at our prom, surrounded by red and gold balloons," he sighed wistfully. "And suddenly you look around and it's twenty-five years later, and everything's different, everything's changed."

He had a far-away look in his eye that I'd never forget. It made my heart hurt. Even if I couldn't understand exactly why.

"Life's a lot like that roller-coaster," he said, pointing upward. Almost on cue the Hurricane rushed by, in a whoosh of funnel cake-scented wind and heat. "Your childhood is that big, seemingly endless hill, thrusting you into the sky," he pointed. "Getting you all amped up for the ride ahead."

I stared up at the giant chain, constantly moving, ready to drag the next line of cars up the hill. Surrounded by sights and sounds, everything seemed so big, so loud, so crazy. But also, so very thrilling.

"For your mother and I, all the biggest twists and turns are over," my father went on. "There's still some track ahead of us, but it's mostly little hills and bumps. And then eventually, the track goes straight again... and you can see the exit. Only the end and the beginning of this ride are kinda the same, you know?" He shrugged and smiled. "The bar comes down and you go another round. Maybe you just get in a different car with different people, and you take the ride all over again."

I stepped out of the shower, wrung out my hair, and wrapped the robe around my still-wet body. I knew what I had to do. It couldn't wait another minute.

I found Shane in the basement, taking stock of the new area we'd uncovered by throwing a whole bunch of broken furniture away. There were two big fermenting tanks down there, connected via a diamond plate platform. And they were newer ones too, with custom piping and a digital control box.

"You know, these are for brewing *beer*," Shane said offhandedly. Somehow he knew I was there without turning around. "And they're not original to the winery. Your uncle put these here."

"Beer?" I repeated, not really paying attention. "Shane, listen—"

"Darius needs to get a look at these," he went on. "The stuff he craft-brewed when we were holed up in Kandahar was better than anything I've ever had statesid—"

"Shane, I'm sorry, but you have to go."

He turned around, still holding a notebook in one hand and a pencil in the other. I was standing there in my robe only, both hands on my hips. His hungry eyes devoured me for a long moment, before his brain finally caught up to my words.

"Wait… *what?*"

"You're going to Montana," I said firmly. "You said it yourself, your mother needs you."

Shane bit his lip and grunted. "That was before three strange guys showed up and jumped you in your bedroom."

"They didn't jump me," I said truthfully. "More like I jumped them."

"You sure did," he smiled. "But things might've been different if we weren't here."

"Yes," I acknowledged. "And I appreciate that. I love that you care for me. But you also need to care for your mother and father. Especially now, while they're still here."

I saw a flash of trouble on his handsome face, but only a flash. It appeared and disappeared with the discipline of a hardened soldier.

"Trust me," I said, uncrossing my arms. "Everything will be fine while you're gone. I'll have Darius. I'll have Christian."

"Christian." He rolled his eyes.

"Yes. And you should feel safer about that."

"I'd feel safer about everything if Darius had run a little faster last night," he grumbled, "and dragged one of those animals back to the house."

"Darius was smart not to chase them into the woods,"

I countered. "He was alone. It was dark. They ran past the tree-line, and they could've been armed."

"Maybe, but—"

"You know the difference between bravery and stupidity," I told him. "Way better than I do."

Now it was Shane's turn to fold his arms. And they were beautiful arms too. Almost as beautiful as the smile he eventually gave up, as he realized I was right.

"Come with me," he said.

"I will," I promised. "Someday soon. In fact, I can't *wait* to meet your family. And the way you talk about home, Montana sounds incredible." The smile on my face felt warm as the sun. It faded slightly, as I watched him realize what was coming next. "But I can't go now."

I stepped into him, admiring his height, his build, his squared-off jaw. Looking up into those gorgeous green eyes, I placed my hands on either side of his two iron-like arms.

"Go home Shane," I said again. "I'll still be here when you get back. And we'll have this whole place cleaned up by then. Darius can take inventory of what we have, what's available."

"Promise me you'll stick by them," he relented. "That you won't ever let them out of your sight."

"I'll sleep with them on either side of me if I have to," I said truthfully. Suddenly, there was a tingle in my stomach. The prospect of the situation was rapidly growing on me.

"Hmm…" Shane mused. "That's not exactly making me want to leave."

I laughed as Shane's mind began wandering again. He was still mentally undressing me, which in my robe wouldn't take very long. His eyes shifted to scan the room, perhaps wondering where he would take me first, which piece of equipment would be most comfortable to bend me over and have his way with me. If we had more time, I'd take him up on it. This was one of the few places in the whole vineyard I hadn't had sex yet.

"The sooner you leave, the sooner you get back," I said, planting a gentle kiss on his lips. I smiled playfully, slapping one side of my ass as I turned away.

"And of course, the sooner you get back to *this*," I winked over my shoulder.

~ 32 ~

AUTUMN

At first I thought working a vineyard would be easy. I mean, the soil was rich, and the plants were already there. The sun came up every day, without fail. All I really needed to do was add water. The grapes would grow, and I'd harvest them all in the fall, right?

Boy, was I wrong.

I had to learn about flowering, and fruit-set, and veraison, where the berries softened up and changed from green to red and purple. There was soil acidity and Ph to consider. Watering requirements for different varieties. The ripening period, as it turned out, required constant care. And that wasn't even considering the business dealings I had lined up with buyers, fermenters, wine barrel technicians, and every other aspect of vineyard maintenance I didn't even know about yet.

Shane booked a flight and left for the airport, and we spent the next two days in the field, trimming and pruning and caring for my first budding crop. Darius and Christian took the job of helping out very seriously. They kept up with every aspect of my daily routine, even the tedious parts, and never once

197

voiced a single word of complaint.

There were no more intruders, no unwanted visits — at least for now. So the three of us worked hard all day, made something to eat, and watched TV or movies until we all crashed out.

By Shane's order I took them both into my king-sized bed, and it was wonderful, sleeping between them. We curled up exhausted at the end of each night, too tired to do much except cuddle up and talk softly, before the spooning of their hard bodies on either side of me sent me into a dreamless, blissful slumber.

By the end of the third day however, I was *more* than rested. Not to mention feeling hot, horny, and wanton as fuck.

"We're taking showers," I said, as we came in from the field. "And then I'm taking us all out to dinner."

Darius nodded happily as I took each of their hands, leading them in the direction of the stairs. Christian however, looked intrigued.

"Are we celebrating?" he asked.

"Of course," I said without hesitation.

"And what exactly are we celebratin—"

"We're celebrating me fucking your brains out," I cut him off. "The both of you. If you'll ever get up the stairs, that is."

I detoured them out of the hallway, pulling them greedily into my bedroom. Once there I stripped the clothes off their hard, sweaty bodies, piece by piece. And then I did mine.

"We're dirty," Christian squinted at me.

"Um-hmmm," I said, kissing his bare chest. "And about to be dirtier."

One by one I took them between my legs, all sweaty and wet and smelling like earth. I fucked Darius first, as Christian's eyes followed every move of our writhing, glistening bodies. I was sure to make plenty of eye-contact with him too, because I knew he loved watching.

"Fuuuuuuck."

It wasn't long before Darius finished inside me, pumping me obscenely full as I grunted some even dirtier encouragement. I squeezed his perfect ass with both hands until I was sure he'd given me every last drop, then I kicked him in the direction of the shower and chuckled.

"Next!"

Christian reached out for me, his dick jutting from his body like a railroad spike. But before he could even touch me, I shoved him onto his back. Mounting him was the quickest way to get him off, I well knew. And right now I was hungry for more than just sex.

"Do you feel your friend?" I purred wickedly, as I bottomed out on him. "All hot and sticky and warm inside me?"

I whispered the words into his ear while biting it, tonguing it, and grinding him deep. I saw his Adam's apple go up and down as he swallowed hard, then nodded.

"Now give me *yours.*"

I rode him hard, impaling myself on his pulsating shaft, taking exactly what I wanted. In no time at all we were climaxing together. I threw my head back in ecstasy, bucking and groaning, rolling my ass tightly against him. Wincing from the pain-pleasure of my nails raking across his perfectly sculpted chest, he filled me from within for the second time in less than ten minutes.

We passed Darius in the hallway, on his way out of the shower. Still wrapped in a towel, he only shook his head.

"Infuckingsatiable."

We cleaned up together, Christian and I, kissing beneath the shower steam. Sharing the hot water, soaping each other's backs and backsides, I reveled in the thrill of it all. I was the luckiest girl in the world. Not just for the sex, not just for the help, but for the friendship, the closeness, the gratitude. These men cared for me deeply, more than anyone since my parents had. And yet somehow it wasn't awkward, it wasn't strange. In fact, the comfort level was off the charts.

We parted on the way to our own respective bedrooms, then met up again downstairs. I'd told them both to dress to impress, because I sure as hell was.

In the end I didn't have much, but a good part of what I did have was owed to these men. They'd come out of the clear blue sky, helping me for no good reason. They'd swooped in and rescued me. Saved me from something terrible.

For tonight at least, I wanted to pamper the hell out of them.

AUTUMN

My pussy is full of two loads while we have dinner. Nobody knows. It *feels* like they know, especially as the night progresses and I flirt shamelessly with both my lovers. I also get a few furtive glances, mostly from women.

Maybe they're jealous. Or maybe they suspect that I've slept with one, or maybe both of the gorgeous men at my table.

Just not at the same time, though.

Darius looks incredible in his shirt and tie, his brown, Italian skin glowing with work, with sex, with raw; animal attraction. Beneath the table, his hand hasn't left my leg all night. He keeps riding it higher, shifting the hem of my slinky black dress ever upward as I spread to accommodate him.

He still hasn't touched me yet, though. Not like Christian has.

Holy fuck.

The booth is circular, and tucked away in a shadowy corner of the restaurant. That, plus the tablecloth, are the only things keeping us modest. We start at our own sides of the table, but creep ever closer during the course of our dinner. By the time dessert arrives, their thighs are rubbing against mine.

We leave early though, because all of a sudden none of us are interested in coffee or dessert. And the reason for that is simple:

I'm the dessert.

"Check."

It felt nice to get out of the house, even though we were leaving it alone and vulnerable. It felt normal, for once. We felt like a normal couple, or throuple, or whatever you wanted to label the thing we had going on. Up until now, I hadn't had to think about appearances when it came to something like this. Everything that happened between us, had happened behind closed doors.

But damn...

I'd completely underestimated how exciting it would be to flaunt my lovers in public.

Kissing them. Nuzzling them. Even the simple act of laughing with them on either side of me had me wet with the idea that *both* of these men were all mine. I was the one taking them home with me, sauntering in front them, giving them a full view of my ass in this dress everywhere that I went. And when we got home? I was the one who would pull their ties off. I was the one who would hand them some drinks, put on some soft music, and then push the pair of them gently back into the couch...

It all happened exactly as I wanted it to, right down to the thrilling but teasing car ride. We got back to the winery. They went ahead, checked the place out, made sure the coast was clear...

And then we were in the living room, where the fire had been resurrected from embers. It was roaring steadily now, flicking shadows everywhere, filling the room with a warm, soothing heat. The men had drinks in their hands as they sat side by side on the couch, their hungry eyes glimmering in the firelight. Their ties were undone, their shirts unbuttoned. Belts and zippers too.

It was the perfect end to a perfect night, or at least it was about to be.

The perfect backdrop for what I was about to do...

$\sim 34 \sim$

AUTUMN

The music was soft, the lights were low. I stood on my toes in a satin green G-string, with matching halter top that left my smooth, quivering belly exposed. I had my hands on my hips. They were resting there, casually.

"You know what you're going to do for us tonight, right?"

Darius's voice was stern and deep. Exactly the way I wanted it.

"Yes," I said breathlessly.

"Tell us, then."

I bit my lip. My entire body was in heat now, and not just from the fireplace.

"I'm going to do everything you say," I murmured softly. "I'm going to suck your cocks. I'm going to beg for it..."

Staring back at their hard, masculine bodies, the intensity was overwhelming. I inhaled a long, shuddering breath, then let it out with a wistful sigh.

"… and I'm going to fuck you both."

My whole body was alive and tingling; every nerve ending, every goosebump stood on end. Between the wine and the heat and the memory of the two loads they'd put in me earlier, the excitement was almost too much to bear. I was practically vibrating.

"Why?" asked Christian, sitting with his knees slightly spread. The hand on the arm of the couch rotated slowly, swirling his whiskey around the glass.

"Because you *own* me," I said huskily. "Because you bid on me. You paid for me…"

I turned around, placing my hands on the fireplace mantle. I spread them wide: arms, legs, everything.

Then, slowly, I reached back and pulled my G-string off to one side.

"This is all yours," I told them, flipping my hair over my shoulder. "It belongs to the both of you."

Christian shifted uncomfortably as something strained to break free of his slacks. Darius actually licked his lips.

"You *do* want this, don't you?" I teased. Bending further forward, I swayed my ass left and right.

The question was entirely rhetorical. I answered it for them by turning around and spreading my arms outward, my finger crawling across both sides of the mantle.

"How many times do you boys think I can make you come?"

There was the jangle of one belt buckle, then two. Both men dropped their slacks and stepped out of them, revealing two pairs of smooth, muscular legs. Their boxer briefs were already tented outward.

"These flames are making my ass *hot*," I breathed, moving it even closer to the firebox. I remained in that position, slightly bent over, until I couldn't take another second of it. "Wanna see?"

Strutting over, I spun to give Darius my ass first. His hands slid across my hot bare skin, and for a moment I let him enjoy it. Hell, I was enjoying it too.

Then I sat myself down on those big thighs, and screwed my ass into his crotch.

"Mmmmmm…"

Kinsley and I had taken a lap-dancing class once, for shits and giggles. It seemed like a hundred years ago, and by now it probably was. Still, I remembered some of the better moves.

And damn it felt good to finally use them.

I spent the next minute or so grinding Darius's lap, sliding the crack of my warm, cherry-red ass up and down along his growing erection. By the time I finished, it was standing straight up, straining to break free of its cotton prison. I smiled evilly, bent to kiss him, and gave it an affectionate squeeze.

"Soon, baby," I said, kissing the head of it through his boxers.

I spun to the other side of the couch, where Christian was already rubbing himself with the palm of his free hand. I wagged a finger at him, indicating he was naughty, then lifted his whiskey and took a long pull from it.

"C'mere," I crooked a finger.

He leaned forward, and I bent to kiss him. Our eyes met, and our faces came together. My hair fell down either side of our cheeks, as my tongue slipped into his mouth.

"Mmmmmm…" I moaned again.

Our kiss was slow and molten, with vanilla and caramel undertones from the bourbon I'd poured him. I savored the taste as Christian's hands slid over every inch of my ass, absorbing the heat there as he sucked gently on my tongue.

Reluctantly I broke our amazing kiss, if only to give him the same treatment I'd given Darius. Grinding into his lap, my hands on his thighs, I gyrated my hips in slow, sensual circles until he too, was fully hard.

"Boxers off," I demanded.

They didn't have to be told twice. By the time I'd turned around and dropped to my knees, both men were standing before me, fully aroused. I wrapped my hands around my two thick prizes and began blowing them, turning my head to each side. I did it sloppily too, with lots of whimpering and moaning and wet, sticky kisses as I passed my mouth back and forth from shaft to beautiful shaft.

Between the fire and wine and the two beautiful bodies at my disposal, I was already soaked and breathless. But the idea of being owned by them was an additional turn on. Playing on the auction was always fun, but tonight I really wanted to serve them by rewarding them with anything and everything they fucking wanted.

Even deeper than that, I wanted a night of total submission. I couldn't wait to be carried upstairs and thrown roughly around the bed. I needed them over me, on me, inside me… pulling my hips up and flipping me over, only to push back inside and plunder me again.

There was nothing I wouldn't do for these men tonight. I was theirs, wholly and completely. Ready and willing to suck them, to fuck them, to let them use me from both ends. I wanted to be their lover, their wife, their girlfriend, their whore...

I wanted to fulfill every last fucking fantasy they ever had. To be the wild, willing outlet for every thrilling depravity their little hearts' desired.

All these things and more swirled through my mind as I knelt before them, alternating taking each of them down my hot, hungry throat. The fire crackled. The music played. The warmth in my stomach grew to an all-consuming heat, leaving me desperate to either bring them off or bring them upstairs, and hopefully both.

That's when Christian took over, pulling me back to the couch.

We were facing each other, kissing fiercely until we leaned back with our thighs still touching. As I watched, totally transfixed, he pushed his rock-hard dick forward and just held it there, right up against my throbbing entrance.

My mouth dropped open as I realized what he was giving me.

I began grinding on it, rotating my hips again as he pushed it through my folds. But it was just the outer folds. Just the shallows. Christian held himself perfectly still as I grinded upwards and downwards, dragging myself along the strong top of his impossibly hard shaft. And through it all, Darius remained on his feet. He continued feeding me every inch of his hard, throbbing manhood, while also giving me something thick to hold onto as I rode myself into an absolute frenzy.

One of them undid my halter, and I gasped as two hot

mouths closed over my breasts. I was bucking and churning, dragging my clit forward and back. The heat, the pressure, the feel of their tongues... it was all too much, the intensity, too overwhelming. I cried out as I finally gave in to it, rolling my chin toward the ceiling as I shuddered through a rapid-fire series of short but savage orgasms.

And then something awesome and miraculous happened.

The boys came at exactly the same time.

Christian's shaft began thumping hard against my folds. He pulled it upward and outward, spraying jet after jet of hot, sticky seed all over my thighs, my stomach, my trembling, heaving chest. I watched him guide it with his fist, as simultaneously, I felt the heat of Darius's own load, spraying my mouth and chin. He pushed forward, past my lips, and I welcomed him in with a whimper. I reveled in his sweet taste as he continued filling my mouth, the underside of his manhood pulsing thickly against my tongue.

When I finally looked up again, Christian locked eyes with me. Down below, my flower felt teased and still hungry. Taking matters into my hands, I guided him inside me and screwed my hips all the way down. He was buried to the hilt and I could still feel him twitching inside me. The sensation of him emptying the last of his balls triggered yet another flood of heat in my womb.

I bit my lip again, shifting my sex-sleepy gaze back and forth between the both of them. I never looked away, never broke eye contact.

And in that exact moment, I knew I was hooked.

~ 35 ~

AUTUMN

"And how's dad? Doing well?"

I was flat on my stomach, naked as the day I was born. My body was still buzzing — especially the part between my legs. But I was content. Sated. Happy. The sun coming in through the window felt warm on my skin.

"Dad's amazing," Shane reported happily. "I took him fishing, and he caught a pike as long as my arm. He's in his glory, believe me."

Christian walked by, wearing only a towel. He reached out and slapped my ass so hard, so perfectly, it would undoubtedly leave a handprint.

"I love it!" I half-exclaimed, half-jumped. I stuck my tongue out at Christian. "He was happy to see you, I'm sure."

"He was," said Shane. "I mean, he is. But I also told him this has to be a short trip. That I have to get back."

"Shane, you don't have to—"

"And he understands," Shane cut in. "I promised my

parents a longer trip later."

Darius finally stirred, somewhere beside me. He swung his legs from the bed, got up, and slapped the *other* side of my ass.

Reaching back to rub it, I playfully flipped him off.

"How are things going over there?" asked Shane. "No more trouble?"

"Not so far, no."

"And you're sticking close to the guys, like I told you to?"

My eyes shifted unconsciously to Darius, who was naked and yawning before the window. He stretched his sculpted arms upward and outward, extending his fingers. The move accentuated every delicious muscle of broad, beautiful back.

Not to mention what it did for his tight, perfectly symmetrical ass.

"Autumn?"

"Umm... something like that, yeah," I finally answered. "And I promise. I won't let them leave my sight."

Shane chuckled. "More like they won't leave your pretty ass alone, if I'm guessing correctly."

I shrugged and pulled an errant piece of hair from my mouth. "Well it *is* a beautiful ass. You said it yourself."

"True."

"And if you were here..."

"I'd be glued to that pretty little ass," he admitted. "Among other places."

I rolled over and scissored my legs, reaching down to feel how swollen and wet I still was. The guys had *really* put me through the paces last night. They'd torn me up. Thrown me around. Taken me in every possibly place, position, and combination, until the whole bedroom was spinning around me.

Last night I'd become theirs, wholly and completely. The warm, willing center of their filthy little universe.

And it was *exactly* what I'd so desperately needed.

"When you get home," I purred to Shane, "I promise you and I are going to have some alone time. Some making up for lost time, time."

I closed my eyes and imagined dragging Shane into my bedroom, then locking the door behind us. The image came with a gratifying bolt of heat.

"Home?"

My eyes blinked open. "Oh. Umm… yeah, sorry. I meant—"

"I know what you meant, Autumn," he interrupted me quickly. "And I like it." Then, after a pause: "Actually, I love it."

The heat was spreading. My belly felt warm, and not just from the sun.

"Shane…" I said. "I—I really need you to know how much—"

"I need to tell you something too," Shane interjected. "Something important. Once I get back."

"Shaaaaane!"

The sound of a middle-aged woman's voice calling his name broke through over the phone. I couldn't help but smile, picturing him sitting in his childhood bedroom, as his mother called him down for breakfast.

"I'm sorry baby, but I've gotta run. Dad's doctor's appointment. I'm tagging along."

Baby.

"Oh. Okay."

"I'll call you later," Shane blurted. "By then I should have info on a return flight."

He called you baby.

"Give my best to your mom and dad," I said, the words feeling a bit foolish. "Not that they know me or anything, but—"

"I will," said Shane. Somehow, although I couldn't see him, I could perfectly envision his boyish grin. "Besides, they know you. I've already told them about you."

He hung up. I sat there for several seconds, with the phone still to my ear.

He told them about you.

The idea was endearing, scary, a little bit weird. But also, so totally, totally Shane.

The phone suddenly rang again, so loudly against my ear I nearly jumped out of my sun-kissed skin! I pressed the button to pick it up without even looking.

"Did you forget something?" I teased.

"Autumn..."

The voice was different. Not Shane's.

Not anyone's.

"Yes?"

213

"It's me. Edward."

For some reason the name didn't register right away. It should've, but after my conversation with Shane I was too distracted.

"Edward?" I repeated numbly.

"Yes, Edward." The voice was low. Solemn. Serious. And then I knew.

My eyes widened, and I bolted upright.

"Edward, your *cousin*."

~ 36 ~

AUTUMN

Realization stole over me, and everything in my world grew suddenly colder. Naked and vulnerable, I stood up and began pulling on clothes.

"W—Why are you calling me?" I stammered, silently cursing myself for sounding weak. "What do you want?"

"I want you to give the place up."

A few seconds of silence slipped by. He was so matter-of-fact about it, I had to laugh.

"Give it up," I repeated.

"Yes. Please."

I couldn't believe the balls on this guy!

"And why the hell would I do that?" I spat back. "Simply because you *told* me to?"

"I'm not telling you," Edward corrected me. "I'm *asking* you."

His voice was identical to brother's voice, which of

course made sense. They were twins, after all. But in some way I couldn't quite put my finger on, it also *didn't* sound like Emmitt.

"He's *our* father, Autumn," Edward went on. "Not yours. The place belongs to us. It's only right."

"Your father..."

"Yes."

Fully dressed now, I peeked into the hallway and could hear the shower running. For some reason, I closed the bedroom door.

"You realize that as my uncle, he left it to me," I told him. "That it's rightfully mine."

"Legally, maybe," he answered cautiously. "But that doesn't make it right."

Alarm bells were going off in my head. The conversation we were having was too calm, too civil. Pinching the phone to my ear with my shoulder, I folded my arms over my chest.

"Did Emmitt put you up to this?"

Edward's voice went lower. "My brother knows nothing about this. I called you on my own."

"To ask me to give up the property," I snapped. "The one I've called home for an entire year. The one I sank every last dime of my savings into."

"I'm sorry you did that," he said, and he sounded genuine. "But it's still—"

"I gave up my family business to do this," I cut in. "Everything I own is on the line, here."

For a few moments, there was only silence. Was he

actually empathizing with me? Or just trying to make it seem that way?

"You know we could've had this conversation in person," I told him. "You and your brother could've told me who you were in the first place. We could've sat down and talked this out."

"I know, but—"

"Instead, you showed up and tried to take my property by force," I snarled back at him. "You broke into my place when I wasn't there. You sabotaged it while I was sleeping." My anger was back, and full force too. "You're even suing me for fuck's sake!"

"Autumn…"

"Who were those assholes who broke in here the other night?" I demanded.

"Those guys… they were nobody," he answered awkwardly. "That was a huge mistake."

"Damn right it was."

"You don't understand," he pleaded. "Emmitt, he—"

"Emmitt's a fucking maniac!" I practically shouted. "Get *him* on the phone. Let's see what he has to say about you calling me and trying to work out a peaceful—"

"No."

The voice was a little sterner now, a little more forceful. I could hear a hint of Emmitt in there, too.

"Autumn, listen," he pleaded again. "Our father, he actually meant something to us."

"Please," I laughed. "Spare me."

"But our mother..." The words trailed off, and his voice changed again. It was softer now. Almost regretful.

"She kept him from us," Edward went on. "There were times when we could've had something together. When we *should've* had something." He cleared his throat. "But then, well, I don't know what happened. We were so young, and she told us these terrible, terrible things, and—"

He stopped talking, and the phone went abruptly silent. Listening intently, I could hear distant voices in the background. They sounded angry for several long moments. Then they faded away, as if he were moving.

"How many more scumbags are you and your brother going to bring up from Blue Ridge?" I demanded fiercely. "And are you going to cut more stuff down? Burn it up? What's the plan here, Edward? At least let me know, so I can prepare for it."

The phone remained so silent, I actually checked it to see if he'd hung up. Then, in a low voice:

"You're my *cousin*, Autumn."

I let the words sink in, to see if they made me feel anything. Anything else but anger.

"In blood only, maybe," I allowed him.

"Yeah," he said bitterly. "I get it. And I know this might seem pathetic, but outside of Emmitt, well..."

I knew what he was going to say before he even said it.

"You're the only other family I have."

He let out a short laugh, but not in a joking way. This laughter was bitter and awful.

"I know that sounds pretty sad—"

"No," I jumped in quietly. "It doesn't."

For a long, quiet moment, neither of us spoke. Like two waiting soldiers, on respective sides of the battlefield.

"Autumn, my brother's not going to stop," Edward said softly. "Emmitt's like a robot: once he gets something in his head, he won't deviate from it until it's accomplished. Our mother knows this, and she's taking advantage of it. She basically programmed him with her own instructions."

"Oh really?" I challenged. "And what about you?"

Silence stretched out before us. It said everything.

"Emmitt's my brother. He's still—"

"You know I appreciate this call," I cut him off, "as well as the head's up. But you're wrong about one thing though, Edward."

"What's that?"

"We're not family." The words were cold, and intentionally so. I could almost feel him shrinking away, at the other end of the phone.

"You and Emmitt might be the only blood I have left, but you'll *never* be a part of my life."

~ 37 ~

AUTUMN

Telling the guys about the phone call was non-negotiable, of course. What I wasn't prepared for, was their level of disappointment. Darius simply couldn't believe it. Christian was borderline angry.

"I'm sorry, the call came in and I answered it without thinking," I told them. "It just all happened so fast."

"You should've gotten us," demanded Darius. "We could've talked some sense into him."

"That's the weird thing," I shrugged. "He actually *was* making sense."

We were at breakfast, which was usually a fun time of the day. Right now, the guys were on edge. I knew it was because all they really wanted was to protect me. That their frustration was more the result of a missed opportunity, than anything else.

It still didn't make me feel any less guilty, however.

"Look, I'm not condoning anything, but Edward seems fairly rational," I told them. "It's his brother who's the crazy one."

"They're dangerous," Christian growled into his coffee. "The both of them."

Darius nodded in agreement. "He's not wrong."

"I'll bet the whole call was to ruse, too," he added.

"A ruse?"

"A bullshit reach-out, to lull you into a false sense of security." He shook his head. "They planned this. The both of them."

I considered it, but only for a moment. "I don't think so. Nothing about our conversation seemed scripted. Everything Edward said seemed genuine to me."

"Genuine, sure," scoffed Darius. "He'll genuinely destroy this place rather than let you have it. He'll genuinely set the house on fire, while we're still—"

"No, I'm serious," I protested. "He wasn't... Well..."

"Wasn't what?"

"I don't know. Something about their mother." I shook my head. "Almost like she's behind this."

"Their mother is a terrible person," Christian agreed. "That much we know, from everything we learned about her."

I pushed my eggs away. They weren't nearly as fluffy as when Shane made them. They tasted flavorless today, anyway.

"Look, I reasoned, "his brother might very well be psychotic, but Edward wasn't really into this at all."

"You think so, huh?"

"Yeah. I could just tell."

Darius leaned back in his chair, cradling his own coffee. He looked thoughtful.

"If that's really the case, maybe we could crack him."

"Who?"

"Edward. We could bring him around to our way of seeing things. Use him against his brother."

I shrugged, not really knowing what to say. The whole thing felt shitty to me, even under these circumstances. I had so much pent-up anger, I wasn't sure I was ready to let go of it yet. Not to mention, sympathizing with someone who was actively trying to destroy your life seemed like a terrible idea to begin with.

I scraped my plate, gave each of them a kiss on the cheek, and walked out into the morning sun. Was there really so much to be upset about? It was already a bright, beautiful day. I'd woken up between two gorgeous, slumbering giants, and a third one would be on the way home to me soon.

On top of all that, last night's lovemaking had been damn near apocalyptic. It set all new sexual records for me, and somehow *still* had me wanting to stretch those boundaries even further.

Seriously, a girl could have worse problems.

I took a slow sip of my coffee, then walked barefoot into the beautiful rows of well-kept vines. The greenery was blooming in every direction, and some of it was teeming with grapes. It was going to be a good crop. A great harvest. I'd get some work done, then go food shopping a little later on. I might even call Kinsley, and tell her who—

"Excuse me?"

I whirled, hands up, ready to defend myself. Standing just behind me, between the rows, was a woman in an immaculately tailored suit.

"Is Christian Gardner here?"

She looked absurdly out of place, standing there in the wet grass. The woman was exceptionally tall, with striking, angular features. Her jet-black hair was pulled backward into a tight ponytail, just above a pair of clear, wide-rimmed glasses.

"C—Christian?"

"Yes." Using her middle finger, she pushed her glasses higher on the bridge of her nose. "I've been tracking his phone. It says he's somewhere nearby."

I was still stunned, still taking her in. "He's here."

Folding her arms, she stared back at me impatiently. "Well, are you going to take me to him? Or should I just keep wandering these—"

"And who exactly are you?" I blurted.

The woman sighed in exasperation. With every last ounce of willpower, she appeared to be fighting the urge to roll her eyes.

"I'm Jacqueline," she said. Then, after a pause:

"Christian's *partner*."

~ 38 ~

AUTUMN

"Christian's your... partner?"

I should've been warm in the morning sun, but an icy chill stole through my entire body. My throat went instantly dry.

"That's right."

I stared at her some more. Head to toe, top to bottom, this woman was flawlessly put together. In the meantime I was half-dressed, messily barefoot, and sporting the worst sex-hair I'd had since college. I felt utterly ridiculous.

But the worst part was the pain. The betrayal. The disgusting lies that I'd fallen for...

"He's not my *partner*, partner," the woman amended quickly. Apparently she could sense my conflict. Hell, the international space station could sense my conflict.

"He's my partner at the firm."

A tsunami of relief blasted over me, washing away the pain, the uncertainty, the silliness of my knee-jerk accusations. The smile painted across my face in its wake must've looked absolutely maniacal.

"O—Oh, sure," I eventually stammered. "Come with me."

I led her back to the house, hyper-aware that she was probably ruining a five-hundred dollar pair of designer shoes. I could tell this wasn't the type of woman who cared, though.

"Christian!"

He came out a few seconds later, wearing the same thing he'd worn to breakfast: a pair of sweat shorts he'd 'borrowed' from Shane, and a T-shirt without sleeves.

"Jacqueline." He uttered the name without a hint of surprise, though I could detect a quiet sigh of resignation. "I guess it was only a matter of time until you showed up."

"A matter of time?" Jacqueline demanded. "Christian, you've been gone for weeks! You barely call to check in, and when you do I conveniently miss you!"

What I imagined to be her courtroom voice was intimidating for sure. Not to Christian, though, who only shrugged and said nothing.

"Miles and Carmen have taken over the bulk of your case load," she went on, "but there's still tons of work to be caught up on. We filed for court dates to be moved of course —"

"Good," he said, taking a casual sip of his coffee.

Jacqueline's eyes seemed to get even prettier, the angrier she got. *"Good?"*

"Great, actually," he agreed. "Nice to see Miles and Carmen stepping up."

"But—"

"And you give the next two week's worth of my cases away as well," he said nonchalantly. "Call it…" he glanced my way momentarily. "Family emergency."

Jacqueline squinted back at him, rather than respond. The shock of the situation had worn off, and she was already shifting gears.

"You really do need some time away, don't you?"

"Yes."

"It's been years, I suppose, since you took any kind of actual vacation." She cleared her throat and straightened her stance. "Alright, how much—"

"I don't know."

Jacqueline shifted her weight from one foot the other. His casual approach was infuriating her. Even so, she remained calm and cool, as lawyers are trained to do.

"Well, you can't stay here forever," she said, matter-of-factly. "We're *senior* partners. We've got a firm to run, and trials already on the schedule. You've missed important depositions, and—"

"Jacqueline, you're not getting this. I don't care."

Her head snapped my way, and she gave me such a venomous look of contempt I felt like shrinking away. Instead, I took a step forward and crossed my arms.

"This isn't my fault, if that's what you're thinking. He came on his own."

"He came because you called him," she shot back. "He flew all the way here, on zero notice, without any thought to the schedule, or—"

"Schedule?" I laughed, then shrugged, casually.

"Sometimes life happens. Friends drop things to help each other, believe it or not."

She turned her nose up at me. "Friends?"

"Jacqueline," Christian butted in. "ENOUGH."

He finished his coffee, then set the mug down in the grass beside him. A bird flew by, chirping merrily. When it landed on a nearby branch, Christian actually turned to smile at it.

"I'm assuming you brought a stack of files for me to review?" he asked, without looking away.

The tall brunette nodded curtly. "Yes. In case I couldn't convince you to come back immediately."

"You can't," he admitted. "But I will take the rest of the day to sit down with you and go over them."

It wasn't the answer Jacqueline wanted, but for now it was the best she was getting. She took the win.

"Fine," she said. "Get dressed and come with me. I've conscripted an office a few miles from here. We can use it to go over—"

"No."

"No?"

"We can go over the case files, but we're doing it here. There's a table on the back patio we can have all to ourselves." He turned to face me. "Right Autumn?"

"Sure is," I smiled happily. "Play your cards right, I might even make lunch."

Jacqueline wrinkled her nose at the both of us. "You want to do this *outside?*"

Christian chuckled. "You're surrounded by walls and windows all day, Jacqueline. The fresh air will be good for you."

There was a moment of silence as she considered this, then she shook her head in acceptance. Defeated for now, the lawyer stormed back in the direction she'd come.

"It bothers me how flippant you are about this," she called back loudly.

Christian's only answer was a shit-eating grin. It was the purest, happiest expression I'd ever seen on his face.

I went to him, sliding my arms over his shoulders as I went though a whole gamut of emotions. I felt happiness for his freedom. Gratitude for his loyalty. There was some guilt for the apparent sacrifices he was making at work, but it was quickly overshadowed by the pure serenity of the expression on his face.

"Hey…"

Christian looked down at me with those smoldering brown eyes.

"You thought we were together, didn't you?"

I shrugged a shoulder. "Well she said she was your partner, so I just naturally assumed…"

"Jacqueline?" he smiled. "Does she strike you as my type?"

"Do you even *have* a type?" I quipped.

"I mean, the two of us once got drunk at a Christmas party, and took each other for a test drive. But it didn't stick."

I felt a flash of intense, unwelcome jealousy. The sheer magnitude of my envy was shocking.

"Really?"

Christian smirked. "No, not really. For one, Jacqueline would never get drunk. She abstains from everything fun: alcohol, dating, taking time off — anything that might draw her away from work." He shrugged. "I've never seen her go out with a man, and I don't think she's into women, either. Her first and only love is work. She's all about the next case, the next litigation, the next trial."

I shook my head slowly. "I don't see how someone can live like that."

"I do," said Christian. "I've been living like that for years."

Sliding in close, he crushed me against his chest and gave me the best hug in the universe.

"Up until now."

~ 39 ~

DARIUS

"Three... two... one..."

I tugged at the knot at the back of her neck, and the blindfold fell away. Her eyes were still closed, though.

"Alright. Open your eyes."

Autumn's excitement and curiosity had been fighting it out for what seemed like forever, but somehow she'd restrained herself. Entrusting us with the design of her tasting room had been a pretty big ask. Several times she'd threatened to sneak in here and check the place out. She'd even tried bribing Shane and I with sexual favors, just for a sneak peek.

And now here she was, finally beyond the plastic curtain. Taking in everything we'd been working on for these past few weeks, while she worked in the vineyard.

The anticipation was killing us as her eyes fluttered open. Autumn blinked a few times, before her hands shot up to her mouth.

"HOLY FUCKING SHIT!"

Shock and awe lit up her beautiful face like fireworks, making the whole thing finally worth it. Every day, every hour, every last minute we'd spent making this place great again — it was all paid in full by this one singular moment.

"I... I can't BELIEVE this!"

Shane was beaming, too, having arrived home earlier. We'd really gone all out. The two of us had cashed in favors with several vendors in order to get everything we needed in such a short span of time. But the end result had made the whole effort worthwhile.

"There's still lots to get done," I admitted. "You need glassware, plumbing fixtures, bar accoutrements. And there's plenty of decor to figure out, including finalizing where you'll put the cash-wrap for all the merchandise you plan to sell, along with—"

Autumn kissed me so hard she nearly knocked me over. I stumbled backwards, directly into the bar. The U-shaped slabs of beautifully-polished maple would ultimately seat dozens of people. Once she got the place open, that is.

"Obviously you still need to pick your choice of seating," said Shane. He pulled out a chair from one of five different sample tables. "But we brought in a few ideas to get you started."

She ran over and kissed him too, then sat down excitedly in the chair he'd pulled out for her. Autumn leaned back to admire our handiwork, tears streaking her face as she took the place in. Her glassy eyes shifted from the high-flung rafters to the polished oak floors we'd meticulously finished beneath her feet.

"We rode around a little too," I added. "Pindar, Pugliese, Jason's vineyard... we stole a bunch of ideas from other places."

"Some very good ideas," smiled Shane.

He swung smoothly into the seat beside her. Stepping around the table, I took the chair on her opposite side

"You wouldn't believe the kind of money you can make with outdoor seating over the summer," I added. "And your asshole cousins already made plenty of space for that, by cutting down the closest row of vines."

Her tears were still flowing. But they were good tears.

"You can set up picnic areas," Shane continued. "Bring in some live music on the weekends. Pop up some tents. Throw down some horseshoe pits and cornhole boards."

"And you can brew craft beer in those fermenters downstairs," I pointed to the floor. "Do you have any idea how big *that* market is?"

Autumn was quivering now, shaking all over. I realized how very long she'd been alone. How many empty years she'd had to be stronger than strong, because there was no one else to rely on but herself.

"The two of you did all of this," she practically cried. "For... for..."

"For you."

I reached out and laid a hand over her trembling arm. She moved to interlace her fingers with mine.

"In the interests of full disclosure, the lawyer helped too," I added. "He's not nearly as handy with a drill or a saw, but he did what he could. He's also been expediting all of the permits and licenses your uncle had started on. You're not going to be able to open *this* year, of course. But by next spring you'll be all set up and ready to go."

"Not to mention fully stocked up on last year's

vintage," Shane nodded through the window.

Just outside, the wind was blowing the vines gently in the afternoon sun. She looked out at them for a moment, her porcelain face perfectly framed by her golden blonde hair.

Shane glanced at me, and I gave him the nod. This was the time, this was the place.

It was now or never.

"Autumn," I said gently. "We need to talk to you. The both of us."

Oddly, she didn't move at all. She continued staring out the window, her expression entirely changed.

"I know," she said softly. "Your job here is done. You've done everything you can for me, everything possible and more."

"Autumn..."

"But you have your business to take care of," she went on. "Your own lives to get back to. "But this..." she tapped the table with one delicate finger. "THIS? This is the greatest gift you could've ever given me," she murmured. "Outside all the love and support you've already given, of course."

I reached out and wiped a tear from her cheek. "Are you done?"

"Yeah, I guess," she chuckled. "I don't know. I'm just so happy and sad at the same time. It's bittersweet."

"Why?" asked Shane

"Are you kidding?" she laughed through her tears. "My whole life's been a fantasy camp lately, but I always knew the end would come. That eventually you boys would fly back to Hollywood and this whole wonderful thing would come to an end."

"You did, huh?"

"Sure. It's been weighing on me the whole time."

I couldn't take it another moment longer. She was laughing, crying, hugging us across the table, which was rapidly becoming stained with her tears.

"And what if we told you none of that is going to happen?" I murmured.

The look in her eyes told me she didn't understand. Not even a little bit.

"Autumn…" Shane offered, taking her other hand in his. "What if you didn't have to be alone?"

She cleared her throat, or at least she tried to. "You mean you'll stay even longer?" she croaked. "I can't ask you to do that. I can't keep you away. Besides, it'll make it even harder when you do eventually leave—"

"What if we didn't have to leave you at all?"

Autumn's lower lip quivered. As the sun kissed her glistening cheeks, I realized I'd never been more attracted to her than in that moment. Her confusion was adorable. But I couldn't let it go on.

"We considered asking you to come back to California with us," I told her. "Hell, we considered throwing you over our shoulder and *dragging* you back. But it wouldn't be fair. Not after all the work you've put in here, and how much you love this place. Look at you. You're thriving. You *belong* here."

I paused, caught her gaze, and smiled.

"And we were thinking, well… maybe we do too."

"But—"

"We love you, Autumn. That's non-negotiable."

I leaned in and kissed her right on her stunned, quivering lips. After a second or two, she began kissing me back.

This is it...

Her mouth was warm and welcome, her resulting sighs soft and delicate. A hand went to her face, pulling her away, and then Shane was kissing her too.

I watched, strangely aroused, not the least bit jealous as he drank from her lips. Shane and I had talked it over so many times, while building this place. Neither of us wanted to give her up. Neither of us was willing to step back and let the other one have her.

The situation seemed impossible, and destined to end badly. Until one day we both came to the same conclusion, at the same exact time.

Her mouth came back to me, and I kissed her some more. She was utterly breathless now, those blue eyes glazed over with lust and confusion.

"We didn't expect to fall for you, Autumn," I murmured against her mouth. "But we have. We have, and neither one of us has a single regret."

"So... so you'd *both* stay?" She hesitated. "You'd both... want to..."

"Share you?"

I could practically hear the butterflies bouncing around her stomach. She swallowed hard and nodded.

"Yes."

"Do you want to share *us?*"

Her lips were all wet and swollen.   I wanted desperately to kiss them some more.

"Are you kidding?" she finally breathed. "I haven't had to share anyone. If anything, I've been the greedy one."

"You've shared your love," said Shane. "You've shared your life with us."

I smiled in agreement. "You've opened your heart and home to us, and in doing that you've bared your soul. You've shown us every last bit of Autumn Holloway. Physically *and* emotionally."

She was breathing heavy now, her mind moving a million miles an hour. Her eyes searched us, moving back and forth. Perhaps trying to figure out if we were serious.

"B—But how would that even *work?*" she pleaded. At the same time, she looked ready to bite her tongue as she said the words.

"Exactly as it *has* worked."

"But there are two of you, and just one of me." She paused, tilting her head.   "You can't *really* be happy with splitting my attention, can you?"

"Do you feel like you've been splitting your attention between us?" I asked simply. "Or rather, giving all of yourself to the *both* of us?"

She had to think about that for a moment. But in the end, the answer was easy.

"The second one, actually."

Shane grinned. "Then what's the problem?"

She was in a corner now, with no real way out. The ball was in her court.

"Look, I know it sounds crazy," I helped her out. "But we don't want this to end. *You* don't want it to end. So why end it? Why couldn't we be happy here, sharing you in every way?" I nodded toward Shane and smiled. "The two of us have shared *much* stranger things."

Autumn was in total disbelief now. But there was a hopefulness and excitement behind her trepidation.

"But your company back home," she murmured. "Your projects. All that you've built—"

"We'd build it again," I shrugged. "Here. On Long Island. There's a building boom right now on the east end that rivals anything we're doing in the valley. And no shortage of veterans that need help, of course."

"And we'd still run things out there," said Shane. "Just not in person. You don't build what we have without competent people, and many of those people are itching to move up anyway."

We'd discussed this at length, of course. The very minute Shane got back and told me everything he felt for her. It was a welcome relief, because I'd felt those things too. Up until that moment, I'd been terrified to tell him I wanted to stay here with her.

"Of course we'd still travel back and forth," I finished. "Probably a great deal in the beginning. But we'd alternate, so one of us would always be here, of course. We never want to leave you alone again."

Her eyes welled with even more tears. It was our intent, but I guess it couldn't really be helped.

"I... I don't know what to say."

"Say you want us," said Shane. "Say you'll be with us."

"I want you," she said, looking up again without hesitation. "I'll be with you. I *love* you…"

She looked down at her lap again. I sensed the other shoe about to drop.

"But?"

"But… But *Christian.*"

Shane and I looked at each other. We knew she and the lawyer were close. As close as we were.

"I love him too," she murmured. "I— I can't help it. I—"

"Christian has his own life back home," I consoled her. "His own path to choose. And yes, he's grown on us too," I said softly. "Even for a lawyer."

"Especially for a lawyer," Shane admitted.

"But—"

"But what?"

A new voice boomed loudly from across the room, echoing amidst the overhead rafters. As a trio, we looked up together. And there was Christian, standing near the plastic curtain, his arms folded across his chest.

"If the three of you think I'm going *anywhere*, you're out of your damn minds."

~ 40 ~

CHRISTIAN

I unfolded my arms and crossed the room, anxious to get near her. She was crying for them, and that was okay. By now I'd seen what I wanted to see. What I'd needed to see:

She was crying for *me*, too.

I spun one of the wooden chairs around and sat down in it backwards, resting my arms on the back of the seat. The others were staring at me in surprise. Probably because it was a very unlawyerlike, unChristian-like thing to do.

"Seriously. I'm here to stay."

Autumn's tears made her pretty face shiny. I wanted to scoop her into my arms and crush her against me. I wanted to kiss those cheeks until they were dry, then bury my face in that soft blonde hair.

"What do you mean *stay?*" she sniffed.

"Everything Chandler and Joey just said," I shrugged, indicating the others, "is exactly how I feel. Autumn, I *love* you. I know that now. I think I've known it the whole time, actually. And up until this moment, it's scared the shit out of me."

Her eyes gleamed with new tears. "Why?"

"Because I didn't know how you felt," I said honestly. "I didn't know if my feelings would be reciprocated, or if this were something finite and temporary. I didn't know if I could open myself to something like this, without knowing for sure that your feelings were real."

"Christian, you *have* to know I love you," she murmured.

"Trust me," I smiled. "I do."

"But I also… I also love…"

"You love us all."

She nodded slowly, almost guilty.

"Hey. Look at me."

I reached across the table with both arms, holding my palms out. Meeting my gaze again, Autumn placed her hands in mine.

"Loving us all is totally nuts," I told her with a smile. "But considering how this whole crazy thing went down in the first place, I guess it can't be helped. You were put into a position where you never had to choose. And so you didn't. Not even once."

She opened her mouth to say something. The look in my eyes stopped her.

"Still, you've never held back your affections, not from any of us." I nodded toward Darius. "And like he just pointed out a minute ago, you've never divided your attention between us either. You've given *all* of yourself, all of the time. And that says everything."

The other two had some kind of planned or rehearsed

speech, or at least it seemed that way. I, on the other hand, was shooting from the hip. As always, I went with my gut. In all my trials and arguments and deliberations, it still hadn't failed me yet.

"At first I thought I was competing with these assholes," I went on, "vying for your affections. But now I see differently. I'm not competing with them, I'm loving you alongside them. And... well..." I shrugged. "Maybe they're not such assholes, either."

"Oh, believe me, we're assholes," Shane spoke up.

"Yeah," laughed Darius. "Don't take that away from us."

"Fine," I smirked back at them. "Duly noted. But my point is this: I went to that auction to broaden my horizons. To push the boundaries of my non-existent personal life, and maybe to find someone new and interesting to share my world with." I squeezed her hands in mine. "I *found* that person, Autumn. I followed her across the country and I fell in love with her."

She looked at me dazedly, and I saw the same love that I felt for her reflected back in those shimmering blue eyes. I felt the depth of it in my heart. The warmth of it in my soul.

"The last thing in the world I'm going to do now, is fly away."

Autumn stared at me for a long time. I couldn't even imagine what she was thinking.

"You're not just a lawyer, you're a *partner*," she finally said. "You have cases, trials, an entire practice back home."

"I do."

"So you're willing to just... just—"

"Autumn, simply having these things doesn't make my life meaningful. It took me thirty years to realize that. All this time I've been spinning my wheels. Moving without direction, without purpose, without a sense of *family*."

My thoughts floated back to where they always went: my mother, my father. All the missing time we could've had together. All the time we *should've* had, if not for ceaseless, never-ending work.

"Without you, there's nothing for me back home," I told her. "An empty house. An empty life. Chaining myself every day to a chair in some stuffy courtroom, or worse, some wood-paneled office surrounded by books of meaningless jargon."

"But your sister," she murmured. "Anna…"

"Anna's getting married, and to a good man. She's finally moving on. She's carving out her own life."

I let go of her, but only long enough to take her delicate face in my hands. Leaning across the table, I kissed her soft, beautiful mouth, then put our foreheads together.

"I'm thinking it's time I carved out mine."

~ *41* ~

SHANE

"Are you... are you sure you don't want to..."

I breathed the words as her head bobbed up and down, somewhere between my legs. I had both hands buried in her cornsilk hair. My fingers sifting, searching, as her wet lips traveled up and down the full length of my shaft.

"Because if you want to climb on it," I murmured hotly. "If you still want to... ride it..."

My resolve was quickly draining. If she'd heard me at all, I couldn't tell.

"You'll need to stop... because... if you don't..."

Autumn paused for a moment to look up at me, with the very tip of my manhood still in her mouth. She winked, chuckled, then went straight back down.

All the way down.

Well, I guess that answers that question.

I sighed happily, sinking back into my pillow to enjoy the last few seconds before oblivion. Autumn's mouth was so hot it felt molten. Her tongue swirled, her lips locked tightly around me as she whimpered and moaned and pumped with one hand.

With the other, she gave my balls a firm, encouraging squeeze.

FUUUUCK!

I erupted down her throat, spewing my own lava deep into her warm, willing mouth. Autumn took it all, pumping me throughout as she swallowed the entirety of my load.. In the meantime, my mind rocketed off to other planets. It shot through distant galaxies of pure, liquid rapture, twitching and pulsing as I clawed at the sheets beneath me.

She was still whimpering softly by the time she finished, giving the still-throbbing head of my swollen member one final, sticky-wet kiss.

"Are we happy?" she smiled up at me, with lips a lot fuller than they were ten minutes ago.

"*Very* happy," I sighed back. "I really fucking needed that."

"I could tell," she chuckled, rubbing her belly. "And to think, that was just a small *part* of your welcome back present."

She winked again, and blew me a kiss. I couldn't stop staring at her ass, though.

"Bring that thing up here," I told her.

"Why?" Autumn teased.

"I need it."

I inhaled her sweet scent as she climbed over me, stopping to kiss her way up my chest along the way. Pulling her G-string to one side had become of my favorite things in the world. I'd had to move pretty fast to get that honor lately, because the others were always ready to beat me to it.

"Tell me how much you missed me," she whispered wickedly, into my ear.

"So fucking much."

She pulled a blanket over us, from the waist down. In the dim light of the bedroom, it made things cozy.

"Now tell me how much you missed *this.*"

She placed my hand over her sex, so warm and soft and ready for me. As always, she was drenched. She bit my lip, then groaned as I slipped two fingers inside her.

"I missed this…" I murmured against her mouth, while cupping her gently. "But I also missed *you.*"

I kissed her mouth. Her face. Her cheeks and forehead.

"I missed holding you," I admitted, cuddling her closer. "I missed the sound of your voice. The music of your laughter." Our tongues touched lightly, as I kissed her some more. "I missed being pressed against you in the night, and feeling your warmth. I missed watching the rise and fall of your chest as you sleep."

I began gliding my fingers in and out of her. But slowly. Tenderly.

Autumn's eyes was half-lidded, but no less beautiful. I kissed those too, just before my lips found hers again.

"The moment my plane took off, I realized that I'd fallen in love with you," I told her. "And it was the best feeling in the world." I paused, mischievously. "Well… *second* best, maybe."

Her face softened and a smile emerged, as her lips grazed mine.

"What's the first?"

I curled my fingers straight into her G-spot. She jumped, adorably.

"This."

All the breath left her lungs, as she cooed into my mouth. I kissed her some more. I just couldn't get enough. I'd dreamt of this moment, ever since I'd left. It had only been days, but they felt like months.

There was no way I could be without her. No possible world in which she didn't exist. Autumn had come into our lives with all the speed of a fighter jet, screaming her way across the sky of our lonely existence. It wasn't at all surprising that Darius and I would fall for her. The only real surprise was that we were both willing to share.

"Did you really tell your parents about me?" she murmured softly into my neck.

"Yes."

"What did they say?"

"They were happy for me, although I don't think they fully understood." I pulled her closer. "They will, though. You'll see when you finally meet them."

"I can't wait."

"My mother's an open-minded person, and an ex-hippie at that. And my father... well..."

"He just wants you to be happy," she guessed.

"Yes."

We stared at each other for a quiet moment, enjoying the closeness of our bond. Our bodies were warm. The smile on her face was beautifully serene.

"I want you to be happy, because I love you too," Autumn whispered. "It was insane to admit that, at first. Even to myself. But the three of you have made it easy for me. You've given me every avenue I need to express that love. And I plan on doing just that," she breathed. "In ways that are going to make your head swim."

She shifted a leg upward, sliding it along mine. It gave me better access as she squirmed against my already soaked fingers and palm. I fingered her some more, playing a whole symphony against her warm, inner folds. Every time my thumb brushed her swollen button, she squealed a different noise.

"Now... *fuck* me."

I looked down into the face of the woman I'd come to love, and her sapphire eyes had changed again. They were dreamy now. Pregnant with arousal. One delicate hand gave me a squeeze beneath the blankets, and I was shocked to find myself fully hard again.

"Your wish is my command," I smiled, as I nudged my way between those smooth, supple thighs.

~ 42 ~

AUTUMN

Three boyfriends.

Not three lovers, three dates, three hookups. Not three 'friends with benefits' either, all being juggled at the same time.

No, I had three separate, individual boyfriends. Three incredible men who not only knew about each other, but who were all willing to share me... and often, simultaneously.

Especially simultaneously.

It wasn't exactly the type of thing a girl ever aspired to, to be honest. Fantasies were one thing, but reality was quite another. In the dead of night, trapped in my own head, I worried that I might not be able to please them. That I might do something wrong; something accidental or inadvertent, to make one or more of them jealous.

Mostly though, I worried that they were giving up their lives for me. That one or more of them could one day resent leaving everything behind, only to travel across the country for one-third of an actual girlfriend.

For that reason, I did everything I could to give all three of them *everything*.

These men had my body, my soul, my mind. Just like the auction that had put me into their arms, I was now theirs completely, in every possible way. That they loved me back was never a doubt: each of them had already given up so much to enmesh their lives firmly with mine. In turn I loved them back just as hard, opening myself to them in ways I'd never been able to achieve with anyone else.

For the first time in my life there were no walls, no barriers, nothing in the way of hesitation. I knew the only way this worked was to place myself at risk, and lay my heart at their feet. I allowed them to take anything and everything, and was astounded by the depths of my own love and affection. My heart always felt full. It was always brimming with happiness.

And no matter how much they needed, how much they took, there was always enough to go around.

With each passing day I loved them even more. My heart ached when Christian went back for a week to settle his affairs, and surged with joy when he came home early. I made love to Darius for hours before his own trip, laying in bed with him and giving him enough kisses to last three lifetimes. My heart had a hole in it until he got back, but the others were there to console me... every single day he was gone.

My bed was never empty, my nights, never cold. I had help now, where I'd never had help before. I shared my triumphs and accomplishments, rather than keep those things to myself. Every single thing in my world was suddenly the complete opposite of how it had been, only a year ago.

And I could not possibly be happier.

All of these things spun through my mind as I stood

on my newly-supported second-floor balcony, repaired and restored by two of the hottest contractor boyfriends a girl could ask for. I had a mug of good coffee cradled in both hands. Behind me, pressed up against the softness of my robe, a pair of steel-like arms pulled me backward into a strong, loving embrace.

"Are they back already?" Shane asked.

I sighed in contentment and took a slow, delicious sip.

"They shouldn't be."

The arms wrapped around me felt incredible. They went a bit looser, however.

"I think they are."

I squinted into the mid-morning sun, my eyes following the long columns of grapevines out to the edge of the property.

"They couldn't be," I reiterated. "They only left an hour ago. The supply house is at least thirty minutes away."

Christian and Darius had left before breakfast, leaving Shane and I still in my bed. Sleeping this late was a rare occurrence. I wanted to savor every moment of it.

I lowered my coffee however, as my eyes caught movement. Off in the distance, a large pickup was turning into the vineyard.

"That's not them," I stiffened.

"No," Shane agreed. His hands slid to my hips before pushing away. That's definitely not their truck."

He joined me at the edge of the balcony, as if taking another two steps forward might offer him a better look. A plume of dust kicked up, just as it always did at the edge of the driveway. When it cleared, the truck was no longer *on* the driveway.

"Shit," Shane swore scathingly. He pulled on his shoes in record time, then placed a hand on my shoulder. "You stay right here."

I didn't nod, I didn't agree. I was too busy watching what was happening.

And that's because everything was perfect in my world right now. My love, my job, my life.

Everything but the asshole at the edge of my property, steamrolling his giant truck over the most coveted part of my vineyard.

~ 43 ~

AUTUMN

It took me ten seconds to get dressed, but another twenty to find my shoes. Those seconds felt like hours, and they might as well have been. By the time I rushed back out the balcony, everything was in chaos.

Motherfucker!

The oversized pickup with obnoxiously large tires had torn through half a row of vines already. I could hear the engine revving, spinning up in low gear. It kicked up more dirt and dust everywhere it went, leaving a wide swath of destruction in its wake.

Shane's own truck shot out from beneath the balcony, racing its way to an ultimate showdown at the end of the driveway. I was caught between wanting to see, and wanting to *do*. Tearing myself away, I chose the latter.

I flew down the staircase so fast my feet lost all track of where they were. I stumbled through the last few steps and flung myself toward the front door. I was frantic. Desperate. But most of all, frustrated, because I wasn't even sure what I could do to help.

Down at the edge of the property, the situation was accelerating fast. Shane's truck — the beautiful blue vintage one, that he and Darius *just* had shipped across the country — was barreling down in the direction of the saboteur. The offending pickup was tearing through the perfectly straight rows of vines, kicking up mud and clumps of grass everywhere. But now it was mostly stationary, doing tight donuts with its big, knobby tires.

And Shane had veered off the driveway, to put himself on a collision course with it.

Oh no!

I steeled myself for the sound of metal crunching against metal, even as I broke into a run. I hadn't gotten three or four steps down the driveway when something else happened.

CRASH!

I whirled. The sound had come from behind me, but also beneath me at the same time. I stopped, confused, not sure what was going on. And then it happened again, and again after that.

I turned back. The last noise was so loud it shook the floor. And then I knew:

Someone was in the basement.

I ran back into the house without hesitation, and flung open the big door to the fermentation cellar. I could hear the clang of metal against concrete, followed by a tremendous splintering of wood. There was a muffled shout, followed by a scream of abject rage. The latter was so deep and terrifying, it stopped me halfway down the spiral stairs.

But only for a moment.

CRASHHHHH!

I reached the basement landing, where the full scope of the damage came into view. Broken wine casks were scattered everywhere. Splintered staves and bent hoops littered the floor, alongside the shattered remains of spigots and rivets.

"HEY!"

My shout was followed by a momentary span of silence. Then, off to my left, I heard a grunt of exertion... followed by another, resounding crash.

"ASSHOLE!"

I screamed the word as I rounded the corner, where I was met with even more pandemonium. There were several rolling racks for moving and rotating wine barrels down here. But now, nearly all of them had been tipped over. Amidst the chaos, I could see one of my twin cousins, his back braced against the wall. Using his legs, he was shoving another cask from its mount. It rolled free just as he noticed me, skidding noisily across the flagstone floor.

"You..."

He barked the word as he stood up, having fallen down when the wine barrel finally broke free. My would-be cousin was covered in muck. His forearms were scratched and bleeding.

To one side of his vicious snarl, I saw the telltale birthmark on the side of his face.

"Emmitt?"

He took a step toward me. His hands were fists.

"Emmitt what the *fuck* are you doing?" I pleaded.

"This isn't right. This isn't the way to——"

"Nothing's right!" the man screamed. "Nothing's ever been right."

Warning sirens went off in my head as he took another two steps my way.

"But I'm going to change that!"

I took a step backward, trying to put distance between us. But I wasn't going to run. I was tired of running, tired of waiting. Sick to death of sitting around wondering when this whole thing would come to a head.

Part of me was relieved that this was finally it.

"You took everything we had," he said, looking around.

"You never had this," I countered. "It was never yours to begin with."

"Ah, but it was!" he sneered. "Our father once loved us. He wanted us to *have* this…"

"But you're destroying it!" I pointed out.

His eyes were outright maniacal. They darted left and right, shifting randomly. I realized he was still moving forward, bringing us ever closer to an inevitable, physical confrontation. His fists kept opening and closing, his dirty fingers curled in a way that was terrifying.

"We'll destroy it if that's what it takes," he said acidly. "Edward and I will tear this place to worthless pieces. Then we'll build it back, even better than it was."

Edward. A flash of panic settled over me as I realized he was the one out there in the truck, being confronted by Shane. Christian and Darius were off on an errand, which left

Emmitt and I alone down here. Just the two of us.

"Talk to me Emmitt," I said, trying to stand my ground. "What do you want?"

"At this point?" He shook his head. "Nothing."

"You want *nothing?*"

"Well, I want this place," he said nonchalantly. "And I'm *getting* this place. There's no question about that."

I was almost at the row of giant pipe casks, lining the wall. I was running out of room.

"Fine," I stalled. "Let's talk about—"

"Oh, no," he laughed menacingly. "Don't even."

He stuck up a grubby finger, then wagged it back and forth. His eyes still had that wild, far away look to them. Only now, unfortunately, those eyes were locked upon mine.

"We asked you to leave," he said, so calmly that it sent a chill down my spine. "We did it nicely, too. We tried to reason with you."

I took my last step and put up my hands. They were shaking with all the adrenaline surging through me.

"We really tried, cousin. We wanted to do this the right way. The easy way."

Emmitt's nostrils flared, as he halted for a moment. Two conflicting expressions on his face told me he was holding something back.

"Emmitt, don't do this," I warned him. "It doesn't have to go down like this."

Absurdly, it was at that exact moment I realized he looked somewhat like me. He looked even more like my father, of course. Or more accurately, my father's brother. But for a fleeting half-second, I saw facial features in his expression that I recognized as my own.

"I need to make you understand," Emmitt said in a slow, stony voice. "Once you see things our way—"

"AUTUMN!"

My heart leapt. The voices floating down from upstairs somehow belonged to the guys.

"Autumn where—"

"HERE!"

I could hear Darius and Christian, calling out frantically. A moment later I would hear their footfalls, bounding down the staircase.

But they were too far away. Not nearly close enough to prevent what was about to happen.

Emmitt rushed me, arms outstretched, reaching for me with both hands. It happened so fast there was no time to move, and nowhere to go to get out of the way.

I braced myself for the attack, throwing a knee up just before he reached me. With luck, I'd strike him hard in the chest. With even more luck, maybe the groin.

None of that happened, though.

Instead, my knee sailed upward, hitting nothing, throwing me off balance. There was a rush of motion, followed by a thumping noise. When I looked again, Emmitt wasn't there. He was on the floor to the left of me, face down, completely unconscious.

I blinked, and looked up. Edward was standing over his brother's crumpled form. In his right hand, he was holding one of the slats from the broken wine barrels.

~ 44 ~

AUTUMN

"Autumn!"

Christian flew past the wall and into the room, followed closely by Darius. As they skidded to a stop, they were greeted by the sight of Edward standing before me, brandishing a weapon.

"Wait, no!"

I couldn't get the words out fast enough. Christian had already tackled Edward into a stack of barrel debris. The twin dropped the curved wooden plank to the floor with a loud clatter.

"NO!" I screamed again. "Not him! Emmitt's the one who came after me. He's the one who—"

Darius reached down and lifted Emmitt into a sitting position. He did it so roughly, with so much anger, the unconscious man's head rolled around on his neck like a rag doll.

"Stop!" Edward screamed, still pinned beneath Christian's two massive arms. "Stop it, you'll kill him!"

Somehow he twisted free of the lawyer's steel-like grasp. Rather than fight back, he scrambled over to help his brother.

"Emmitt..." he cried, slapping him repeatedly in the face. "EMMITT!"

Unfortunately his brother was in bad shape. He was sitting there limply, with his chin lolling against his chest. Blood from some unseen head wound was running into his eyes.

"We need to help him!" Edward shouted frantically. "He needs—"

"Let him bleed."

The words were angry, and spat with disdain. They also came from somewhere behind us.

"Shane!"

We whirled, and there he was. His blond hair was matted to his head by something reddish-brown and literally all over him. It was too oily and thin to be blood. Thankfully, it also wasn't the right color.

I ran to him, and he swept me into his arms. It got all over me, too.

"Hydraulic fluid," he shrugged.

Back on the cold, cellar floor, Edward was cradling his brother's head against his chest. He was rocking him gently back and forth, almost like a child. I could hear him weeping.

"Please don't hurt him," he begged, softly.

"Hurt him?" snorted Darius, who was rolling up his sleeves. "Are you fucking kidding me—"

"He wasn't always like this," Edward croaked. "He was a good brother, when we were young. We did things together. Protected one another."

He paused, his eyes tearing up. Darius moved to take a step forward, but I put an arm out to stop him.

"I remember our father coming down," Edward went on. "Doing nice things with us. Fun things..."

Tears streamed down both sides of his face. His eyes, I could tell, were turned toward the past.

"But I drove him away," said Edward. "I thought it was what my mother wanted. We both did. But I don't think Emmitt ever got over what I did to make Jeff not come back. And I'm sorry, bro. I really am. I wish things had been different..."

He hugged his brother, who groaned against his chest. The groan was a welcome relief, as far as I was concerned. It was the first sign of life since Edward had nearly brained him.

"My uncle," I fumbled. "I—I mean your father... he spent time with you?"

Edward nodded. "He took us places. Taught us things. Once, we spent a two whole weeks camping together, just the three of us." He sniffed. "It was the best two weeks of our lives."

A vision of my uncle formed in my head. I could see his smile, and his smile was gentle.

"I never knew any of that."

"He loved us," Edward explained further. "I know he did. But my mother got fiercely jealous, and decided she didn't want him seeing us anymore. We moved a bunch of times after that. She made it hard for him. She also took the child support our father sent down, but she kept every single penny from us."

He inhaled a slow, shuddering breath. "It was her way of keeping us dependent upon her. She didn't want us to have our own lives. She wanted to keep us around."

"If you knew all this, why would you stay?" I asked gently.

"Because Emmitt stayed, and he's my twin," answered Edward. "And don't get me wrong, I love my mother. We both do. But Emmitt's more... more trusting of her, if that makes sense."

My shoulders slumped, and a tear formed in my own eye. I was shocked by the realization that all the anger I felt in my heart was somehow, miraculously gone.

Emmitt stirred, groaning again. He reached up, and I saw his arm go over his brother's shoulder. The relief in Edward's eyes was pure and beautiful.

Fuck.

I about damn near melted.

"Alright..." I murmured quietly. "If we're all down here, then who the hell was out there in the truck? Tearing up my vineyard?"

"I don't know," Shane spoke up, "but the guy was *big*. I plowed into him hard enough to bend the axle on that thing, and it didn't even faze him. He jumped out, and took off running."

"And you couldn't catch him?" challenged Darius.

"I'm sure I could've," Shane acknowledged. "But I wasn't about to leave her here alone."

All eyes fell on me. But my gaze was still downward.

"The big guy was Connor," Edward said quietly. "He

262

was just... just a distraction."

"A distraction that destroyed half the crop of black muskats," I said sadly. "Those were some of the oldest vines, too."

"I'm so sorry," Edward sobbed again. "None of this was my idea. I told my brother the whole thing was crazy, and we were idiots to still be here. I begged him not to do this, but he said if I went home he'd just do it without me."

"So now we have to worry about some *third* asshole running around out there?" Darius demanded, adding a sigh. "Stealing trucks, trying to—"

"No," Edward shook his head. "I'm sure Connor's already on his way home. He owed Emmitt a favor, but this was it for him. Trust me, you won't see him again."

"Trust you?" Shane scoffed. "You want us to *trust* you?"

Edward shrugged, then lowered his chin to cradle his brother even tighter. In a moment of silence the boys and I glanced at each other, just the four of us.

"And the others who broke in here?" asked Christian.

"They're gone," Edward swore quietly. "Brooks is all sorts of fucked up. He still can't walk right. Davis got his face sewed up, and Brooks took him back home, right after that whole thing happened."

"Home to Georgia?"

"Yes." He looked down at Emmitt and shook his head. "They're both ready to kill my brother, to be honest."

"Good," spat Darius. "Because if they don't, I will."

As if on cue, Emmitt coughed, then grunted loudly.

This time he actually stiffened, and finally opened his blood-caked eyes.

"Easy," Edward told him. "It's okay. I've got you."

Emmitt looked dazed and confused, and suddenly very, very helpless. His gaze shifted around the room, eventually fixing upon each of us. He was looking at us, but not really seeing us. Not yet, anyway.

Finally, his eyes shifted to me. There was confusion at first, then grim acceptance. He blinked a few times, coughed some more, and leaned into his brother. Side by side, they really did look the same.

"Here," said Christian. He extended his arm and handed me his phone. "Go on. Call 911."

I stared down at the phone for a few long seconds. Eventually I took it.

"911..." I repeated.

"Yes," he said, eying me closely. "You can tell the police they broke in here and tried to assault you. We're all witnesses."

There was a knot in my throat all of a sudden. I tried to swallow past it, but couldn't.

"And I guess that'll help my case?"

"The plaintiffs physically attacking the defendant, on the property in question?" He nodded. "It sure will."

I stared at the phone some more. Edward wasn't looking at me. Neither was Emmitt. They both looked tired, and beyond exhausted. So I did the only thing I could do.

I dialed 911.

It picked up immediately on the other end.

"911 operator, what's the emergency?"

"Hi, we're going to need an ambulance right away," I said smoothly.

Glancing down at the two of them, I felt the knot in my throat slowly begin to unravel.

"My cousin fell and hit his head."

~ 45 ~

AUTUMN

"Seriously. I *still* can't believe it," Kinsley swore. "All three of them?"

"Yes."

"At the same *time?*"

I smiled and took a bite of my cheeseburger. The sandwich had traveled three thousand miles since it was made twelve hours ago, and just spent thirty seconds in a microwave. Even so, it was still the best damn burger I'd had in a long, long time.

"We gotta get one of these out here," I mumbled, pointing to the In-N-Out logo on the white paper bag. "This is so fucking good it's criminal."

"Yeah, yeah," my friend said dismissively. "It's great. Eat up. But you're still not going to avoid my question."

"What question?"

Kinsley looked left and right, then leaned in across one of my new tasting room tables. Her voice dropped to a near-whisper.

"Are they all doing you at the same time?"

I nodded and licked a finger clean. "Sometimes." I thought about it. "Okay, most times, actually."

Her eyes lit up as she slumped back into her own chair. "Holy fucking shit, Autumn."

"Yup."

I stared back at my friend, enjoying her expression. For once it was nice to actually shock Kinsley for a change.

"So what's it like?"

I smiled and winked. "What do you think it's like?"

"I think it's probably pretty fucking amazing."

I toasted her with my half-eaten sandwich. "Well, there you go."

It was true I'd been busy, and in just about every way. There'd been planting, and replanting, and pruning and such. I'd met with buyers, with sellers, with suppliers of all kinds. I was rapidly learning all the different aspects of running this place, year after year. And just outside, every far-flung corner of the vineyard was blossoming beautifully.

Thankfully, the guys had finally finished the process of moving in. Christian was busy wrapping up his caseload out west. Shane and Darius were setting up a brand new shop, not even two miles from here. It was still early to begin thinking about the harvest, but the four of us were more than willing to learn. Best of all, it felt amazing to be doing this *with* someone for a change, instead of by myself. I enjoyed sharing the burden, the tasks, the overall general experience.

Who knew letting go of control could be so fun?

"I— I just still can't believe it."

Kinsley's gaze shifted around the giant room, stopping on all sorts of things I'd been excited to show her. At the moment though, she wasn't seeing any of them.

"And why not?," I asked, gesturing around. "This is all your own fault, actually. You're the one who auctioned me off, remember?"

"I know, but…"

"And have I thanked you for it yet?"

My mischievous grin turned into a chuckle, as I picked at the spill of french fries scattered between us. They weren't nearly as crispy as when they came out of the fryer on the other side of the country. But they were still golden and salty and totally delicious.

"The idea of it is pretty far out there," I admitted. "Three men? One woman? All in a relationship?" I shrugged. "It's radical for sure. Poly—"

"Polyamory?" my friend interrupted. "Autumn, I live in California. I *know* what polyamory is."

"But—"

"I personally know more than a few throuples."

"Actually," I told her, "this would be polyandry."

Kinsley squinted. "Polyandry?"

"That's the more specific term for it. I looked it up."

My friend laughed heartily, then shook her head. "Yes. Yes, of course you did."

Her gaze drifted out the window, to where Darius and Shane were unloading a delivery of seasoned fermenting casks we'd purchased at auction. Another winery had closed down, not that far into Connecticut. We'd gotten lucky.

"So are you shocked by all this?" I asked her.

My best friend played with her paper straw. It had been in her soft drink for so long it was collapsing in on itself.

"Shocked that four people could love each other?" she asked. "No. Not at all." Her eyes flitted to me. "But the idea that it's *you*? That's probably the last thing I expected."

"Oh yeah?" I challenged. "Why?"

"Because all through high school you were the rational one, and I was the crazy lunatic."

"You're still a lunatic," I pointed out.

"Yes, and now you've joined me in the asylum."

Just then Christian walked into the room, stole some of our fries, kissed me, and walked out. All without saying a word.

Kinsley chuckled.

"If this is the asylum, sign me up," my friend sighed.

"Nope, sorry. Get your own asylum," I told her. "This one's mine."

Kinsley pulled at her curls, fluffing them out — a leftover move from high school. I winked at her.

"Besides," I pointed out, "you and Eric have been doing great. From everything you've told me, that is."

"Yeah," she admitted. "True."

"It's good to see you in something solid for once," I told her. "Something real."

"Oh, he's real alright," Kinsley admitted. "Eric's sweet,

he's fun, he's loving. He helps out at the shelter, when he can. He even has a great job." She sighed happily as she sank back into her chair. "What more could a girl really ask for?"

Both our gazes drifted outside, to where all three men were now standing together. The smirk on my face grew slowly wider, until I couldn't stop it. I burst out laughing.

"Oh, fuck you, Autumn," Kinsley laughed with me.

~ 46 ~

AUTUMN

I found Christian in the place I usually found him this time of day. He liked to be outside amongst the vines, walking the long columns as the light of the day faded and the shadows deepened. If there was one thing I'd learned about Californians, they really valued their sunsets.

"Hey, princess."

He heard me well before he saw me, even though I'd tried sneaking up on him from an adjacent row. It didn't stop me from sliding my arms around his thick waist, and molding myself against him from behind.

"Is your friend gone already?"

"For now," I sighed contentedly against his back. "She's not flying back for a couple more days, but she wanted to spend a few nights with old friends."

Christian looked to the sky and nodded. "Your old neighborhood stomping grounds."

"Something like that," I chuckled. "You know, Kinsley always *did* do a lot of stomping."

He pulled me even tighter against him, letting his giant hands settle entirely over mine. "She strikes me as the type."

The wind picked up a bit, wafting the sweet scent of the vineyard beneath our nostrils. I could smell earth, and grass, and something I now knew were called terpenes. The latter were given off by the plants to attract pollinators, like bees.

"You feel… not tight," I told him. "Not tense."

"No," Christian agreed. "Not at all."

I kissed his back. "This place is good for you," I said softly.

Taking in a deep breath, the giant lawyer eventually nodded. "Beats the hell out of wearing a suit and tie."

"And shoes," I noted with a chuckle, nodding down to his bare feet.

Christian broke my grasp and twisted to face me. Settling his hands over my hips, he planted a sweet kiss on the top of my head.

For a while we just held each other, enjoying the warmth of our bodies. The shadows grew even longer, as the sun began setting over the slight rise at the end of the property. When I looked at him again, his expression was serenity and contentment. But there was also a wry smile painted across his face.

"What are you thinking about?"

He paused for a moment, then looked down at me.

"A memory."

"Which one?"

He scratched at his five-o'clock shadow, and his smile grew even wider.

"Well, there was this one day my mother was picking me up from preschool," said Christian. "It was raining hard, and there were these huge puddles of mud at the back end of the parking lot. They were glorious mud puddles. Magnificent mud puddles."

"And four-year old you wanted to jump into them," I chuckled.

He let out a huge sigh filled with heady nostalgia. "Like a starving man eying a juicy steak."

"So did you?"

"Well, I would never have done it on my own," he admitted, "but for some reason this one time was different. I'll never really know why, but my mother took one look at me and said: 'Go on. Take off your shoes and do it.'"

His eyes took on a very happy, far away look.

"And for the next five minutes I had the time of my fucking life."

I followed his gaze, and together we looked down at his bare feet. They were totally covered in mud, top to bottom. Thick, squishy gobs had even caked up between his toes.

"Looks like that day stuck with you," I noted.

Christian grinned happily. "I jammed an entire childhood into those five little minutes. And it's one of the only times I can remember seeing my mother smile."

"That's nice," I sighed.

"Yeah."

He squeezed me even tighter. The lightning bugs had just begun blinking yellow, all around us.

"So the moral of the story is: sometimes you need to stop and jump in the mud puddle," I chuckled.

"No."

I tilted my head. "No?"

"The moral is, sometimes it's okay to go outside of your comfort zone," said Christian. "You say yes to things you normally wouldn't."

Slowly, he lifted his gaze back to the darkening sky.

"Ten minutes' worth of cleanup and an extra bath is a small price to pay for a legacy memory," he murmured softly. "Especially one that lasts a lifetime."

I stared at him, and he looked so happy in his memory it made my heart ache. But in a very good way.

"Speaking of doing things you normally wouldn't…"

His trip down memory lane finished, Christian's gaze eventually found mine. He knew what I was going to say before I even said it.

"You still want to do that thing, don't you?"

I nodded slowly. "Yes."

His expression was stoic now. Not judgmental, but not encouraging either.

"You know, once you do this, it can't be undone."

I swallowed, dryly. "I know."

"It's a big decision. A huge step."

"A huge step *forward*," I added. "Or at least I hope so."

His head bobbed up and down, his expression still entirely impassive.

"Yeah. Me too."

Taking his hands in mine, I squeezed them tightly.

"Christian, I *need* this. It's who I am. And it's a decision I'd rather make and be wrong about, than to regret never making at all." I paused, looking down at my feet. "I know that doesn't make any sense or anything, but—"

"No," he stopped me cold. "The reason you're doing it makes perfect sense… in an imperfect way."

Sliding an arm around me, he guided us back in the opposite direction. An army of shimmering lightning bugs stood between us and the house.

"We're going to help you and support you on this," he went on. "We'll do it exactly the way you want."

"Thank you," I said, choking back tears. "That means the world."

"Autumn, you *are* our world," Christian sighed, squeezing me tightly. "And you're a much better person than I am."

Scooping me into his arms, he planted a fiery kiss on my eager lips.

"It's one of the reasons I love you so much."

~ 47 ~

AUTUMN

They crossed the field side-by-side, looking exactly the same. Their strides, their movement, the way they lifted their legs to sit down on the opposite side of the picnic table — all of it was so perfectly identical. If not for the birthmark on the side of one twin's face, I still wouldn't be able to tell one from the other.

In time though, I was hoping that might change.

"Again, thank you for coming," I told them. "I know it probably took a lot to come back here."

We were in the most public of places; Osprey's Dominion Vineyard. Summer was in full swing. Hundreds of people milled around bright green grass, sipping beer or wine against a sky of pure, cerulean blue. There were tables and tents and corn hole boards. Frisbee and Spikeball and Can Jam games, going on all around us.

I'd wanted it to be public because I'd wanted *them* to be comfortable. I, on the other hand, was already comfortable. Especially with Darius and Shane seated on either side of me, and Christian standing with his arms crossed, just behind.

"Hi Autumn," said Edward.

"Hi Edward," I smiled. "Hi Emmitt."

The ensuing silence was every bit as awkward as I imagined it might be. I offered to buy them drinks, but both twins refused. Emmitt looked impassive, but also a bit subdued. He still gazed in my direction, but he wouldn't look me straight in the eye. Edward however, couldn't hide his nervousness.

"I'm going to make this short and simple," I told them. "I'm running a winery. Your *father's* winery. I know that's a tough pill to swallow, but I've never run a winery before and I don't know exactly what I'm doing. I'm getting a general idea of it though, and I'm going to need help."

"Help?" Emmit finally spoke up. He was doing his best to hide his disdain, but it wasn't working. "You're really asking for our *help?*"

"Maybe," I allowed. "Possibly."

"You called us all the way back from Georgia to offer us a job?" he tried not to sneer. "Working for *you?*"

Even Edward seemed somewhat underwhelmed by the offer. I looked down at my half-empty glass and swirled the dregs of my wine around.

"Or maybe I'm offering the two of you more than just a job."

The live band started up just then, the microphone crackling as the singer made a couple of announcements. As they launched into their first song, I folded my hands in front of me.

"I never really had much in the way of family," I said,

"and what little I did have was taken from me far too soon. But as of now I'm building a new family. A hopefully big, beautiful, indestructible family, so I'll never have to be alone again."

Both twins looked left and right and behind me, their eyes flitting from man to man. They didn't look all that surprised. I hadn't really expected them to be.

"The two of you have always had each other," I went on, "and that's a bond so amazing I can't even imagine it. I'm sorry you didn't have a relationship with your father, though. If you had, we might've grown up around each other. We might even be family ourselves."

"Family…" Edward repeated. He jerked a thumb across both sides of the table. "Us."

"Yes."

Emmitt squinted. "You're saying—"

"I thought about this a lot," I broke in. "And then I realized… what's stopping us? Why shouldn't we have the chance our parents never gave us? Why should we suffer the sins of our fathers, or be bound by their own petty differences?"

There was silence from the other end of the table. The twins still weren't sure what I was saying.

"My father cut off his own brother, over a disagreement so obscure, so long ago, I don't even know what the hell it was about. But we don't have to go down that road. We can throw our own disagreements away, and call each other family for the first time in our lives."

"Autumn…"

Emmitt was speaking to me directly, now. It was the

first time I could remember him using my actual name.

"These weren't just disagreements," he said quietly.

"No, they weren't," I agreed. "You invaded my home. Tore up my vineyard."

"And that was wrong," he admitted quietly. His expression actually softened. "I'm... I'm sorry for that. But we saw the place as ours."

"I know you did. And maybe, on some level, I don't entirely disagree with you."

Emmitt blinked a few times, and now his eyes did meet mine. I could tell he was shrewd. The wheels in his head were already turning.

Peripherally, I looked to the boyfriends on either side of me. Shane and Darius watched vigilantly as I reached across the table and laid my hand over Emmitt's.

"I don't want the two of you to work *for* me," I told him. "I want to work alongside you. With you. As partners."

"Partners..."

"Yes."

Edward's eyes narrowed in confusion. "In what way would we be—"

"I'm willing to give up forty percent of the vineyard," I told them. "You'd each get a twenty percent ownership stake. I'll still keep the other sixty, of course. I *am* a control freak, after all."

Emmitt stared at me for a long, quiet moment. His look was absolute incredulity. Somewhere beneath that though, I saw excitement. Maybe even some gratitude.

"Seriously?" he breathed.

"Yes, seriously," I smiled. "You boys move up here. Settle in. Help me build this place out, make it into something like this."

I extended my free hand and swept it out over the broad, beautiful fields of Osprey's Dominion.

"We'll make wine, and of course we'll have tastings," I said. "But we can also brew craft beer. We've already amended our permits for it. Do either of you know anything about brewing?"

To my surprise they nodded in unison, making them look even more like twins.

"We've home-brewed since... well, pretty much forever," said Edward.

"Perfect!" I said. "Of course, we'll hire an experienced brewmaster to show us the ropes, teach us the equipment, and run things when we can't be there. Because believe me, we're going to be busy. Extremely busy. I mean, just look around."

I didn't even have to gesture this time. I watched as their hazel eyes scanned from one end of the field to the other, stopping on everything in turn.

"And since you boys had the foresight to destroy the row of vines *closest* to the main house, we can set up picnic tables, lawn games, and everything else there, including a small stage. Eventually we'll have food trucks. Or maybe we'll run a kitchen. Honestly, I don't even know. These are the types of things I need partners for, you know?"

"What about them?" asked Emmitt. His eyes shifted to the left and right of me.

"If you're asking about us," said Shane, "you should know that we strongly advised her against all this." He stiffened a little as I bumped his leg, under the table. "But your cousin is stubborn. She doesn't give up."

"In that regard," Darius added, pointing a finger, "she's a lot like the two of you."

"Ultimately," Shane went on, "we support her decisions. And you will too, if you want to work with her."

They twins fell silent once again. As I watched, they leaned in and murmured something amongst themselves. Eventually Emmitt raised a hand, and called for drinks.

"You'll really do this?" he asked, as a server in a burgundy apron began making his way over. "After everything we've done?"

"Yes," I said definitively. "In fact, my lawyer's already drawn up a preliminary contract."

I reached back, and Christian handed me a plain manila folder. I dropped it to the table and slid it forward, along with the pen clipped to the top of it.

"Maybe I was wrong to dismiss you off the bat," I said. "But also, I'm doing this because I was wrong about something else, too."

The eyebrow above Emmitt's birthmark arched upward. "And what's that?"

"I said you were nothing more than my blood, and that you'd never be family." Very slowly, I shook my head. "That was narrow-minded thinking. Especially coming from a girl who could use all the family she can get."

The server arrived, and Emmitt ordered a bottle and some more glasses. Eventually he poured enough for all six of us — a gesture that was not lost on the others.

"I really don't know what to say," he shrugged awkwardly, hoisting his glass. His skin was about three shades redder than before he'd arrived. "Other than, well…"

"We're in," Edward smiled cheerily. He raised his own glass.

We toasted, and even the guys joined in. They'd had their reservations, of course. But with my parents gone, they knew what this meant to me. How important it was that we'd at least give it a try.

"One last stipulation," I added, waiting until their attention was focused upon me. "If you want your cat back, you'll have to be the ones to break the news to him. Because he's pretty much made the tasting room his home."

Emmitt and Edward both looked at each other.

"Cat?"

"Yes."

"We've never owned a cat," said Emmitt. "Not in our whole lives."

"Yeah, right," I scoffed at him, adding a chuckle. "So this random stray cat just *happened* to show up on the night you took over my place?"

"I guess so," Edward admitted.

I studied their twin faces carefully. "I don't believe you."

They didn't laugh. They weren't joking.

"Wait, seriously?"

Edward opened the folder and picked up the pen. Before looking down at the paperwork, he gave me a wink.

"If we're going into business together, you probably need to trust us, right?" he asked.

"Sure," I replied. "Of course."

He set the tip of the pen against the signature line without even reading it.

"Then we're now the proud owners of forty-percent of a soon-to-be amazing winery," he said, signing his name. With a charming smile, he passed the pen to his brother.

"And you're the proud owner of one free cat."

Epilogue

AUTUMN

I waited until halftime, then I came out. It was a longer wait than I thought. Two minutes in a football game could sometimes take twenty, depending upon penalties, commercials, and God knew what else.

Lucky for them, I'm a patient woman.

Sometimes.

SCREEEEEECCCCH!

I blew the whistle so loudly Shane dropped his bowl of popcorn. It hit the floor in front of the couch and exploded upward, showering everyone with freshly-popped microwave kernels with extra butter flavor.

Dropping the whistle back between my exposed breasts, I giggled.

"Alright, that's it!" I shouted. "The referee is here, and she's ready to start calling penalties!"

My three boyfriends whirled, spinning in my direction. One by one their mouths opened. The jaw-dropping part was always my favorite.

It made all the effort I'd put into the costume worthwhile.

"So... which one of you went offsides?"

Darius was the fastest. His hand shot up immediately.

"Fine. Sit there and keep your hands in your lap."

I sauntered over in my sexy referee's outfit, which didn't consist of all that much. I wore a black-and-white vertical striped shirt of course, like the employees of *Foot Locker*. Unlike the employees of *Foot Locker* however, mine was only a half-shirt. A half-shirt with a radically plunging neckline, that left my entire midriff exposed.

"If I can't use my hands, do I at least get to—"

"Stop talking and lay back."

The bottom half of my outfit consisted of white socks that were knee-high, and a pair of black boy shorts so skin-tight they looked painted on. Fortunately, there was a zipper down the front, to free me when the time was right. It was the only thing keeping me from being a forever prisoner.

Shane was picking up popcorn while staring at my ass, which I knew from the mirror in my bedroom looked absolutely phenomenal. In the meantime, I straddled his friend and began making out with him. Darius moaned as I grinded my ass into his lap, letting my hair hang down to tickle the sides of his face. He was growing harder with each passing second. With my shorts so tight, I could feel every last inch of him.

Eventually he couldn't help himself, and began using his hands. The second his fingers pierced the waistband of my shorts, I pulled back and blew the whistle again. This time much less loudly than before.

"Neutral zone infraction!"

He laughed into my mouth. "You really looked these up, didn't you?"

"Maybe."

"Well then…" he began kissing me some more. "Damn good job."

I'd been looking forward to this day all summer long, and into the fall. Halloween was coming up fast. I wanted them to have me in this outfit now, because I had an even sluttier costume all planned out for *that* holiday.

"This isn't fair ref," I heard Shane say. "I… I think I should be penalized too."

He was seated on the couch beside us, rubbing himself through his jeans. Watching as I basically got his friend off with a lap dance.

"Quiet!" I told him. "Or I'll toss you out of the game."

Highlights from the other games played, as I kissed and rubbed and brought Darius almost all the way there. In time, I worked his pants and boxers downward. His erection sprang free, jutting toward the ceiling.

I kissed it once, swirling my tongue around the head.

"I dunno…" I purred. "This might be an equipment violation."

Darius was glassy-eyed and totally subdued. He just shrugged.

"We'll have to come back to it."

I leapt over to Christian's lap, and began giving him the same treatment. When Shane protested again, I just giggled.

"Trust me, you'll all get your own turns in the penalty box," I promised, with my face buried in Christian's deliciously-scented neck.

"But there is no penalty box in football," said Shane.

I turned to look at him over my shoulder. "You wanna argue? Or do you want a lap dance blowjob?"

Shane smiled back at me and began unbuckling his jeans. The way his hands moved over his zipper made me want to jump him on the spot.

"Arguing with the referee is always a bad idea," Darius chastised. "Besides, I really want to see the inside of that box."

Christian was kissing me fiercely now, and sliding his hands all over my breasts. We were grinding hard, in slow circles. Every time I rolled my ass into his lap, his hips bucked upward to meet me.

I was getting so hot in my boy shorts, I knew they were probably soaked through. One of them would have to peel them off me. I decided that whoever that lucky man was, he'd get to fuck me first.

Beneath me, Christian was so big he was bursting out the top of his boxers. I was riding him forward and back, gliding myself against the underside of his pulsating shaft. If I didn't do something soon, he'd probably come all over his ripped, beautiful stomach.

Which, I decided on the spot, might be something worth seeing.

Instead, I grabbed him by the wrists and pulled him out from under my shirt.

"Illegal use of hands!"

"What?" he protested. "But you *put* my hands there!"

"Too bad. I'm still calling you for it."

I slid downward and over his thighs, giving his throbbing manhood somewhat of a break. Besides, I wanted to kiss that beautiful stomach. Just the scent of his skin was giving me the full body shivers.

I was stretched out like a cat, his thick shaft nestled snugly against my cheek, when I finally felt Shane. Unable to control himself, he'd placed both hands on my hips. Rather than fight it, I slid further backward until our bodies made contact. The heat and electricity between us was off the charts.

"Illegal block in the back," I murmured, rolling my ass into his pelvis.

Shane's hands settled over my hips. "Hey, you're the one grinding on me."

"I'm the ref. Are you gonna argue?"

There was a short pause. "No, ref."

I pushed myself up, grabbed his head, and began kissing him hotly over my shoulder. Our tongues danced as I murmured softly, into his mouth. "Good man."

By now I was already in heat, and my will to resist was fading fast. It had been a long, arduous week. The grape harvest was in full swing, and the vineyard was rapidly changing from green to gold and even red. The whole thing was beautiful, even if it was a ton of work. But I had help in the way of Emmitt and Edward — who were turning out to be solid and enthusiastic partners — as well as a few pickers from nearby sister vineyards who'd agreed to buy a good portion of our crop. All after pressing and filling our own casks, of course.

With the money we made, we'd prepare for an even bigger and better next season. And with everything the guys had fixed up around the old place, I knew next year would be absolutely badass.

Right now though, I wanted to reward my boyfriends for all their hard work, dedication, and selflessness when it came to supporting me. And in the process of doing that, if I happened to have a few monster orgasms of my own? Well, all the better.

"So... when do I get to score?" Shane murmured. He was naked now, and thrusting behind me. Even with my shorts still on, the feeling of him gliding through my thigh gap was absolutely incredible.

"We might need... to call... for a measurement."

I reached between my legs and hefted his thickness. I couldn't hold back much longer.

"I'm sure I made the first down at least," he played back.

"Maybe..." I teased.

"Or maybe—"

I whimpered as a hand went into my hair, pulling me forward and against something hard and warm. Christian was apparently done waiting. He pushed himself past my lips, and straight down my throat.

Mmmmm...

The move created a virtual flood between my legs. I was suddenly desperate to be taken, used, utterly destroyed.

"This zipper... it's stuck."

An instant spike of panic shot through my brain. It didn't stop my enthusiasm for going down on Christian, though.

"What kind of a penalty would I get for—"

"Just do it," I mumbled around a mouthful of warm, beautiful man-flesh.

Two pairs of hands moved to grasp the back of my shorts, from either side. There was a short, violent tug, followed by a satisfying rip as Shane and Darius tore the fabric to shreds.

So much for wearing it twice, I thought, headily.

I was bent over and completely exposed now. The boy shorts had been so tight, there had been zero room for panties.

Not that I needed much in the way of panties around the house these days.

Two faces buried themselves between my cheeks, alternating kissing and tonguing me until my eyes crossed. I could tell them apart by the softness of their facial hair. Darius's was courser, his stubble even sharp at times as he devoured me whole. Shane's on the other hand was softer, and his tongue more daring in its exploration of *all* my nether areas.

Holy fuck...

I was moaning and groaning, crying out in soft, delirious ecstasy. Simultaneously, my hands and mouth were pumping and churning, working to give Christian the blowjob of his life. I was grinding my ass backward, trying to take them even deeper. In the heat of the moment, I wanted so desperately to be fucked. For one or both of them to just grab my hips, surge into me, and start plowing away at me until I saw stars.

Instead, just when I was about to beg for just that exact thing, they abruptly stopped.

"Where…" I murmured. "What the—"

"We're trying to get called for delay of game," Shane teased.

I popped Christian from between my swollen lips and turned around. "If you don't finish what you started, I'm red-carding the *both* of you!"

"Red card?" Darius laughed. "That's soccer."

"Whatever."

I turned my full attention back to Christian, and began really putting it to him. I was on my knees now before the couch, rolling my head around in his lap. I wriggled my ass enticingly backward, as he let out a hiss and sank his hands into my hair.

"Fuck…" Shane swore.

One of the men shoved the other out of the way, and the next thing I knew I was getting deeply, blissfully fucked. A new set of hands sifted into my hair and pulled firmly, arching me backward. Soon I was bouncing happily between them, my eyes screwed involuntarily shut. I welcomed my onrushing climax with a rapturous sigh, while still pumping Christian with both hands.

"Yesssssssss…."

I hissed as everything contracted all at once. I could feel my insides pulsing, thrumming, melting into oblivion. And in the hazy background of my delirium: two of the most gorgeous men I loved most in the world. Pumping me. Filling me. Using me from both ends. My release was sweeter and more total than I could ever remember, and over the past half year I could remember quite a lot.

They were still using my body as I collapsed around

them, the referee's whistle bouncing against my chest as Shane continued surging into me. They weren't nearly done, and neither was I. But the good thing about having three boyfriends was, I always had backup.

"Get over here," I demanded of Darius. "I need you."

He was sitting back with his beer, pretending to casually watch the action. But the lust in his eyes was unmistakable.

"You sure?" he quipped. "I won't get called for too many men on the field?"

I grinned sexily and bit my lip. "Not *this* field."

Shane generously gave up his spot. He slapped my ass on the way out, leaving a handprint that I knew his friend would match on the other side. Because sometimes, I'd learned, having a boyfriend with OCD could be fun.

Darius passed his beer to his friend and took my hips in his hands. He entered me slowly, as I watched the cool liquid slide down Shane's beautiful throat. It was a magic moment, made even more magical by Christian leaning forward. He brought his face to mine, and kissed me so slowly and beautifully I wanted to freeze time.

Family.

There were so many things great in my life now, but nothing felt better than the love and intimacy that came with being the center of the guys' world. I had a relationship so incredible it couldn't be described or understood. Three men, three lovers, three lifelong mates who wanted to build an entire future with me. Men who enjoyed sharing a woman, a girlfriend, and eventually a wife. I wanted to spend my whole life with them, to share every beautiful experience from this point forward. I wanted to build a family so full of love, so closely bonded, that not one of us would ever be lonely again.

Darius slapped my ass exactly where I expected, just as Shane's handprint was no doubt appearing on the opposite side. It felt amazingly good, especially with him buried so deep inside me.

"Harder."

He leaned over my back to nuzzle my neck. "Yeah?"

"Oh fuck yeah."

He slapped me again on the rump, and Shane joined in. Back and forth they traded blows, until I could feel my ass glowing a nice, numb, cherry red.

"Be careful man," Christian chuckled. "You'll get called for unnecessary roughness."

He was kissing the other side of my neck, now. So softly and slowly it was giving me goosebumps.

"I haven't been properly spanked in weeks," I sighed, only now remembering just how much I loved it. "Trust me. It's necessary."

Someone dragged me to the floor. There was blankets there now, and pillows, which were always on hand. I fell to my back and parted my knees, letting my legs fall open for whichever one of them wanted me next. The thrill of not knowing who would fuck me next was something that never got old. Not in a million years.

Christian took me next. Then Shane again. Then Christian a second time, followed immediately by Darius. They were kissing and holding me. Pinning my legs back over my shoulders, to give each other better, deeper angles. And they were egging each other on, too. Daring each other to go even harder, or bragging about what they'd do when they took their next turn.

I came again, screwing myself all the way down on Shane's beautiful shaft while raking my nails across Christian's chest. There was nothing I wouldn't do for these men. My heart was filled with more than enough love for all three of them, and I knew that no matter what challenges we faced there would always be enough to go around.

"Halftime's almost over," I heard one of them say. "Better finish the ref off."

"The ref finished twice already," I sighed, my body rocking beneath long, deep strokes. "Maybe you should finish off *in* the ref, so she can jump in the shower."

I had errands to run, and Sunday dinner to plan. I was meeting my cousins for coffee, and I wanted to pick up a few pumpkins for our jack-o-lantern contest. It was incredible how busy my life was now, compared to before. And it was even more incredible — not to mention sensuously hot — that I'd do these normal, everyday, public things... while the combined loads of my three hot boyfriends were swimming around inside me.

"Come..." I whispered into their ears, one by one. "You don't want to miss the second half kickoff."

The three of them did just that, roaring like lions, flooding me as I locked my legs around their powerful flanks. I took them all, whispering dirty promises into their ears. Cooing and kissing their warm necks, as I gently grazed their broad backs with the very tips of my fingernails.

The game started again, and the boys pulled on their clothes and went back to their seats. I lay there for a few happy moments as they toasted with fresh beers, looking like a referee that got totally laid out by a bunch of linesmen. Which, pretty much, was exactly what happened.

"Fifteen thousand dollars at auction, huh?" I heard one of them say.

I looked up sleepily, to find all three men smiling down at me.

"Yeah," grinned Shane. "I'm pretty sure we got our money's worth."

Bonus Epilogue

Wanna read the ULTRA-HEA, sugary-sweet,

super-sexy, flash-forward

BONUS EPILOGUE?

Of course you do!

TAP RIGHT HERE TO SIGN UP!

Or enter this link into your browser:

https://mailchi.mp/kristawolfbooks.com/bonus-
epilogue-the-auction

to have it INSTANTLY delivered to your inbox.

Need more Reverse Harem?

Thanks for checking out *The Auction*. Here's hoping it knocked your socks off!

And for even *more* sweltering reverse harem heat? Check out: Best Friends Never Kiss. Below you'll find a preview of the sexy, sizzling cover, plus the first several chapters so you can see for yourself:

* * *

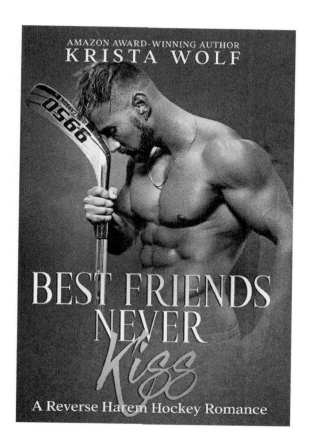

AMAZON AWARD-WINNING AUTHOR
KRISTA WOLF

BEST FRIENDS
NEVER
Kiss

A Reverse Harem Hockey Romance

~ 1 ~

ARIANA

"Sooo… are you finally going to tell me what it is you do for a living?"

My date blinked back at me from across the table, not exactly sure how to respond. He'd answered the question twice already. Neither answer was to my liking, however.

"Well, as I told you, I'm a freelance publicist."

I held out a halting finger as I finished draining my beer. As the last of the suds slid down my throat, my date was regarding me curiously.

"What?" he tilted his head. "You don't believe me?"

"Oh, I believe you," I said matter-of-factly. "It's just that those words don't have any true meaning. Not in the sense that it conveys anything real, I mean."

He was cute, my blind date. Handsome, too. Maybe a tiny bit on the shorter side, but he was well-dressed enough to make up for it. His hygiene was good, and he was groomed past my usual point of satisfaction. Which in this day and age, was a sliding scale.

Still, he'd ridden up to our date on a bike. Not a motorcycle either, but an actual bicycle. A mountain bike, to be more accurate. One with big knobby tires that seemed oddly incongruent with Seattle's smoothly-paved streets.

"Alright, what do you do as a freelance publicist?" I prodded him. "And don't use the words 'freelance' or 'publicist' in your answer."

The man's mocha brown eyes flitted upward, as if the answer were somewhere above him. When he spoke again his voice was more monotone, more mechanical.

"Well, I drive progress," he started.

"Ah, progress," I chuckled. "Always good."

"And I support influence marketing initiatives," he went on. "I nurture client relationships. I provide strategic, team-based oversight..."

It was like he was reading directly from a book. Or from his resume. Which was probably directly from a book.

"I also develop systems and tools, to optimize synergy and enhance media outreac—"

By now I was already distracted, and taking in other stimuli. I scanned around, soaking in the sights, the smells, and the atmosphere of the place he'd chosen for our rendezvous. Three waiters were serving up frothy pitchers of amber-colored beer to a dozen or more high tables scattered throughout the open room. The place wasn't a restaurant — well, not technically anyway — although it did have food. But it had axe-throwing, which was apparently good for building upon my already significant appetite.

"So is this your go-to first date, Chris, or what?" I asked.

Chris stopped talking immediately.

"Hmm?"

"I mean look around," I waved an arm. "It's pretty specific. Axe-throwing bars and restaurants are pretty trendy right now, don't you think?"

He looked suddenly uncomfortable. "I— I guess."

"So I'm thinking you bring a girl here, you ply her with booze, you throw a few axes around… it becomes your thing, right? Your lead-off first date?"

Chris's face was expressionless now. Utterly blank.

"Hey, I'm not saying it's a bad one," I said quickly. "It's clean, it's casual, it's fun…" I picked up one of the onion rings from the basket we were sharing and crunched into it. "Kinda noisy though," I added. "But a lot more unique than, let's say, dinner and a movie."

"Would… would you rather we went to dinner and a movie?" he stammered.

I shrugged. "No, not necessarily."

"Then what—"

"I mean dinner and a movie is a lot more intimate," I went on. "It's conversation-driven, too. Then again, spooning me from behind as you show me how to throw axes is intimate also. In a different way, of course."

"It—It is?"

"Of course it is," I answered, as if the observation were obvious. "But then you have the added danger of competition, too. I mean, what if you beat me and I resented it? Or even better, what if I beat you?"

"But you did beat me."

I smiled prettily. "See? There's my point."

My date looked around again, as he had when trying to find the server who brought us our drinks. His eyes were different this time, though. They were shiftier now, almost panicked.

"As a freelance publicist, I'm not sure how you synergize the intimacy of physical closeness with the pitfalls of a competitive—"

"Can you excuse me for a second?" Chris asked abruptly. "I… I need to run to the men's room."

"Sure. Knock yourself out."

Chris left, and I resisted the temptation to drain his beer as well. He'd barely touched it, and after a minute or two the beads of condensation running down the sides of his pint glass were outright beckoning to me.

Relax, Ariana.

It had been a tough week. The coffee shop was busier than ever, and people seemed to be on edge. I was looking forward to this date, as random as it was. Meeting people online could be like that, though. No matter what their profile looked like or how many interests and hobbies you lined up on, going out and sitting across from a perfect stranger was always a roll of the dice.

"Umm, excuse me, miss?"

Our server was back. I tilted my head in the direction of the restrooms.

"I'll wait for him before ordering, thanks."

"Yeah, umm…" His expression was troubled. "That's what I was going to talk to you about. I'm afraid your friend left."

I sat up a little straighter. "My... friend."

"Yes."

"What do you mean he left?"

The man gripped his serving tray a little more defensively against his chest. "Well I don't know how to say this —"

"Just say it, then."

"He climbed out the window," the server said apologetically. "The bathroom window."

There was a second of confusion, followed by two seconds of shock. Then my brows came together.

"Wait... what?"

"We only know because there was a commotion, and the window shattered," he explained. "It was a small window. Really small, actually. I still don't know how he managed to get out. But there was a lot of glass, and there was some blood too, and—"

"Blood!?"

"Not a lot of blood," the man added hastily. "I don't think so, anyway. They're cleaning it up now."

A resounding cheer went up from one of the axe-throwing stalls. Either someone had scored a bullseye, or a group of six or eight fraternity brothers were celebrating my latest dating disaster in unison.

He climbed through a window.

Holy fucking shit.

A tiny window...

I didn't know whether to freak out or start laughing

hysterically. I wanted to do both. Neither seemed strong enough a reaction, though.

"I'm really sorry," the server said again.

The man's look was a mixture of apology and restraint. I wondered if he wanted to break out laughing as well, but protocol wouldn't allow it. In truth, I wouldn't have minded.

"Alright then," I said, trying to gather up the last scraps of my dignity. "I guess I'll take the check."

Awkwardly, the man fumbled with his server book. Eventually he tore one out and laid it gently on the table.

"Again, I—"

"Forget it," I told him. "It's not the weirdest date I've ever been on, anyway." Now I did laugh, and it felt surprisingly good. "Not by a longshot."

His eyes went a little wider at that, which brought an even bigger smile to my face. The server smiled back, albeit weakly, then hurried off.

"Fuck you, Chris," I said, reaching across the table and toasting my date with his own beer. I was suddenly more determined than ever to salvage the night.

"Fuck you and the mountain bike you rode in on."

~ 2 ~

ARIANA

GreatSkates was the type of place that looked totally closed down, at least from the outside. The half-moon-shaped building was comprised of mostly dilapidated and crumbling cinder-block, with a roof that was patched in so many places it looked like an art project. The paint was chipping away in layers, and the sign's electronic letters flickered, noisily. The parking lot was cracked and pitted, with entire swaths of grass growing through the once-sealed asphalt.

Finally, if the building appeared to be tilting to one side, that's because it was. Engineers had determined the west side of the foundation was sinking at least a half-inch per year, which meant that no matter how much lipstick you slapped on this pig, GreatSkates' days were ultimately numbered.

"Axel?" I inquired, on the way through the door. Two hockey players in red-and-black jerseys nodded and pointed. "He's over there, feeding the puck-bunnies."

The first player laughed, while his friend gave him an admonishing shove. I smiled to let them both know it was alright.

"Thanks."

They shuffled off, still wearing their skates, and I turned left at what used to be the snack bar. Once upon a time, GreatSkates had been a roller rink — and a glorious one at that. I'd seen photos of it back in its heyday, and by the smiles on the faces of the 1980's mullet-wearing, high-haired, neon-wearing crowd, it had apparently been *the* place to be.

Sometime in the early 2000's it finally closed down, only to be bought and refitted as a flea-market venue. When that eventually failed it was left abandoned and rotting… at least until a few fiscally reckless investors bought the building, gutted it down to the cement walls, and turned it into an ice rink that was as much nostalgia as it was actual profit.

"Axel! AXEL!"

Two girls bumped me on either side as they went flying by, bounding over to the boards. And there, at the edge of the ice, was Axel. There were three other girls surrounding him, and a fourth had ventured onto the ice with nothing but a pair of flats on. He was holding her up with one arm, and balancing his helmet on his stick with the other.

I stopped short on the dirty, threadbare carpet to admire my friend since the seventh grade. Axel was of course *ridiculously* hot and handsome, with model good looks and a panty-dropping smile. His thick brown hair and stunning blue eyes captivated anyone who saw him, but it was his charisma and charm that really sealed the deal. Simply put, Axel had an energy that could not be explained. His voice, his mannerisms, his killer eyelashes — all of these things were wrapped up in a cool confidence that made everyone want to be around him, guys and girls alike.

The man was a god, at least amongst hockey players.

Not to mention his many, *many* female fans.

"Axel, AXEL!" I mocked, using my best teasing voice. "Can I have your autograph?"

The girls surrounding him gave me a dirty look as I approached. Especially the one clinging to him on the ice.

"Or could you maybe sign *these?*"

Laughingly, I pushed my tits together and sauntered over. I had some really great tits, actually. Three of the girls wrinkled their noses at me, including a bleach-blonde with a skirt so tight she could barely even move.

When Axel saw me his whole face lit up. In hilarious contrast, his fans all wore insta-frowns.

"What the hell are *you* doing here?" he asked cheerfully.

"Coming to find you, so you could take me to dinner."

"But I thought you had a date?"

An image of Chris climbing through a tiny broken window floated to mind. I fought the urge to roll my eyes. "Yeah, let's just say that ended early."

He shrugged off the girl who was still clinging to him, handing her his stick and helmet. She was still holding them, open-mouthed, as he skated over to me.

"Yeah? You're hungry?"

"Starving."

Before I knew it he'd reached out and lifted me onto the ice with two corded, powerful arms. It occurred to me that there'd once been a 'nobody on the ice without skates' rule, but the days of enforcing the rules at GreatSkates had long-since passed.

"Good. Me too."

The kiss Axel planted on my cheek happened quickly, much to the dismay of the puck-bunnies. They gave up a collective groan and slowly began to shuffle away.

"Umm… your stuff?" I chuckled.

Axel glanced back. The girl still holding his stick and helmet looked frozen, like a deer caught in headlights. He nodded in a certain direction.

"You can put that down in my locker if you don't mind."

She nodded mechanically as he led me away, slipping a friendly arm over my shoulder. I could feel his pads shifting beneath his jersey. The scent of him was overpowering; a heady but familiar mixture of moisture, musk, and sweat.

"Ugh. You really need a shower."

I teased him and others all the time like this, but in reality I didn't mind. Over hundreds of games in dozens of arenas, I'd grown to sort of like it.

"Tyler and Zane hit the shower ten minutes ago, so I'll make it quick."

He gathered up his duffel from the other side of the boards, and together we walked the length of the once-proud, but now ramshackle building. Before he ducked through to the showers however, I squeezed his hand.

"Sorry if I just ruined your night," I apologized, nodding toward the line of girls at the exit.

Almost on cue Axel's phone buzzed and lit up. He pulled it from the side pocket of his bag, then checked it with a laugh and a grin.

"Night's not ruined yet," he winked.

I felt a strange stab of jealousy, which was odd because that sort of thing had never happened before. I'd born witness to dozens of Axel's many conquests, and some of those women had been damn near close to perfect. None of them however, had made me feel like this.

"Be back in ten," he grinned, as his hand slipped from mine. "And whatever you do, don't let Tyler pick the place."

~ 3 ~

ARIANA

"And he escaped through the fucking *window?*" Zane swore incredulously. "Just like that?"

"Just like that," I smiled sheepishly.

"Broken glass. Blood…" Tyler tilted his head. "Totally gone?"

"Totally gone," I agreed. "Like some asshole magician."

The guys set their beers down, utterly astonished, but they also looked like they were holding back. More than one of them was stifling a laugh, which of course would've been at my expense.

"So what did you do?" asked Axel.

Looking down, I stirred the deflated remains of my whipped-cream into the rapidly-melting amalgam of my hot-fudge sundae.

"I paid the bill," I said with a shrug. "Then I came

310

looking for your sorry asses."

It was definitely getting late, but the sports bar we'd agreed upon was known for its late closing times. It sure as hell wasn't known for its food.

"Why didn't he just use the front door?" asked Tyler.

"Or the back door, even," Zane added.

Once again, I shrugged. "Maybe he thought I might see him? Who the hell knows?"

The table before us was scattered with the remains of our late-night feast: cheeseburgers, fried pickles, and a three-quarter eaten poutine pizza, half of which had been downed by Axel. Not a single busboy had come to remove anything, in all the hours we'd been here. The waitress had come five times with more drinks, however.

"Look, this is the third and last time I'm telling the story," I chuckled. "Whether you believe me or not—"

"Oh, we believe you," Tyler cut in. "It's just... well..."

He hesitated, searching my expression to make sure he could go on. I tightened my mouth into a smirk and gave him the go-ahead.

"It's just that no one's ever *bled* themselves to get out of a date with you, before."

If we weren't so many beers in, I might've kicked him under the table. Instead, I joined in on their laughter. I was buzzed. Happy. Sated. Lazily dissecting the remains of a hot-fudge sundae, while surrounded by my three best friends in the world.

Told you that you could salvage the night.

I looked at Axel, who'd been on and off his phone all

night — presumably with puck-bunnies. It was hard not to smile. The jealousy I felt before was gone now, and I was actually happy for whatever midnight hookup he might be arranging.

Tyler was staring at his phone just as much, but I didn't envy his messages at all. If I had to guess, his overly-controlling girlfriend was firing off an endless stream of nonsensical bullshit, mostly aimed at getting him home. Not that he ever lived with her, mind you; he lived with Axel. As always though Lexus just wanted him anywhere but out.

I hated to see it, too. Tyler and I once lived next door to each other, and I'd known him most of my life. We'd grown up together, braved the perils of puberty together. As friends we'd fought each other's battles and stood up for each other through thick and thin. I'd watched him grow from an awkward, gangly boy into this tall, gorgeous man who towered over me at six-foot-four. We were connected on levels only childhood friends understood. I'd always felt like a part of Tyler belonged to me, and vice-versa.

That left Zane, who spent the night throwing me the usual side-eye and flicking pickle chips my way. I spent equal amounts of time sticking my tongue out at him and admiring his deeply-tanned, Italian frame. His chestnut eyes and sexy stubbled goatee made him easy to look at, all throughout high school and beyond. He'd also been my hometown buddy sticking around Seattle those few lonely years when Tyler and Axel were off doing the college thing.

"So did you win tonight?" I asked, having missed the entirety of their game.

"Nah," Axel grumbled. "We lost by a goal."

He shot a semi-accusatory glance at Zane, who of course was goaltending. As usual, Zane didn't even acknowledge him.

"I guess we're all losers then," Tyler winked at me. "Right?"

"Well, not necessarily..." I teased.

The guys leaned back in their chairs and regarded me curiously.

"This particular date might've bombed, but I've got another one lined up for tomorrow night," I explained. "So there's always redemption."

"Oh yeah?" challenged Zane. "A date with who?"

"Garth."

I dropped the name and then quickly sipped my beer, waiting for the other shoe to inevitably drop. I didn't have to wait long.

"Garth?" Tyler repeated. "That blond defenseman on the Mother Puckers?"

"Yup."

"*That* Garth?" Axel swore.

"So?" I demanded, trying to keep my voice from becoming too defensive. "I like Garth. He's kinda cute."

"That guy's a duster!" Axel cried loudly. "He never leaves the bench!"

"Yeah, well he asked me out the last time you guys played him," I explained.

"Probably from the bench," Zane grumbled. He grunted and rolled his eyes. "Look, if you're going to date a hockey player at least date a successful one. Not some guy who only comes over the boards once or twice a—"

He stopped mid-sentence in a wince of pain. I knew immediately that Tyler had come to my rescue, kicking him under the table.

I cast my gaze down for a moment, trying to remember what Garth actually looked like. Were they right? Had I taken the date just because he asked me, without even knowing whether or not I even liked him?

When I glanced up again, Tyler's eyes locked on mine. All three of my friends knew my love life had been full of land mines, but Tyler knew more than the others that casual dating just wasn't my thing. Half the time I was uncharacteristically and almost painfully shy, and the other half I just couldn't shut myself the hell up. No matter who it was that took me out, most of my dates ended in disaster. I really seemed to suck at it.

"Look, Garth's okay from what I understand," Tyler spoke up. "So go out and have fun. You have our blessing."

His brotherly speech elicited an awkward laugh from me. "Uh… thanks."

"Yeah, what Tyler said," Axel finally nodded. He grinned and toasted me with his beer. "Stick to the basics and you'll do just fine."

I raised my own glass in salute, and the others joined in. Across the table however, Zane's smirk was wider than ever.

"Whatever you do, just don't let him go to the bathroom," he winked.

~ 4 ~

ARIANA

Working at the coffee shop was one of those jobs you took to pay your bills for a while, as you searched for your true career. You never really expected to stick around very long. It was a mere pit stop in the race of life.

That's what I told myself four years ago, anyway.

In reality though, being a barista at *Java Queen* wasn't a bad gig. The hours were good, the pay was adequate, and the tips could be outstanding at times. The place was clean, the work was honest, and it smelled heavenly every single time I walked through the door and tied on my apron.

On top of all that, I was entitled to all the free coffee I could drink... which as a consummate coffee drinker, saved me a small fortune by itself. They even threw in some pastries, too. I also got to practice my coffee art, which admittedly was pretty impressive. Instagram and TikTok accounts included.

No, the place was generally alright, even on the bad days. And today, I was in a really good mood. A spectacular mood, actually. The kind of mood that nobody could mess with, except for—

"Ummm… *Ariana* is it?"

The way he said my name was uncomfortable enough, but the man's eyes still lingered on my name tag. As if he needed to explain how he knew my name.

"Yes?"

"There's something wrong with my latte."

'Franklin' — or at least that was the name I'd scrawled across his cup fifteen minutes ago — had been sitting in the corner, watching videos on his laptop. I knew he was watching videos because he didn't have the common courtesy to use earbuds or headphones. Right now, he was holding the lid to his coffee in one hand, while tilting the beverage my way.

"What's wrong with it?"

"It's… well… something's just not right," he said, struggling to summon some frustration. "It's not as *creamy* as it usually is."

I nodded apologetically. "Yeah, sorry about that. The milk foamer's been acting up all week."

"Oh."

"We've been trying to lock down the problem, but sometimes it works and sometimes it—"

"Don't you think I should get another one?"

My mouth went instantly tight. Under any other circumstance, I would've poured him a new one right away. But it was the snotty, snobbishly effete *way* in which he asked the question that sent my hackles up. Not to mention how casually and unapologetically he'd interrupted me.

"Well… you did already *drink* this one," I said with a sigh. "Didn't you?"

It was true. At least three-quarters of his latte was gone.

"Not all of it," he said defensively.

Rather than answer him, I smiled and shrugged.

"If your milk foamer is broken maybe you shouldn't be pouring lattes at all," he grumbled. "And if you think for one second—"

"You know what? You're right," I cut him off. "Hang on sir. I got you."

I plucked the cup from his hand, tossed it away, and grabbed one of *Java Queen's* proprietary ceramic mugs. A minute and a half later I was handing him a hot, steaming latte. Freshly-poured milk foam and everything.

Franklin accepted it graciously. He was halfway back to his laptop when he stopped dead in his tracks.

"You're kidding, right?"

The disgusted way he was staring down at his mug made me giggle. "No. Not really."

"I think you need to get me the manager."

I paused for a moment, then shrugged one shoulder. "Sure, no problem."

As the man returned to the counter I ducked behind the cappuccino machine. When I stepped out again, I had a much brighter smile and an ear-to-ear grin.

"Hi, I'm Ariana! How may I help you?"

The man's lip curled back in repugnance. "*You're* the

manager?"

"I sure am," I said cheerily. "Supervisor, too. And head barista. And—"

"Can I speak to the owner, then?"

I motioned, and somehow caught Katie's attention. She put down the broom she'd been sweeping with and glided over.

"Can I help you with something, sir?"

Franklin squinted skeptically at the curly-haired blonde. "Are you the owner?"

"Yes, why?"

Katie shot me an inquisitive glance. I shrugged in response, and her eyes rolled.

"Alright," she sighed heavily. "What'd she do this time?"

The man was speechless for a moment. He was still staring down at the coffee art I'd so thoughtfully provided him.

"Did she draw an asshole again, or—"

"Well no, not exactly."

"Did she write a curse word then?" Katie frowned. "A bad one?"

"No," the man admitted. "Here. Look for yourself."

Holding the mug out, he rotated it so that she could finally read it.

"What does that say?" Katie squinted through her glasses. "T-E-A-M G-R-"

"It says Team Grumps!" the man exploded, rather grumpily.

Katie let out a sigh that was half-relief, half-frustration. "Ah, yes. Team Grumps. I can totally see it now." Her frown deepened. "Is *that* all?"

"Wha—"

"You're angry about *that*?" Katie pointed. "Seriously?"

The man began turning a shade of red. It wasn't an angry red, either. It was more like the crimson of deep embarrassment.

"She could've drawn something terrible," Katie explained. "And I mean *really* bad. She's done it before. Trust me, she's got the chops for it. But all she did was put you on Team Grumps. Which, quite honestly..." she leaned in confidentially, "... you might actually deserve."

By now I'd taken the broom and was sweeping furiously. It was the only way I could stop from breaking out in laughter.

"And look at it," Katie said, tapping the mug. "I mean, it's so well *done*. Don't you think?"

His astonishment complete, the man said nothing more. Eventually he wandered numbly back to his seat, taking his latte with him.

"Some people," Katie smirked. "They just don't appreciate an artist at work."

"I know, right?" I chuckled.

"Of course... it *would* probably be better for business if you don't insult the customers," she added casually. "Not too many of them, anyway."

I nodded sheepishly. "Right. I'll be more... selective."

"That's all a girl can ask," she grinned, adding a wink.

The door jingled as a trio of new customers came in. The place was mostly empty, though. The morning rush was over, and the afternoon lull was here.

"Hey, you've got class today, don't you?" Katie asked.

I stopped sweeping and nodded. "Three of them, actually. And then afterwards, I've got a date."

She smiled and nodded approvingly. "A hot date, eh?"

"Well that part remains to be seen," I admitted. "But I'm always optimistic."

Katie looked me over for a second or two, and her smile widened. The owner of *Java Queen* had always been cooler than cool. It was just one more perk — pun definitely not intended — that came with the job.

"Why don't you knock off early then," she suggested. "You could stop at Pagliacci and grab yourself a slice, or something else to eat."

I pointed at the pastry case. "Well... I was going to grab those scones."

"*Other* than my scones," Katie admonished.

I untied my apron, then bunched it up and threw it at her.

"Yes boss," I said, kissing her on the cheek before bouncing away.

~ 5 ~

ZANE

The ice-resurfacing machine hummed beneath me, grinding away the day's grooves and gouges. The augers were set to the perfect depth. The board brush rotated at the just the right RPM's, as the spray bars put out new ice behind me.

"Move the fucking Zamboni, jackass."

I guided myself smoothly through another one-hundred and eighty degree turn. As I swept back up the ice from the opposite direction, the asshole in the blue jersey dropped a puck at his feet.

"Did you hear what I said?"

I responded by flipping him off. He responded by winding back and taking a slapshot.

THWACK!

I didn't even flinch as the puck ricocheted off one of the screw conveyors at the front of the machine.

"You missed, dickhead."

I rumbled by, skirting closely around the asshole who was still leaning on his stick. A part of me wanted to play chicken with him, to see if he moved out of the way. But it would've been messy if he didn't.

"Why are you doing this?" the red-bearded goalie demanded. "I've still got ten minutes left."

"We close at eleven," I told him. "It's well past that."

"Yeah, well I didn't get started until late. Locker jammed."

"Sounds like a whole lot of your problem."

He'd been skating around in full gear, flicking wrist shots at an empty net for the better part of an hour. Most likely because his teammates hadn't shown up to practice shooting at him.

"The stuck locker's *your* fault," he insinuated. "Or at least the owner's."

"Take it up with him then."

The asshole ripped off his helmet and spat. "Shit, I don't even know why we practice here anymore," he seethed, "much less play. This place is such a shithole. The roof looks like it's going to collapse at any second."

I shrugged. "All the more reason you should go home."

I couldn't argue with the shithole comment, but I certainly wasn't going to give him an inch. We remained at a stalemate, glaring back at each other with equal amounts of disdain.

"Look man, just hit the showers already. I gotta take the nets down." Under my breath, I stifled a curse. "I'll tell Greg to credit you for fifteen minutes."

"Screw that," he spat again. "I want an hour."

I shook my head. "You're not getting an hour. It's not our fault your teammates didn't show up. You're lucky you're getting anything at all."

The flame-haired asshole's name was Devin, or Devon, or something equally ambiguous. I'd hated him since the moment I'd met him, which was unfortunately some time ago. He had a point about the lockers though, and maybe even the roof. Hell, the whole place was falling apart and the owner wasn't doing jack shit about it. It didn't make the guy any less of a dick, though.

"Fine, I'll give you a half hour," I relented. "Just get your shit and go."

The old Zamboni ran pretty decently when you got it started, but it was a bitch to get it going again once you stopped it. You had to set all the dials correctly, and run it at just the right speed. It didn't have any fancy digital gauges, or a laser-leveling system to keep the ice even. Everything was done by feel, by gut, by instinct.

And I'd been doing it way too fucking long.

Eventually the asshat relented, and began gathering his things. He skated up to me one last time before leaving the ice, however.

"You know… it's not my fault you didn't make the cut," he smirked.

My hands balled into fists. Somehow, I willed them back open again.

"You just need more practice, that's all," he taunted, adding a shrug. "Maybe next season."

Grimly I looked over my shoulder, wondering if Greg

had left yet. We were probably alone. Anything could happen.

"Then again…"

No one would hear his screams. Especially over the sound of the Zamboni.

Easy, Zane. Don't blow this.

"Then again, you can't teach speed," the asshole pressed onward. "Or flexibility. Or hand-eye coordination." He paused to scratch at the back of his head. "Those things are gifts, I guess. Either you have them or you don't."

The words I could ignore, but it was the smile on this prick's face that made me want to punish him in the worst possible way. I wanted to launch over the front of the machine and grab him by the head.

"And from what we've seen as a team…"

If I pressed hard enough, I could use his front teeth to carve my name into the ice.

"… I guess you don't."

I jumped down, landing nimbly in front of him. I could see in his eyes that he wasn't expecting it. But he dropped back into a fighting stance anyway.

"There you go, loser," Devin or Devon chided snidely. He tapped his ugly bearded chin with a gloved finger. "Go on. Take your shot."

I reached out with one hand… but instead of grabbing him, I pushed past and detached the nearest goalpost from its moorings. I had to take the nets down before the Zamboni stalled out. And if there was one thing I was sure of, it *would* stall out.

"Yeah," he chuckled. "That's what I thought."

I watched as he skated away; a giant dick holding a garishly-painted goalie mask and wearing overpriced pads. He was a douche for sure, maybe even the king of all douches. But he had one thing I didn't have, and the both of us knew it:

A starting spot on the River Kings.

About the Author

Krista Wolf is a lover of action, fantasy and all good horror movies… as well as a hopeless romantic with an insatiably steamy side.

She writes suspenseful, mystery-infused stories filled with blistering hot twists and turns. Tales in which headstrong, impetuous heroines are the irresistible force thrown against the immovable object of ripped, powerful heroes.

If you like intelligent and witty romance served up with a sizzling edge? You've just found your new favorite author.

Click here to see all titles on

Krista's Author Page

Sign up to Krista's VIP Email list to get instant notification of all new releases: http://eepurl.com/dkWHab

Printed in Great Britain
by Amazon

40553469R00189